"Annja, come on! Move!"

Annja watched the water. It rose noticeably in the passing of a few heartbeats.

She cursed silently. When she started out that morning, it hadn't crossed her mind that all the rain would affect her exploration of the caves. She should have considered the possibility. She should have realized there could be flash floods. Being on vacation had made her mind numb.

She glanced at the nearest coffin, then back at the water. The river could conceivably reach the coffins or perhaps completely cover them.

No doubt this chamber had flooded in the past what with the annual rainy season and the monsoons. Perhaps the rising river was the explanation for no bodies…the water had washed them away and left behind only the heavy teak coffins and the most cumbersome pieces of pottery. Maybe the water had even rearranged where the coffins had originally been placed.

She hadn't imagined the voice. She heard it distinctly now. It hadn't come from the coffins, though. It was as if it had traveled through the very stone of the cave and seeped into her head. It echoed like a child calling down into a canyon.

Free me…

Titles in this series:

Destiny
Solomon's Jar
The Spider Stone
The Chosen
Forbidden City
The Lost Scrolls
God of Thunder
Secret of the Slaves
Warrior Spirit
Serpent's Kiss
Provenance
The Soul Stealer
Gabriel's Horn
The Golden Elephant
Swordsman's Legacy
Polar Quest
Eternal Journey
Sacrifice
Seeker's Curse
Footprints
Paradox
The Spirit Banner
Sacred Ground
The Bone Conjurer
Tribal Ways
The Dragon's Mark
Phantom Prospect
Restless Soul

ROGUE Angel™

Alex Archer

RESTLESS SOUL

A GOLD EAGLE BOOK FROM

WORLDWIDE®

TORONTO • NEW YORK • LONDON
AMSTERDAM • PARIS • SYDNEY • HAMBURG
STOCKHOLM • ATHENS • TOKYO • MILAN
MADRID • WARSAW • BUDAPEST • AUCKLAND

Recycling programs
for this product may
not exist in your area.

First edition January 2011

ISBN-13: 978-0-373-62147-7

RESTLESS SOUL

Special thanks and acknowledgment to
Jean Rabe for her contribution to this work.

Printed in U.S.A.

The
LEGEND

...THE ENGLISH COMMANDER TOOK
JOAN'S SWORD AND RAISED IT HIGH.

The broadsword, plain and unadorned,
gleamed in the firelight. He put the tip against
the ground and his foot at the center of the blade.
The broadsword shattered, fragments falling
into the mud. The crowd surged forward,
peasant and soldier, and snatched the shards
from the trampled mud. The commander tossed
the hilt deep into the crowd.
Smoke almost obscured Joan, but she continued
praying till the end, until finally the flames climbed
her body and she sagged against the restraints.

Joan of Arc died that fateful day in France,
but her legend and sword are reborn....

PROlogue

Vietnam, July 1966

At first, he hadn't minded the sound of the place.

He was Bronx born and raised, and the constant insect chorus of the Vietnam jungle was an interesting oddity and an almost welcome change from the frequent sirens and ever-present racket of traffic back home.

The birdsong, the swish of the big acacia leaves in the breeze and the occasional chatter of monkeys…it was all a pleasant diversion from orders barked by commanding officers and the grumbles of the men in his rifle company. He even liked the smell.

But that was more months ago than he cared to count.

Now the sounds blurred into a hellish cacophony that he had to pick through to listen for branches snapping, footfalls that weren't from his men, the metallic click of machine guns and rifles ready to fire. Now the place reeked…of mud and rotting leaves, of things his imagination wasn't vivid or brave enough to picture, and sometimes of decomposing bodies that neither side had retrieved.

Sergeant Gary Thomsen had learned to hate summer and the jungle. He hated the trails tangled with plants that grabbed at his heavy pack and all his weapons. He hated the sweat running down his face as plentiful as rain. He hated the fear twisting in his gut that someone was hiding around the next tree ready to kill him. He hated everything about Vietnam and the goddamn war that the politicians in the States wouldn't call a war. A police action—was that the latest term?

He hated the leeches most of all.

He knew that they were clinging to him now. They were somehow always able to find their way up his pants and under his sleeves, into his boots, so they could gorge themselves on his sweet American blood. He'd led his men through brackish ponds and across streams and along a riverbank that morning and well into the afternoon, so there would be leeches on everyone.

He wanted to strip and pull the leeches off, but that would have to wait. There was another three hours or so left of what passed for daylight…the canopy was thick and not much sun was getting through. He had his orders to reach the firebase before dark and regroup with the rest of the platoon.

"Sarge…"

Gary scowled that someone had broken the relative silence. He turned to Private Wallem, a gangly hawk-nosed Texan who was pointing to just north of the trail. A body, mostly bones and scraps of dirty cloth, lay under a big fern.

"It's one of theirs, Sarge. See? You can tell by the

boots. Wonder if we got him or the jungle did? Guess it doesn't matter. As long as it's one of theirs and not…"

Gary shut out the rest of Wallem's words and fixed his eyes on the body, angry with himself that he hadn't spotted it. Not that it was all that interesting or all that important. But nothing used to get past him.

He'd set himself as point man for the patrol. The squad leader wasn't supposed to walk point. He was supposed to take the second position. But Gary thought he had the keenest, most experienced eyes, and he wanted to be up front.

There was just too much green. He'd spent too many days in the jungle, and there were all those leeches, attached to his flesh, distracting him.

A good point man should have seen the body and not let anything distract him. What else had he missed? he wondered.

"War is always the same," Gary thought, quoting President Lyndon Johnson. "It is young men dying in the fullness of their promise. It is trying to kill a man that you do not even know well enough to hate. Therefore, to know war is to know that there is still madness in the world."

The quote had stayed with him because Gary was sure he was going mad.

Johnson had said the words six months earlier, back in January, shortly before Operation Masher, a large-scale search-and-destroy operation against North Vietnamese troop encampments, began. Johnson had then changed the name to Operation White Wing, which didn't sound quite so aggressive.

Gary and his men were a part of it, in the Bong Son Plain near the coast. A little more than two hundred

American soldiers had died, but almost six times that many North Vietnamese. Gary thought maybe he'd get to go home after it ended, but his sergeant was one of those Americans killed, and he was assigned another tour, promoted to E-5 and given his rifle squad of ten to lead.

The leeches would get some more of his sweet American blood.

"Leave it alone," he said of the corpse. Sometimes the enemy rigged trip wires and explosives around bodies. "Keep moving," he ordered.

He checked his compass. West, definitely. They were humping due west on an established trail. It took too much effort to hack straight through the jungle; everything grew too tight.

He'd look at the map again in another few minutes. They were hard to read, the maps. He navigated mostly by gut instinct and the compass.

He heard the steady tromp of the men behind him, the annoying but comforting buzz of insects. The insects rarely quieted. They didn't seem to mind the presence of soldiers from either side. When they did go quiet, that was when fear seriously twisted in his gut.

God, but he wanted to go home.

A sound like thunder, muted and distant, rumbled. It was a bomb, he knew, from a B-52. The planes carried up to a hundred, dropping them from as high as six miles up. The U.S. regularly bombed North Vietnam and lately had been hitting oil depots around Hanoi and Haiphong.

Gary had read somewhere that Senator Robert F. Kennedy had criticized the president for the bombing, saying the country was heading down "a road from which there is no turning back, a road that leads to catastrophe for all mankind."

As far as Gary was concerned, there'd been no turning back since the U.S. brought the first planeload of soldiers. He wished they'd bomb the whole damn country into oblivion so he could go home.

There was the thunder of another bomb, coming from even farther away.

Wallem started to speak again, but Gary cut him off with a quick chopping motion of his hand.

Between the sounds of marching and insects buzzing, he'd heard something else, a spitting sound, a sustained whisper that he recognized as machine-gun fire. It wasn't terribly close, but he prayed it didn't come closer.

He held his breath and sensed that his men were doing the same, and he gripped the stock of his rifle tighter. He didn't want to engage any Vietcong, but those were part of his orders—dispatch any VC patrols on the way to the firebase.

The sound came again. Four or five machine guns, he guessed from the bursts. He couldn't tell which side was doing the shooting. Didn't matter, did it? The enemy was involved, to be sure.

It suddenly became quiet again...quiet except for the insects.

"Move out." His voice was so soft the men directly behind him had to strain to hear.

Gary picked up the pace. His legs ached with the punishment of too many miles, but he forced the pain to the back of his mind. Just another hour, two at the outside, to reach the firebase.

Maybe he should call for a five-minute rest, get rid

of some of the leeches. Then it would be easier to press on to the base so they could regroup with the others, get rid of more of the leeches, sleep before falling out the next day on some new asinine mission the higher-ups had concocted.

He cut through a particularly tight weave of trees where the trail narrowed, led them through a stretch of marsh and was just about ready to call for that blessed five-minute rest when he spotted something that hadn't been marked on his map.

"Sarge, what is it?" Private Wallem said. "Sorry!" he added when he realized he'd spoken above a whisper.

Gary glared at Wallem, then turned back to what he'd seen.

Right in front of them was a building of some sort, definitely an old one. The jungle had practically swallowed it. Vines were thick on the columns and what was left of the walls. Most of the stone was stained green, but there were patches of white here and there, and he could see worn symbols that he suspected had once stood out quite prominently.

"Maybe a shrine," Gary said. The country certainly had enough of them. They were Buddhist, right? They worshipped the smiling fat guy with the bald head, he thought.

Almost half of the building looked intact, and there was an opening midway down the greenish stone. The door, if there had been one, had been eaten away by time and the jungle, and the opening that was left looked like the yawning mouth of a serpent.

They probably had an hour or so left to get to the firebase, if he wasn't off course. Maybe a little more than that, maybe two at the very outside he was sure.

He knew he shouldn't take the time to investigate the place, but God, his feet and legs ached from all the walking. And the wide-open stone mouth beckoned.

He edged forward, straight toward the opening, gesturing for Wallem to come behind him. His curiosity tugged him, but it was also his responsibility to make sure no enemy soldiers were hiding inside. Checking would just be following orders.

He held up his fist for his men to stop and wait, then he stepped through the serpent's mouth. His mouth dropped open.

"Holy spit!" Wallem said when he poked his head inside. He stretched to see over Gary's shoulder. "Sweet Mary, mother of…"

Gary was so surprised that he didn't even frown at Wallem for speaking.

Sunlight was shining through a sizable hole in the roof, illuminating gold figurines, several of Buddha with emeralds set in his earlobes and where his belly button would be. There were pieces of ivory, bowls that he figured might have some sort of religious significance because they were so delicate and beautifully painted, jade and coral carvings, and more. It was too much for him to take in.

His gaze flitted from one piece to the next, pausing on a pair of jade koi with intertwined tails before settling on a small Buddha with jewels draped around its neck. The light dimmed, as if the sun was behind a cloud, plunging everything into shadows.

Still, he could see well enough. There was a bird the size of his hand, probably carved from ivory, perched on a shiny black pedestal. It made Gary think of Operation White Wing.

"This is creepy," Wallem said. He held a covered bowl with dark symbols etched everywhere. He put it down and picked up a fist-size jade turtle. "This is better."

The treasure didn't belong there. It didn't have the mossy green film of the jungle, nor any vines growing on it. And it was polished as if it had just come from a temple or museum. It had to have been put there fairly recently. Maybe by thieves, maybe by monks who, fearing the invading Americans might destroy their precious antiquities, moved them to the middle of nowhere.

Would it hurt to take some of the smaller pieces? There were things that would easily fit in pockets and packs. The jewels draped around the Buddha alone would buy him a Mustang when he got back home. Hell, with that, he could buy a house. Maybe get his mother one, too.

"Sarge?"

Gary didn't answer. He reached behind his back and eased his pack off, flipped it open and started filling the crannies with pendants and thumb-size jade carvings, taking the small things that looked the most valuable.

There was a ring with a diamond in the shape of a sunflower seed. He'd give it to his girl as an engagement ring when he popped the question after he got back home.

He looped a string of gold beads around his neck. They felt heavy and cold, but they quickly warmed against his skin.

After only a moment's hesitation, Wallem joined in the looting, snatching the ivory bird first and discovering the wings detached, which made it easier to fit in his pack.

"What about the rest of the men? Should they come in, Sarge? There's enough for everybody."

Gary didn't reply. He was filling his pockets with anything that fit, shoving jade and silver rings on his fingers as he went. His mind raced to figure out how to take one of the golden Buddhas.

He heard muted thunder, and at first thought it was another distant bomb. But it was followed by the patter of rain, some of which found its way inside.

Real thunder. That explained the light slipping away on him. Storms sprang up quickly in Vietnam. The frequent rains were proverbial mixed blessings—they cooled the men off, but they added time to any mission. And worse, the rain smeared all the greens together and made it more difficult to see the enemy.

He muttered a string of soft curses. It would take them longer to reach the firebase now, slogging along a muddy trail through a wet jungle, probably slowed a little bit more by the weight of the treasure. A good weight, he thought. The only good thing about this god-forsaken country was this room full of treasure.

"Get Sanduski and Moore," Gary said. "Mitchell and Everett and Seger, too, for starters. Those guys go first. Tell 'em all to load up whatever they can. Everybody can take a turn."

Some part of Gary knew he shouldn't be doing this, and he knew he'd have a hell of a time trying to get the stuff back home. But he just couldn't get past all the gold.

"I'll take it home," he whispered. "I'll find a way." He was nothing if not resourceful.

Besides, his orders never said he couldn't pick up

abandoned treasure. In fact, his orders never mentioned treasure at all.

"This ain't stealing, Sarge," Wallem said, as if reading Gary's mind. "This stuff is just—"

"Lying around," Gary finished as thunder shook the small building.

"Sanduski and Moore for starters," he reminded Wallem. They were on their second tour, too, and deserved something for it. Moore, the radio man, had twin boys who'd just turned three. "Then the rest. There's enough for everybody."

Wallem managed to stuff the tail-touching koi into his pack after taking out some probably necessary supplies. "We'll take it all, Sarge. The slope heads just left this unattended. Maybe the owners are dead. It's all ours and—"

"We can't take it all. There's too much," Gary said sharply as he tried to heft one of the small Buddha statues and discovered it was made of solid gold. "We'll only get out of here with some of it."

"A king's ransom," Wallem gushed.

Gary heard some of the men talking outside, and then felt a faint vibration through the stones when thunder sounded again.

"Gotta get going," Gary said. "Gotta get to the firebase. Probably have to clear some ground there tomorrow for a helicopter pad. Gotta get there before dark."

Wallem called for Moore and Sanduski. "In a few minutes, Sarge. Give us a few more minutes. It'd only be fair for everyone to get something."

Lightning flashed and thunder followed closely. Then another sound came that Gary didn't place at first. The rain pelted through the roof and *rat-a-tat-tatted* on the stone and the golden statues. The light turned gray, but not so dim that the golden statues couldn't be seen.

Moore gave a whoop and brushed by Gary.

Sanduski stopped in the opening and gaped. "Fort Knox!" He shouted back over his shoulder. "Load up."

The rest of the group squeezed past Gary.

More than satisfied with his share of the haul, the soldier stepped out into the downpour. He tipped his head back to let the rain wash the sweat off.

His pack felt heavier, and his pockets bulged. He fought the grin that spread across his face and lost, letting out a whoop. He wished he could take one of those Buddhas.

"Grab fast and move out!" Gary called back to his men.

No use looking at his map in this dreary muck. He'd rely on the compass and his gut instinct.

Lightning flashed and the ground rocked again. Above the patter of cleansing rain, the whisper-hiss of machine-gun fire stole his breath. Mud spat up around his feet. Hot fire slammed into his legs.

Gary screamed.

"Wallem!" he managed to call out as he fell. "Company. Moore, get out here. We've got—"

1

"Company. Such beautiful company you are, Annja Creed. And I am very much enjoying the pleasures of it." He stood behind her at the sliding glass door and slid his fingers through her silky chestnut hair.

She leaned against him, happily discovering he hadn't put on a shirt. At five feet ten inches, Annja was nearly his height.

"And I am so very much enjoying this vacation, Luartaro."

"Lu, please." He leaned around her and softly kissed her cheek. "How many times do I have to ask you to call me Lu? It's what my family calls me. And it's much easier for you to pronounce."

"Lu." She blew out the breath she'd been holding, fluttering the hair that hung against her forehead. "Lu. Lu. Lu. This vacation was long overdue."

He brought a long strand of her hair to his nose and inhaled. "I wish it could go on forever, Annja, this vacation."

"But we've only got another four days," she said.

"Maybe we should leave this bungalow and see a bit of the countryside? We didn't travel halfway around the world to Thailand to spend all our time in bed."

"Speak for yourself." He chuckled.

Annja reveled in his voice, throaty and rich with a sensuous Argentine accent. She waited for him to speak again, but when he didn't, she edged away and pressed herself against the glass door. It was cool with the rain that had blotted out the July sun. She followed a rivulet with her finger as it slithered down the pane.

The patter was gentle, like his breath on her shoulder, and it made the green of the trees beyond their cabin more intense.

They'd found this resort on the internet, though there were no public internet connections available in the lodge or any of the cabins. Wireless service didn't exist here. Neither were there television sets, nor telephones, save an old rotary one in the office. With that they had both immediately agreed on the place, as they could keep the world at bay for a while.

Annja had been in South America, filming a segment for *Chasing History's Monsters* on the fossils of ancient penguinlike creatures that had been discovered in the mountains. She'd met Luartaro Agustin at one of the dig sites there.

He was charming and smart, and when he'd surprised her by suggesting that they spend some more time together, she'd hesitated only a moment.

She desperately needed time off—from the show, from her life, from everything. So right there in his lavish office, she'd twirled the huge globe that took up most of one corner, closed her eyes and pointed her finger.

Luartaro had come over to see where her finger had landed. Northern Thailand. She'd surprised him by walking over to his immense oak desk and calling the airline to make a reservation. For two.

As she watched the rain, she thought that perhaps Luartaro had fallen in love with her, though he wisely hadn't said the words.

Would those words frighten her away? Did she love him? Not yet. But perhaps…with time… She'd only known him a handful of days before they'd recklessly packed their bags and flown here. She'd learned through difficult circumstances that life was terribly short, and she decided to take a chance on joy for once.

Could she love him? Perhaps if she let herself. The attraction, physical and otherwise, was strong.

She watched the way the rain distorted his handsome reflection.

He had a rugged face weathered by long days in the sun, a shock of black hair with the faintest hints of silver at the temples, broad shoulders and considerable muscles from years spent digging at sites throughout the mountains and foothills of South America.

He had flashing eyes that she could easily lose herself in. *Had* lost herself in, she corrected herself. He was intelligent—in addition to being an archaeologist, he taught at a college during the regular academic year, had written three textbooks and was fluent in half a dozen languages. Though, unfortunately, Thai was not one of them. They had a lot in common.

Perhaps she was reading too much into his actions. After all, he knew very little about her, which was a plus, as far as she was concerned.

He didn't know that danger too often surrounded her

and that some mystic force seemed to have chosen her to battle evil.

She hadn't told him that she was an orphan with little sense of a real connection to people. Nor had she told him—and never intended to—that on a whim she could summon Joan of Arc's sword from some nether-dimension to fight whatever malignant force had crossed her path.

She had been on a dig in France when she found a piece of the legendary sword. She didn't know how, but in a heartbeat, magically reformed by her touch, it had appeared in her hand, whole and shining, more than five hundred years after its famous wielder had been put to death by fire. Now the sword was poised just beyond this world, waiting for her call. She sometimes thought of it as waiting in a closet in her mind, though *armory* might be a better term.

Because of the sword and her risky life, she never allowed herself to become too attached to people. She had Roux and Garin, but they were associated with the sword, Roux claiming they had witnessed Joan's hor-rific death and had existed in a kind of decadent limbo in the centuries since.

Luartaro was different. Like so many others, he wasn't a part of that life. Normally, she would have kept her emotions in check. But there was something special about him. She felt things for him that she hadn't intended.

And what does he think of me? she wondered. Did he consider her merely a television personality with a flair for archaeology? Or was she just another woman who had quickly succumbed to his boyish grin?

She watched his reflection in the window again. He

had moved close enough that he was stroking her hair again, but he, too, was staring out at the rain and the mountains beyond.

The view was the reason she was paying eight hundred baht a night for their cabin, four times what the average room cost. It was more lavishly furnished than most of the other accommodations at the lodge. It even had its own bath and shower. But best of all, it offered an incredible view of the lush countryside.

Beyond the sliding glass doors was the path that led to the swimming hole and another that wound its way to the small restaurant that served only native Thai dishes. The rain was slowly turning those paths into mud slicks.

In the distance, the mountains that ringed the place disappeared into the gloom. "Complicated mountain ranges," one of the locals had called them on the bus ride to the resort. Misty clouds hung halfway down them, and the rain was blurring the rest.

Mae Hong Son was called the City of Three Mists because no matter the time of year, there were always low-hanging clouds present. "Three" because the mists were different—the forest-fire mist of the summer, the rainy mist in the monsoon season and the dewy mist of their mild winter.

The area had long been considered a "land of exile" because it was largely inaccessible, but tourists had eventually found the place, and buses and rental cars brought them in from larger cities. She and Luartaro had opted for a bus, the seats of which had not been very well padded.

Mae Hong Son claimed a hot spring, small and large crystal clear streams and a magnificent cape—none of which Annja had seen. There was an elaborate Buddhist temple nearby, so the brochures said, and a tribe where the women elongated their necks with a series of rings—the Karen of the Pa Dong.

"I think we should do something touristy," she said, breaking the silence that had settled comfortably between them. "Maybe we could take an elephant ride or do some mountain biking. The pamphlets—" she pointed at the nightstand "—say they have meditation classes in the mornings, rafting and—"

"If you want to venture outside," Luartaro interrupted, "why don't we visit a spirit cave?"

A shiver raced down Annja's back, and she bit back a *No!* before it could escape her lips.

She couldn't explain what brought on the touch of dread, not to herself and not to Luartaro. She could just claim that exploring a cave was too close to her real life as an archaeologist. That wasn't too far from the truth. She hadn't planned to let real life interfere with this long-overdue vacation.

She shook her head and turned away from the window. He wrapped his arms around her and held her close; he couldn't see the sour, conflicted expression on her face.

"I saw a flyer about it in the lobby—a spirit cave," Luartaro continued. "And I remember it was also mentioned on the internet when we found this place. Ancient coffins carved from trees, burial grounds inside the mountains. There's such a cave less than a day's hike from here, and a guide takes you out in the morning. This area is known for its spectacular limestone caverns. There are hundreds of caves in the mountain ranges. It would be a shame not to visit at least one while we're so close…especially since you want to venture outside."

She could tell by his voice that the prospect enticed him.

"All right," she said after a moment. "A spirit cave. First thing tomorrow morning." Another shiver coursed through her.

"Wonderful! And we'll manage to make time for an elephant ride or some rafting before we leave," he added. "And maybe see the long-necked women and that big Buddhist temple. But for the moment, since it's raining…" He drew her toward the bed.

2

At first glance, Annja couldn't tell whether the guide was thirty or fifty. His eyes were bright, hinting at youth, but his skin was tanned and leathery from the sun, the wrinkles deep especially at the edges of his eyes. Careworn, she judged his face. His black hair was thin and short, slick with either sweat or oil, and his shoulders hunched slightly.

He smiled broadly and nodded to their little group. "Zakkarat," he said, holding his index finger to his chest.

He wore khaki pants, frayed and stained green and brown at the ankles as if he'd never bothered to hem them, instead letting the ground and his heels wear the fabric down to a more suitable length. He had a faded polo shirt with an illustration of a gibbon on it, and over that an unbuttoned short-sleeved shirt that was a riot of color—red, blue, green, with birds and flowers. He also wore a cord around his neck with a whistle dangling from it and old black-and-white tennis shoes.

"Zakkarat," he repeated. "Zakkarat Tak-sin. Your guide to Tham Lod Cave."

Luartaro reached for Annja's hand and swung it as if he was a child. He was smiling, too, obviously happy to be off to the spirit cave, as the pamphlet called it. His skin felt warm against hers, and she intertwined her fingers with his and reveled in his boyish attitude.

With them were two other couples, one in their twenties—on an ecohoneymoon, they'd proudly announced. The other was a middle-aged Australian pair who were on their third trip to Thailand.

"Comfortable shoes, all?" Zakkarat looked at everyone's feet.

"Comfortable shoes, yes," Luartaro replied. The others nodded in agreement.

"Five, six miles to the cave," Zakkarat said. "Two hundred baht now, more later for extras. Not much more. This is one of the cheapest trips for tourists."

Luartaro was quick to pay the guide, whispering to Annja that the pamphlet said there would be a charge to enter the cave and for the raft.

After passing out small water bottles, Zakkarat led the way. He had a quick gait and was nimble, ducking under branches and stepping over ruts, and Annja put him closer to thirty for it. He chattered as he went, pointing first to the tops of the mountains and mentioning the mist. They were unlike other mountains she'd traipsed through, certainly unlike the familiar Rockies and the mountains she and Luartaro had combed through for the ancient penguin remains. These peaks had been weathered away into twisted shapes and odd-looking knobs largely covered by jungle. They were beautiful and ghostlike in the mist.

She regretted not bringing her camera. Luartaro wasn't taking as many pictures as she would have, or from what she deemed the proper angles. The path Zakkarat took was wide and flat from the traffic of countless tourists. To the sides stretched swaths of dark green moss, still shiny from yesterday's rain.

Though practically everything was green, there were remarkable variations, Annja noted. Some of the leaves were so pale they appeared bleached bone-white by the sun. Others were a deep green that looked like velvet. Shadows were thick near the ground where the large leaves reminded her of umbrellas. If there were patterns to the colors and light, she couldn't discern them—everything was a swirl.

Had someone taken a picture of the scenery and turned it into a jigsaw puzzle, it would be one of the most difficult ever to assemble, she thought.

Annja listened intently to hundreds of tiny frogs that chirped like baby birds. After a mile, she spotted a fence far to her left, and a tilled field beyond. On the opposite side the ground rose at a steep angle, and she wondered if there were caves beneath.

A bit farther along, the Australian man drained his water bottle and looked at his watch. "My feet are hurtin', Jennie," he said. His wife smiled sympathetically and pointed to a thin river that meandered out of the fields to their left. It widened as they kept walking, eventually paralleling the path, which had started to narrow.

"More than two hundred caves in Pan Mapha in Mae Hong Son alone," Zakkarat announced. He numbingly rattled off facts about their length in meters and feet with so little inflection that Annja guessed he'd been repeating his speech and leading tours so long that he was bored by it all. "This cave we go to, a most popular spot. Tham Lod Cave does not need climbing equipment. Easy on the feet, yes?"

Good for most of the tourists, Annja thought, wishing for something a little more adventurous and taxing.

The path narrowed to the point they had to walk single file, and Annja noted faded signs tacked on trees written in Thai and English advertising a bird show. They'd obviously been posted years earlier, and she wondered if the show still continued and, if so, what it entailed.

They came to a fork in the trail. Zakkarat pointed to his right and said, "Temple. Tours available there, too." Through the mist, Annja could barely make out a large stone building with hints of ornate corners. The other course, the one they followed along the river, led to an old wooden gate that hung off its hinges and which they easily stepped through.

The path became rougher, and gnarled tree roots poked through here and there. Zakkarat slowed his pace and jabbed his finger at the largest roots.

"Take care," he warned. "Take care that you do not trip." He nodded to another sign advertising a bird show. "Going out with a big group tomorrow night for the birds."

"So there *is* a bird show," Annja mused.

"Ain't there birds out now?" This came from Jennie, who was looking up into the trees and alternately watching her husband, who was still grumbling about his feet.

Apparently, she'd not noticed the other bird-show signs.

"Ah, there's a red one with black streaks on its wings." Jennie pointed. "And there's another red one. So what's with the bird show? Are they trained? Parrots?"

The ecotourist wife answered before Zakkarat had a chance. "We're in the bird group tomorrow night," she said. "At sunset, all the bats fly out of the cave we're going to right now and a colony of swifts fly in. Trading places, if you will. There are supposed to be three or four hundred thousand of them. The swifts have adapted to living in the cave and hang on the stalactites like they would tree branches. This is the only place in the world this happens, I've heard. We bought some ultra-high-speed film for it. No digital camera for me." She pointed to the expensive-looking camera around her neck.

"You can come back tomorrow to see the birds if you want, Jennie. I'm not walking back out here again," the Australian husband announced. "I'm too old for this nonsense. My blisters have blisters. I'm picking our next holiday. A beach somewhere so I can park my bum. Maybe Hawaii? Or Aruba on some package deal?"

The river practically butted up against the path as they made their way. They stopped at a collection of small huts, one of which offered concessions, another of which shaded a dock. It was thirty more baht per person for the bamboo raft ride to the cave.

Luartaro and Annja were the first couple on board.

Zakkarat used a pole to edge the raft away from the bank. "Not deep here," he said. "But it is wide. Taking this raft is better than wading, yes? Stay dry by taking this raft. The Shan tribe provides the rafts and gets the baht here. That is good."

He pointed to a woman and child near one of the huts.

"Tourism money has cut the Shan's need for slash-and-burn rice farming. That is very good."

"Are you a member of the Shan tribe?" Luartaro asked.

"Yes. All the people in my tribe respect the caves and their creatures—the birds, bats, fish and snakes. The tourists who come to see the caves are helping our community."

The raft floated with the current for several minutes before Zakkarat poled it to a stop against the opposite shore and motioned his passengers to get off.

A young boy collected a few more baht from everyone.

The cave loomed sharply to the right, and Zakkarat took the lead and gestured to a half-dozen crude wooden steps that had been built next to the entrance.

"Follow me, please."

Annja took the first spot in line and was quickly swallowed by a cavern filled with stalagmites, small sinkholes and vents.

The change in temperature hit her immediately. The air was cool from her knees down, closest to the ground. Above that it remained warm and humid. The light had changed, too, and Annja closed her eyes for a moment. When she opened them, they had adjusted better to the dimness.

She looked up, but couldn't see the ceiling; it was lost in overlapping shadows dotted with the tips of stalactites.

"Cave elephant," Zakkarat said, pointing to a formation of rock and limestone that had been fashioned by water dripping across it through the centuries.

Annja could make out the broad shape of it and the outline that could be construed as ears and a trunk.

"Cave dog. Cave monkey." Zakkarat pointed to other limestone formations that were not quite so easy to make out. "Cave crocodile."

The ecowife pointed to one that looked like a snake and snapped a picture of it.

Annja shielded her eyes as the woman took another picture and then another, the flash in the darkness almost painful in its sudden brightness.

"So it's called a spirit cave because of the animal spirits that fill it, right? Spirits in the lime, I guess you could call them," the ecowife said.

She took several more shots of other formations in rapid succession and of the natural limestone columns that extended twenty meters or more to the ceiling.

"Spirits of dead animals? No." Zakkarat chuckled. "Some of the local tribes claim that the souls of the human dead live here. That is why it is called a spirit cave. Those tribes, but not the Shan, will not come here. They fear for their lives. Some other tribes, they are not so superstitious. It is these tribes, but not the Shan, that stole most of the artifacts that were here. But there are some pieces, not so good, for you to see. I will show you."

The group edged deeper into the cave, and bats, hidden by the shadows, started squeaking.

Zakkarat picked up a gas lantern from the floor and lit it. The squeaking grew louder as the light grew brighter. A mud-colored snake slid across the path and toward the wall.

"This is all so beautiful," Annja said.

"Yes," Luartaro whispered. "Though not so beautiful

as you." He took a few pictures of her looking at one of the limestone formations, bouncing the flash so it would not be so disturbing.

They both stared at the immense chamber striped with earth colors and shining in the meager light.

No matter how many caves Annja had traipsed through, she never really tired of them and was always amazed by what magnificent formations nature had sculpted.

Annja felt relaxed in the cave, though she knew from their mannerisms that some of her companions, the Australian husband in particular, were made uneasy by the surroundings. The sense of foreboding she'd had the night before seemed far away.

They walked on, following the bobbing light of Zakkarat's lantern.

Annja could hear moving water a few minutes before they reached another river, or perhaps a branch of the same one.

Zakkarat indicated another bamboo raft.

"More baht, right?" the Australians said practically in unison. "For the Shan."

Zakkarat poled them across to the far side of the cave.

"Follow me, please." He led them up a fairly steep rise to a ledge that overlooked a cavern.

"No rails," the ecowife noted. "We've been to quite a few caves. Not near the safety standards as in Carlsbad Caverns and Mammoth Cave. Or even that Mark Twain one in Missouri. They all had railings."

Zakkarat's course took them around a deep sinkhole and to another chamber from which tunnels branched away. Scattered road cones and faded danger signs blocked off a few of the passages, and Annja suspected there was a risk of cave-ins. Another sign, more recent from its bright paint, dangled from a rusty chain. It read Do Not Pass—Low Oxygen.

"See here? Cave painting. Authentic." Zakkarat pointed to a spot midway up the wall. "One of seven in this cave. But the only one I can show you today. Most paintings are where it is under excavation. Archaeologists from Bangkok found a skeleton under a rock shelf, supposed to be twenty thousand years old. The oldest skeleton found in Northern Thailand. The dig is off-limits, and the skeleton predates the coffins you will see. But this cave painting you can look at. Do not touch, though."

Annja squinted to make out a faded design. At first glance it looked like a shadow or a smudge. Beneath it, affixed to the stone, was a large black-and-white photograph of what the painting had looked like before tourists had rubbed it away by touching it. The photograph clearly showed a deer, an arrow and the sun overhead.

"There's writing on the photograph," Luartaro said. He leaned close and almost touched the picture. "A date. This photograph was taken thirty years ago."

"Pity that people have to ruin things," Annja said. "Inadvertent or no, people don't understand how precious the past is. I wonder what the artist was like. He or she probably painted it with burned bamboo. A lot of bamboo still grows around here."

"The cave paintings off-limits today are in better condition," Zakkarat said. "Perhaps it is why they stay off-limits."

Zakkarat led them up a damp slope, then down, stepping over and through pools of water and past columns that dripped with moisture and glimmered like jewels in the gaslight. They walked down a set of rickety wooden steps, and they reached the river again.

"A beach, I say," the Australian man grumbled. "That's where we're going next. With a book in one hand and a drink in the other. I'll sit on my bum and soak up the sun. Aruba, I think. Or maybe Jamaica. Rum and cola from a bottomless glass with one of those paper parasols in it."

Zakkarat pushed the raft into a darkness that his small lamp couldn't keep at bay. Bats screeched from high overhead and fluttered their wings. The air turned thick with the smell of guano.

"God, the stink. It's incredible. I can't believe we paid to smell this stuff." This came from the ecowife. She doubled over and retched. Her husband hunched over, too, and held his stomach.

"It is the bat droppings," Luartaro said. "That is what stinks so bad. Thousands of bats. Probably hundreds of thousands. Far more than there were in the other chamber. Amazing. The smell is truly amazing."

"Amazingly awful," Annja said. She could tell that even he was affected by the intense smell. She cupped her hand over her nose and mouth and tried not to gag.

Her stomach roiled. She'd been in caves many times before, but none of those had such a large bat population.

Their guide seemed inured to it.

She was grateful when the raft docked and Zakkarat took them up an incline and through a short tunnel that opened into a chamber filled with what looked like coffins.

Though musty and close, the air was considerably better there. No bats were present.

"As I mentioned before, the tribes not afraid of this place stole from it," Zakkarat said. His voice took on a sad tone. "Stole from this chamber and others. Stole some of our history."

He turned up the lantern, and the Australians gasped as more details were revealed.

The coffins were hollowed-out teak logs ranging from seven to nine feet long and were relatively well preserved.

"The pamphlet said they date back at least two thousand years," Luartaro said.

The logs had been intricately carved, and one had deep designs of leaves and vines on it. There were heavy pottery remnants, too, and Zakkarat said the tribes no doubt stole all the good, intact pieces.

Perhaps they'd also stolen the bodies, as Annja couldn't see a single bone left behind. She shuddered as she stepped close to the largest coffin, as if a cold wind had just whipped across her skin. Her skin prickled, as if tiny red ants were crawling over her.

Were there real spirits here? Were they trying to tell her something? Perhaps they were upset at the presence of tourists who had come to disturb their eternal rest. Maybe they were angry that their remains and relics had been stolen and were seeking justice or retribution. She could provide neither for them.

Sometimes she had an innate sense that something was wrong or that a problem needed addressing. She'd thought it came from inheriting Joan of Arc's legacy and the sword, but she'd eventually realized it was more than that. Even when she was growing up in the orphanage in Louisiana, she'd had an uncanny knack for knowing when things were amiss or when something untoward was about to happen.

"What?" she mumbled. "What is wrong here?"

"What?" Luartaro touched her shoulder. "I did not catch what you said, Annja."

"Are there more chambers here with coffins?" Annja directed the question to Zakkarat and hugged herself when she felt the chill intensify. A heartbeat later the odd feeling vanished.

"Not here, in this cave. Not anymore. But there are other spirit caves nearby in this very mountain range," Zakkarat said. "Many more coffins in them. Soa Hin, Tukta. There is a place called 'spirit well,' too, but part of it collapsed and it is not safe. But this cave, Tham Lod, is easiest on the feet and easiest to reach. This is where I take the tourists. It has some of the best limestone formations."

The Australian man snorted, and Jennie patted his back sympathetically.

"Pi Man Cave, too, has teak coffins," Zakkarat continued. "Many, many more coffins there. Ping Yah and Bor Krai, too. Not so easy as this to get to. More climbing and squeezing."

"But you've been there," Annja prompted.

"Yes. Have taken a few people there, to Ping Yah and Bor Krai and Pi Man. But only a few, and that was quite some time ago. There are maps you can buy with directions of how to get there, but I am better than a piece of paper. I am a very good guide."

"Take us there, please," Annja said. "To Ping Yah and Pi Man." The tingling she'd felt moments ago came back stronger and raised goose bumps on her arms.

The cold sensation was almost numbing. She rubbed her arms to keep from shivering. If the answer to her unease was here in this chamber, she couldn't see it. The answer had to rest elsewhere in the mountains.

"Take me to see more of these coffins," she said.

Annja felt for the sword at the edge of her mind, seeking its comfort.

"How many baht, Zakkarat?" she pressed. "For you to take me."

"Us," Luartaro corrected.

"Take us to Ping Yah and to Pi Man and Tukta and wherever else there are more of these coffins. Places tourists don't go." She stood a better chance of investigating without others around.

"You're crazy," the Australian man grumbled.

Zakkarat scratched his head. "Not easy going like this place. We would need a little equipment for steep places. Not much, some ropes and pitons, a safety line. Helmets. Maybe a pulley—"

"Do you—"

"Yes, I have some caving equipment. My father and I used to—"

"How much?" Annja knew the price didn't matter.

"Five hundred baht."

"Done."

"Each."

"Fine."

"Plus extras, maybe. And I will pack a lunch and water bottles for all of us. No charge for the lunch or water."

She realized he was testing her to see just how much she'd spend. "When can you take us there?"

"Tomorrow morning," Zakkarat said. "Very early, we

should start. The day I have free. And tomorrow night I take tourists to the bird show. So we have to be back before sunset. We could get in two caves, I think."

"You're not taking *us* to the bird show," the ecowife said. "Even though I've bought the film, I'm tired and God knows I can't stand this stink."

Her new husband nodded in agreement.

"The limestone caves that you want to go to…" Zakkarat said, moving close to Annja. "They are off any regular paths, as I said."

"I understand," Annja said. "Lu and I are in good shape. Climbing will not be a problem."

"I can see that you are in good shape." Zakkarat smiled. "Tomorrow morning very early we will leave. When the sun rises. Very, very early so we have time to see a lot. As the saying goes, I will give you your money's worth."

Annja continued to feel uneasy as she looked around the chamber and studied the coffins. "You don't mind, Lu? Going to more caves?"

"I would have suggested it if you hadn't. This is fascinating. And I love caving." He reached out a hand, but stopped himself just short of touching one of the teak logs. "Too many people have touched these," he said. "Too many people don't respect the past."

"It's not that," Annja said. "It's not a matter of respect, Lu. It's a matter of ignorance. Too many people just don't know any better."

She searched the shadows, thinking she saw movement—a spirit, perhaps—something half glimpsed or maybe just imagined, something that was tugging her or begging her to solve some mystery.

She decided in the end it was just the play of Zakkarat's light. Still, the troubling cold sensation wouldn't leave her. What was bothering her? What could possibly—

"Did you hear that, Jennie?" the Australian man said.

"Hear what?" Jennie glanced at the coffins, and then at their guide. "Oh, I heard it. Thunder. The man at the hotel desk mentioned that it might rain today."

"Rains come unexpected this time of year," Zakkarat said, frowning. "It is almost our rainy season. Time to leave." He scratched his head. "Let us hope it doesn't rain too much. The paths will be muddy and slippery."

Annja was the last in line this time, taking one final look at the coffins and the shadows and feeling a stronger shiver go down her spine.

Outside, it was pouring.

3

It had rained steadily through the night and was still raining the next morning, though it had turned to a drizzle by the time Annja and Luartaro met their guide outside the lodge.

She'd put her palm-size digital camera and extra batteries in a plastic bag and shoved them in her back pocket for insurance against the weather.

Zakkarat, in the same outfit as the previous day, though with sturdy hiking boots, looked smaller, with his wet clothes hanging on him and hair plastered against the sides of his face. He looked sadder, too, eyes cast down at the puddle between his booted feet, the ball of his right foot twisting in the mud.

"If you do not want to go because of the rain, I understand," he said. "It rained hard last night, and long. Still going. Maybe going all day. The trail will be sloppy and the river swollen."

Annja realized his disappointment was in missing out on the thousand baht he would have earned—

and wouldn't have to share with the lodge or tour company.

"I do not have another free day until early next week," he said. "I can take you then."

"We'll be gone in a few days," Annja said. "Me back to New York." She paused. "But I don't mind the rain, Zakkarat. Maybe Lu does, though, and—"

"I like rain fine," Luartaro said. "When I was a young boy I used to be afraid of storms. But my mother told me that rain is just God washing away some of man's dirt. Rain makes the world clean again."

He tipped his face up and grinned to illustrate the point. "And God knows I want these few days to last forever."

Annja had intended to go to the spirit caves no matter how hard it rained, alone or with a guide. She needed to discover the source of her unease. She'd intellectually accepted that there was a message someone or something was trying to tell her, and she believed that—like it or not—it was her duty to figure out just what that message or warning was and where in the mountains it was coming from.

"Five hundred baht, right?" Luartaro said. "Each? How about six? No. Let's say seven each because of the rain, and that covers all the extras along the way. Half now." He placed some bills into Zakkarat's hand. "The other half when you drop us back here."

Seven hundred baht was almost what they were paying per night for the cabin, which came to a little more than two hundred U.S. dollars. Giving the tour guide twice that amount for several hours of his time was rather exorbitant, especially for this part of the country. But they had only three days remaining of their

vacation, and neither she—nor Luartaro obviously—
were hard-pressed for coming up with the amount. And
judging from his clothes and worn boots, it looked as if
Zakkarat could use the money.

"Seven hundred each." Zakkarat was quick to nod,
his expression visibly brighter. He pointed to an old,
rusting Jeep, which had packs and helmets in the back
and two coils of rope. He'd come prepared in the event
the rain had let up or not deterred them.

"Besides," Luartaro said as he gallantly waved an
arm to let Annja into the front seat. "It'll be cozy and
dry inside the caves." He climbed in the back.

"You think this is a lot of rain?" Zakkarat made a
shrill, forced laugh. "This is nothing compared to our
monsoon season. Good for you that the monsoon season
is a few weeks away. Because Thailand sits between
two oceans, we have either downpours or cool and dry
weather. Wet now, but the jungle and the mountains are
prettiest."

Zakkarat drove part of the way, the tires of the Jeep
easily churning through mud that was several inches
deep in places. The rain both muted and intensified the
colors, and the scenery reminded Annja of chalk sidewalk paintings in Brooklyn that ran like impressionist
watercolors during spring showers. It was a wonderful
blur of green that she found beautiful, and she drew the
scents of the flowers and leaves deep into her lungs and
held them as long as possible.

"Which cave first?" she asked.

"Ping Yah," he said. "It is older than Tham Lod, and
perhaps has the most to see. It is in the same mountain range, and they are not terribly far apart, but it is
harder to get to. Then Bor Krai or Pi Man, as I think

I remember how to get there. We'll have time for at least two. Maybe a third, as it is certain the lodge has canceled my bird-show group tonight. The tourists do not want to walk through all the mud."

"Pity," Luartaro said. "That's too bad about your birding group." His tone was evidence he did not mean the sympathy.

Annja had heard of Tham Lod Cave even before Luartaro had looked this area up on the internet. But Ping Yah and Bor Krai were new to her.

Although a part of her was excited at the prospect of seeing something that an average tourist never would, she couldn't shake her worries over the mysterious sensation that niggled at her brain.

"What?" she whispered too softly for the men to hear. "What bothers me?"

She'd been to Mammoth Cave in Kentucky, which one of her companions yesterday had mentioned. It had more than three hundred miles of tunnels, and she'd walked most of them during her many visits.

Three years earlier in California she'd explored a series of caves created in ancient times by volcanoes and earthquakes. And of course she'd been through the Carlsbad Caverns, which was famous because one of its chambers was larger than a dozen football fields.

In France, she'd climbed through the Lascaux Cave that featured paintings that dated back about seventeen thousand years.

Older still, by as much as fifty thousand years some scientists estimated, were the fossils of bears and other creatures found in Poland's Dragon's Lair.

On the island of Capri off Italy one summer, she'd

journeyed through the Blue Grotto, a four-mile-long cave with breathtaking formations.

Her favorite cave? She thought about it a moment as the Jeep jostled along the road, which was little more than a puddle-dotted path. Perhaps the one in the Austrian Alps, Eisriesenwelt in the Tennengebirge range, one of the world's largest ice caves. Or maybe the Pierre Saint-Martin Cave that stretched from France to Spain, one of the deepest recorded.

In Australia for a *Chasing History's Monsters* special, she'd made a side trip to the Naracoorte Caves, but found them disappointing. The caves were largely a collection of big sinkholes.

Her trip was salvaged when she went to the Waitomo Caves in New Zealand. That had been her favorite, she decided after a few more moments of contemplation, because of the worms.

The same way Zakkarat had poled their group along the river on a bamboo raft in Tham Lod Cave, the New Zealand guide had taken her group in a flatboat into Waitomo.

At various points in their half-hour excursion, the guide had doused the lights. A riot of shimmering stars had appeared overhead. Except they weren't stars; they were glowworms. Annja had counted herself fortunate that day to have seen something so unique and glorious.

She continued to run the names of caves through her head—ones she'd been to, ones she had no intention of visiting and ones she would like to see while she was still young. She couldn't recall the name of the cave system in China that was perhaps the longest in the world. That was on her must-see list.

The mental activity was a reasonable distraction to keep the chill away. She'd gotten goose bumps again the minute she'd sat in Zakkarat's Jeep, and the sensation of ants crawling on her skin had worsened as they'd headed down the road.

It wasn't the rain and the cool breeze that came with it. The sensation was from something else. Maybe, she wondered, the ill feeling had nothing to do with the limestone caves or the spirits of the dead that had been interred in the teak coffins, but instead about their guide.

Worse, what if her nerves were jangling because of Luartaro? Was either of the men in danger—or dangerous? Would Roux know what was troubling her?

No, it's the caves, she thought. Maybe not the caves themselves, but something in the mountains.

She realized Luartaro was talking, and she'd missed most of what he'd said—something about the limestone formations they'd seen yesterday.

Zakkarat chattered, too.

She pretended to be distracted by the scenery and pushed their voices to the background.

Her mind touched Joan's sword—her sword. It waited for her.

But it would have to wait for quite some time, she thought. It had no place in her vacation—especially with Luartaro around. She didn't want him to see that part of her life. Still, its presence reassured her.

The Jeep slid to the side of the trail, the front bumper coming to rest against an acacia tree as mud flew away from the back tires.

The jolt jarred Annja into alertness.

The trail they'd been bouncing along had suddenly

disappeared, as if the jungle had reached out and swallowed it.

"The rest of the way we go on foot," Zakkarat said. He turned off the engine, pocketed the keys and grinned at Annja. "God is washing away a lot of man's dirt today." He eased out of his seat and slogged to the back, fitting the largest pack over one shoulder and a coil of rope over the other. He put on one of the helmets so he would not have to bother carrying it. "Good thing you two wore boots today. And a good thing it does not rain inside the caves. We can dry out quickly inside."

Luartaro took another pack and the second coil of rope, also putting on a helmet and gallantly leaving Annja the smallest pack to carry.

The rain was coming down harder, thrumming against the hood of the Jeep. It splattered against the big leaves and the mud and her shoulders, then against the helmet she put on. She fell in behind Zakkarat and Luartaro and continued to listen to the rain.

"You walk fast," Zakkarat said after half a mile or more had passed. "Good thing, that. It leaves more time for the caves and less time in the mud. Most people, the tourists, they don't walk so fast as you."

Annja noted that Zakkarat was in good shape, no doubt from walking so many miles daily to take tourists to Tham Lod. She could have easily outpaced him, though; she was in that much better condition.

He told them that the last time he brought a few people this way it had taken nearly two hours to reach the first cave. They managed it in less than one, the mountains looming before them. The rock face they started to climb was slick from the rain.

As Annja worked her fingers into a crack, slid her

foot sideways to find a purchase, she grumbled to herself that this was why the typical tourist was not directed this way.

Her foot slipped and she teetered, held in place by just the tips of her fingers and willpower. She fought for balance and slowly righted herself, pressing tight against the cold, wet stone. The rock felt good against Annja's fingers, and her muscles bunched as she pulled herself up behind Luartaro. The exertion was welcome. Even the thrill of almost falling was welcome. It brought a slight flush to her face and chased away the unnatural cold that had been teasing at her gut.

The first chamber was nearly three hundred feet above the jungle floor, and it was a tight fit to step inside, though from the rock face it had looked to have been larger in earlier years. An earthquake or rock slide had narrowed it.

Luartaro had to shrug off his backpack before he could slip in.

Once past the opening, Zakkarat lit a gas lantern and passed Annja a dented flashlight.

"In case," he told her. "You should always carry a flashlight in case something happens to the lantern."

"I have one, too—a flashlight," Luartaro said, slapping a deep pocket in his khaki pants. "And some extra batteries." He stroked his chin and the stubble that was growing there. "So tell us about this particular cave. I find all caves fascinating."

"Fifty years ago," Zakkarat began, "a United States man came to my country to study plants." He chuckled and waved his hand to indicate the high, steeplelike chamber they were in.

"Plants, of all things, led to this discovery. The man

was studying the Hoabinhiam people who lived in this area in ancient times and who were said to favor the limestone caves. The United States man thought they..." He sucked in his lower lip, searching for the word. "Domesticated! He thought they had farmed, not just gathered, vegetables and fruits, but planted them. And domesticated animals. The Hoabinhiam..."

He paused again, grimacing as he obviously searched for the words to phrase his explanation. "My father taught at the university when I was young. Taught history, and so I know about all of the Hoabinhiam because he taught me, too."

"My father was also a teacher," Luartaro said. "Archaeology. I followed in his footsteps, so to speak. He still teaches, guest lecturing mostly at schools and universities in Argentina and Chile."

"You are an archaeologist?"

Luartaro nodded animatedly to Zakkarat. "For quite a few years. Her, too." He pointed at Annja. "A famous one. She is on TV. She is the star of *Chasing History's Monsters*. Ever see it?"

Zakkarat seemed unimpressed about the television mention. "The United States man," he continued, "found this very cave. Burma, we are not far from Burma here. Were it not raining you might see a stream outside through that crack on the other side. Burma is past it. Supposedly the stream was a river in ancient times, and the Hoabinhiam hunter-gatherers lived by it...and lived in this cave."

Still listening to Zakkarat, Annja strolled nearer the closest cave wall. It was covered in drawings of pigs and birds and a trio of images that looked like two-legged lizards. The shifting light from the lamp made it seem as if the figures were moving. Though faded, they were in far better condition than the smudge she saw in Tham Lod Cave.

Zakkarat continued to talk, and she listened closely, about the American fifty years past finding plants—beans, peas, peppers, something like a water chestnut, cucumbers and gourds—all fossilized in this cave.

Annja knew that with a map, she and Luartaro could have likely found this cave with little trouble on their own, but she was glad to have Zakkarat with them, providing information about the ancient-plant discovery.

Zakkarat explained that carbon dating placed all the fossils at roughly 8,000 BC. There had been stone tools, too, which were quickly ensconced in a museum in Bangkok, as well as remains of small animals that suggested the primitive people were not so primitive, after all. They roasted their meat, maybe in containers of green bamboo, a method still used throughout Thailand.

Zakkarat led them into a tight passage with a roof barely six feet high. His voice echoed softly against the stone. "They found pots and pieces of pots, some made with woven cords to make them stronger, some with evidence they were used over a fire. Found lots of tools. My father called them adzes, and they were polished, those tools. You know, the Chinese learned how to polish stones and tools from us, not the other way around."

He stopped when the passage forked, one route rising steeply, the other passage twisting down at a sharp angle. He took off his helmet, scratched his head and then put the helmet back on. "It has been quite some time since I took people here. I'm not sure—"

"I vote for down," Luartaro said. "If it's wrong, we can backtrack and take the other one."

Annja nodded in agreement. She and Luartaro had discussed last night the possibility of going without a guide, as they were both reasonably good cavers. In the end, they had decided to stick with Zakkarat.

"Down, then," Zakkarat said, leading the way with Annja right behind him.

The rock was so thick, she could no longer hear the rain, and they were going deeper still. She tried to imagine what living in these caves must have been like centuries upon centuries ago—without such modern conveniences as flashlights and Zakkarat's gas lantern.

Their course leveled off, then descended again, and the passage became so low they had to crawl. Water covered the floor by several inches.

Annja was struck by the cold air and the stink of patches of guano that floated on it. The floor was alternately squishy and slick with mud, and she struggled to keep her face and shoulders out of the water. Farther, and the air became heavy and saturated with water, the smell of mud hitting her like a wall.

"Underground rivers in these mountains," Zakkarat said. "Maybe they are rising because God needs to wash away still more dirt."

The rock floor was sharp in places, evidence that few people came this way, and it bit into Annja's legs through her now-soggy jeans. Despite it being summer, it was cool in there, and she wished she'd brought a jacket.

"My sister is terribly claustrophobic," Luartaro said. He was a few feet behind her.

Annja realized she knew actually little about him;

she'd never asked about his family. Now she knew his father was a teacher, and he had at least one sibling.

"My sister…she wouldn't… What is the American expression?" Luartaro continued.

"Be caught dead in here?" Annja suggested.

"Yes, be caught dead. Here, or in any of the other caves I've been to. Still, you'd like her, my sister. I hope you get a chance to meet her. Even though she is claustrophobic, you would get along."

Caught dead. Annja froze. She felt certain that whatever was bothering her had something to do with death.

Free me.

She twisted in the tiny space, looking left, then right, then back over her shoulder. Was someone there?

Zakkarat kept crawling ahead, dragging the lantern with him, the jostling and sloshing of the base of it in the water sending shadows dancing maniacally across the walls and reflecting off the wet stone. He was careful to keep as much of it out of the water as he could; if it got too wet, it would go out. Fortunately, the lantern had a reflector in it, which made its light fairly bright.

Annja felt an icy jab rise up from her knees. Had she heard something, or was her imagination dancing in time with the shadows.

"Something wrong? Something I said?" Luartaro asked.

"No, Lu," she said. "Nothing's wrong." She hurried to catch up to their guide.

The passage twisted sharply and, for several yards, Annja and Luartaro had to crawl on their stomachs, their packs scraping against the ceiling, their faces just above the water. Then the passage rose again, and they were back to crawling on dry stone.

"It cannot be far now." Zakkarat's voice bounced off the walls. "I believe we are near. But it has been too long since I've been to this cave. Nothing looks familiar."

"He's earning his baht," Luartaro said. A moment later he added, "I've a thought, Annja. He's taking us to see more of these teak coffins, right?"

She nodded, but realized he couldn't see her.

"But there's no way those coffins could have fit through this twisting tunnel. So the ancient Thai people couldn't have brought them down here. We should have taken the other passage. This is my fault. I suggested we take the downward slope."

"We're all in this together," Annja replied.

A few minutes later they were standing in a chamber that stretched at least thirty yards across and at least twice that high. There was a massive crystal flowstone immediately to their right. It ran nearly the height of the chamber and was dotted with delicate calcite and aragonite crystals.

"This cave," Zakkarat said, "if it is the cave I am thinking of, is known for two different species of blind cave fish. I read about them in one of my father's magazines. They share the same river, and one of them is scaleless and colorless and uses fins to walk up the banks. I have a picture of one at home."

He gestured for them to keep moving. The next cavern was not as physically beautiful, but it contained what they had come to see.

One wall was lined with coffins, and another had larger coffins stacked against it. The air was stale, but clean, and there was no evidence that bats had ever frequented the place. It contained a natural chimney that rose on one end, and Annja would have enjoyed climbing it were it not for the coffins.

"You're right, Lu. There's no way the coffins were carried along that tunnel we came through," Annja said. "All of these coffins had to be brought here another way. They're massive, some of them. And teak is very heavy. Maybe an earthquake changed the passages through the years. Maybe a rock slide. Caves change. Rivers change them, too."

"Change, yes. But—" Zakkarat held the lantern in front of him. The light casting up and out haloed his puzzled face. "This is not a part of Ping Yah I remember. I've seen coffins, but not these. I've not been here before. Perhaps this is not Ping Yah at all. Perhaps we should have taken the other way, and went up. Perhaps that was Ping Yah with the blind cave fish. Not this cave."

He made a tsk-tsking sound, took his helmet off, scratched his head and put the helmet back on. "But you wanted to see coffins, and there are plenty here."

"Yes, we wanted to see more coffins," Annja said softly, gritting her teeth as a wave of cold washed over her.

She stepped to the closest coffin. There were intricate carvings on it, some tugging at her memory, as if she'd seen something similar in a book. She reached into her pocket and pulled out her digital camera. The plastic bag had kept it dry. She took several pictures, and then moved to the next coffin.

What is bothering me? she wondered. Something she couldn't explain had her feeling very unsettled.

Like the coffins from Tham Lod Cave, these held no bodies. Scientists and explorers who had been there before had likely removed them—if there were any to remove. They may even have taken some coffins, too, for it looked as if there were odd gaps between some of them. There were pots inside some of the coffins, probably heavy by the thickness of the clay. They were intact and looked as if they should be in a museum.

"No, maybe this is not Ping Yah at all," Zakkarat repeated. "I am so sorry. The rain, not coming out here for some time…so sorry. I should have looked at a map and my father's notes. I have gotten us lost. Nothing here is familiar to me. I will not charge you so much. We can go back and—"

"I'm not sorry," Luartaro said. "These are magnificent. You did just fine, Zakkarat." He let out a low, appreciative whistle and retrieved his own digital camera. "In fact, you did very well."

Annja's fingers hovered above the teak. She peered inside and used the flashlight to better illuminate a large coffin's interior. Though there was no trace of a body, there was evidence one had been there. The wood was slightly discolored in the shape of a prone person.

What were these people like? What was their view of life and death? And did they believe in an afterlife? How a society treated its dead often reflected the extent to which they valued life. Annja was certain the primitive people placed great reverence on life—or at least on the lives of the people they had interred in the cave.

"So very sorry," Zakkarat repeated, shaking his head. He let his pack slip to the ground. "Should have realized this was the wrong way. These coffins would not have fit in the tunnel we crawled through. *We* barely fit."

"Maybe an earthquake changed things." Luartaro voiced what Annja had said earlier. "There have been earthquakes throughout Thailand and all of Asia. Or maybe—"

"Or maybe they brought the coffins in through there." Zakkarat pointed halfway up the wall, where a wide cleft in the rock looked like the opening to another passage.

Luartaro took a picture of Zakkarat pointing, and then snapped several of Annja and the wall of large teak coffins.

"Let's hope that's a passage," Annja said. She turned away from the coffins and looked back the way they'd come.

Water was spilling into their chamber, meaning the tunnel they'd taken to get there was completely flooded, and the chamber was going to fill next.

"All the rain," she said, her voice cracking with nervousness. "Yesterday, and today. That underground river is rising quickly. We might soon be dealing with a considerable flood."

Again she felt for the sword at the edge of her mind. This time its presence offered no comfort. It couldn't do anything to keep the rising water at bay.

4

"Up! This is flooding!" Luartaro headed toward a section of the chamber wall that looked the most uneven. "Annja, Zakkarat, come on! Move!" Despite his shouts, his voice registered authority rather than panic.

Zakkarat began to chatter nervously in Thai.

It was nothing Annja could decipher, though she felt the fear in his voice. He scrambled toward Luartaro, the light from the lantern he carried bouncing and creating a dizzying effect.

Annja watched the water.

It rose noticeably in the passing of a few heartbeats.

She cursed silently. When she started out that morning, it hadn't crossed her mind that all the rain would affect her exploration of the caves. She should have considered the possibility. She should have realized there could be flash floods—especially since the cave they visited yesterday had a river running through the middle of it, what the pamphlets called "active." Being on vacation had made her mind numb.

They should be reasonably safe, she hoped, as the water likely wouldn't reach the top of the chamber—the roof was so high. Nevertheless, she knew they must look for a way out just to be certain. There was no telling how long the water would remain high and keep them prisoner.

She heard a scuffing sound and turned around.

Luartaro was climbing up the wall toward the dark cleft. The muscles in his back and arms strained and rolled. He glanced back and called to her again.

She looked at the nearest coffin, then back at the water.

The river could conceivably reach the coffins or perhaps completely cover them. Would it damage the ancient teak?

Annja winced at the thought. They should be all right, she decided. No doubt this chamber had flooded in the past, what with the annual rainy season and the monsoons. Perhaps all the rising river was the explanation for no bodies—the water had washed them away and left behind only the heavy teak coffins and the most cumbersome pieces of pottery. Maybe the water had even rearranged where the coffins had been originally placed.

Free me.

She hadn't imagined the voice. She distinctly heard those two words now. They hadn't come from the coffins, though. It was as if they'd traveled through the very stone of the cave and seeped into her head. It echoed like a child calling down into a canyon.

Had Luartaro heard it?

"Lu, did you hear—"

"Annja! Now! We have to get out of here!"

The water swirled around the soles of her boots.

Zakkarat continued to babble in Thai, his words laced with anger.

There was another scuffing sound, and a heartbeat later Luartaro's hand touched Annja's shoulder. He'd climbed back down to get her.

"Annja, we have to leave. It isn't safe here, and that tunnel's flooded. I used to free dive, but not even an Olympic swimmer could hold his breath long enough to get back out that way. Come! The water isn't going to bother the coffins. No doubt they've been flooded before." He shook her. "Please hurry."

She focused her thoughts and turned to face him.

The light was low, as Zakkarat had set his lantern inside one of the coffins by the far wall. Luartaro's face was heavily shadowed, making the angles and planes of it more pronounced and striking.

Did she love him? The question seemed to materialize in her thoughts as mysteriously as the voice did.

His unblinking gaze caught hers.

"The water is—"

"I know," Annja said. "Rising fast. This might as well be a monsoon."

She let out a deep breath and hurried to the wall and started climbing. There were pitons in her pack; she'd discovered that while she investigated the contents during the ride in the Jeep. She didn't need them, however, as she was able to wedge her fingers and the toes of her boots into crevices; natural handholds were abundant.

The muscles in her arms strained as she pulled herself higher. Below her, the water made sounds like the gentle, sonorous noise of a wave meeting a beach.

Zakkarat still chattered, though now she could make out a few English words in the mix. *Hurry. Drown. My fault.* The words were mixed with an interesting mishmash of Thai and English profanity.

Annja certainly understood his frustration. She wasn't overly afraid, but she was disappointed. She would have liked to examine the coffins and the carvings she'd noted on one wall. She could have spent hours ruminating over what the people might have been like. She'd intended to take plenty of pictures. And then there was the echoing voice begging for her help....

Within the passing of a few heartbeats she was at the mouth of the dark corridor, grabbing her flashlight and shining it in.

"This tunnel looks to go on for a while," she called down to Luartaro and Zakkarat. "And it's wide enough that they could have easily brought the coffins in through it and lowered them into the chamber. There's a painting on the wall, too, like the one in Tham Lod Cave. The ancient people came this way."

She turned and peered over the edge. Luartaro grabbed the lantern and waited patiently behind Zakkarat, who had started to climb but nearly slid back down.

Annja cringed when she saw Zakkarat step onto the edge of one of the coffins for a boost.

She'd been so distracted by her thoughts and the water—and the odd, cold sensation that had plagued her off and on—that she hadn't been thinking clearly.

She should have taken one of the coils of rope from the men. She could be lowering it down at this very moment and helping Zakkarat. He was in good shape, but his large pack made him clumsy and off balance.

She should have come out here alone and not put anyone else in jeopardy. "Wake up, Annja," she muttered.

She knelt and extended her hand as far as she could reach. "Grab it!" she called out.

A few moments later Zakkarat did just that, and she tugged him up to the narrow shelf.

She took some rope from him and started to drop it over the side.

"I don't need it," Luartaro said. Pack over one shoulder, coil of rope over the other and lantern in one hand, he managed roughly the same hand- and footholds that Annja had used. He expended more energy than her, however, as the rings of sweat under his arms were deep by the time he reached her.

"Annja, I watched you in my country and thought you were athletic then. Beautifully so. But here…seeing you climb this stone…you are very impressive."

She shrugged. "I like watching you, too. I like the outdoors. And I work out a bit." She smiled and stared down into the chamber.

The water had covered nearly the entire floor and shimmered darkly under the light from the lantern. Annja took a few pictures of the coffins from her high vantage point, knowing they would turn out dark but wanting to preserve the memory of this place.

"After you, Annja." Luartaro gestured at the opening. He smiled. "Ladies first, as they say."

Ladies first just so I'll get going, Annja thought. "How thoughtful, Lu. Thanks," she said. Not that she minded; she preferred leading the way.

She stuffed the flashlight in her pack, camera into

the plastic bag in a pocket, then took the lantern from him and stepped through the opening.

The air was close and musty and she picked up a trace of guano. Bats had been there, but not for quite some time or not in any great numbers.

She ran the fingers of her free hand along the wall as she walked. The stone was smooth and cool, and she would have allowed herself to linger and enjoy the sensation were she not in a hurry.

The ascent was so steep that at first she thought the corridor was an aven, a passage that rises toward the surface. But after fifty or so yards it took a steep downturn and a gentle crook to what she guessed was the east.

"Watch your step, Zakkarat." The guide was right behind her. "The floor's uneven, and there are some hollow spots."

"I have not been here before," he told her. "I would have remembered this. And all those coffins…I would have remembered them, too. I have not been in this particular cave. I took a wrong turn somewhere. Should have brought a map, I know. I should not have trusted my memory. So very sorry, miss. This is not Ping Yah." He rattled off more words in Thai.

She realized he'd never said her name, nor had they ever been properly introduced. He probably never bothered to learn the names of tourists he guided—no practical reason for it, as there were so many and they were only briefly in his life.

"Annja," she said. "My name is Annja Creed. And don't be sorry, Zakkarat. The coffins are magnificent. In much better shape than the ones you showed us in Tham Lod. I hope we can find more."

"I have never been this way, Annjacreed," he said.

He made a worried tsking sound, and she heard him tap his helmet. "Not that I remember, at least. I have gotten us horribly lost and—"

"I say again, I'm not worried," Annja cut in. She truly meant it.

"Me, neither." Luartaro said from behind them. "I consider this just a grand adventure, Zakkarat. Something to make my vacation more remarkable. We'll find a way out of here. Lost is just a temporary condition."

Despite her confidence, Annja's stomach clenched several minutes later when the passage led down into a small chamber flooded with river water.

She couldn't say why, but she instantly thought of Roux as she glanced at the surface of the water. It looked as black as oil, still and mysterious. Annja hadn't seen Roux in quite some time, and she knew that he would admonish her when she met up with him again and told him about her Thailand excursion. And she *would* tell him all about it.

He'd say that she shouldn't have ventured into active caves after there'd been so much rain and that she certainly shouldn't have taken Zakkarat and Luartaro with her, risking their lives. That if she was going to investigate whatever it was that niggled at her brain, she should have done it on her own.

No doubt he'd also grill her about Luartaro, and perhaps scold her for being so impetuous and flying halfway around the world with a man she'd only known for a few days.

The "old man" as she thought of him sometimes took a great interest in her personal life, like a father might. But they were bound together by history and the sword, not by blood. Maybe Roux wouldn't care about her relationship with Luartaro.

She shook her head to chase away the thoughts and tentatively waded forward into the water. It was cool, but not uncomfortably so. She was thankful it was summer, as at any other time of the year she would be shivering from being so wet and so far under the mountain.

The ground continued to slope down and soon the water was around her knees, and then her thighs.

She reached into her back pocket for her digital camera. Even though it was in plastic, she didn't want to take a chance it would get ruined. She put it in her shirt pocket and moved ahead.

Behind her, Zakkarat chattered anxiously and softly in Thai—it had the phrasings and rhythms of a prayer.

"We'll get out of here," Luartaro reassured them. His voice didn't carry quite the confidence it had held before. "We'll find a way out of this. It won't be too long."

Annja moved the lantern in a steady arc as she went, and when the water swirled around her waist she spotted another dark slash in the rocks directly ahead. She took a couple of steps toward it, and the current tugged her gently in that direction.

"Follow me," Annja said as she headed toward the only apparent exit. She went slowly, feeling forward with each step and encountering jagged rocks here and there.

Faint squeaks came from overhead. "Bats." She gestured upward with the lantern. "A lot of them from the sound of it. They got in here somehow, and if they can get in and out, hopefully we can find a way out."

The guano hadn't been fresh enough in the passage

behind them, so the bats had to have flown in another way.

Roux would definitely chastise her about this, she
decided, and it would be justified. But maybe he would
also smile when she told him they'd been saved by bat
droppings.

She ventured into the next tunnel that she came
across, this one wider at the base and roughly egg-
shaped. She thought for a moment the route was taking
her deeper still, but it was only a depression she had
stepped in. After a few more yards, the floor rose again
and the water dropped back down to her thighs.

Bats rustled above her. A good sign, she thought.
Several of them flew away, in the direction Annja was
traveling. A better sign.

Moments later, the water was only to her knees and
she emerged in a chamber. The wider end of it rose
above the waterline, and a half dozen of the teak coffins
were evenly spaced on a limestone shelf.

Annja headed straight toward them, shrugging off
Zakkarat's hand on her arm.

"Annjacreed," Zakkarat said, "the passage continues
over there. See? And we—"

"And we will follow it," she said. "In a minute." She
paused. "Give me just a minute, please."

"These coffins are magnificent!" Luartaro took the
lantern from Annja so she could more easily take pictures of the coffins. He held the lantern high and turned
it up to improve the lighting.

"No bones in these, either. Wait—" He stepped forward, climbing onto the shelf and standing between two
of the coffins. "Here's one, a body! It's small and like
a mummy. A body!"

Annja climbed up next to him and took several pictures. "Mummified," she observed. "Look how tight the skin is…what's left of it. This is amazing. They must have done something to preserve the flesh because otherwise in this damp climate it would have rotted away."

A silence settled, save for the squeaking of bats hanging in crevices in the ceiling and the soft shushing sound Zakkarat made by pacing in a shallow strip of water.

"I don't think anyone has been here for a very long time," Annja said. She pointed to another coffin that held an even smaller body. It was a skeleton with pots arranged around its legs. "Local archaeologists would have moved these things to a museum. The bodies would have been studied and medically scanned."

"Or looters would have stolen them." Zakkarat slipped forward and peered into the far coffin. "Old jewelry here. Ugly, old jewelry. But someone would think it is worth something because it is old and ugly. Historical significance. Maybe we are the first here since…since these people died."

Annja doubted it, but certainly no looters or serious archaeologists had been there. "Thank you for getting us lost, Zakkarat," she said.

She took several more pictures. "Truly, thank you. We'll have to make our own map to this place so people can come back here and get these things to a museum. Maybe get a film crew in here. And so we can come back when it's a little drier. I think my vacation has just been extended." Her mind whirled with the possibilities of bringing in a film crew and taping a special for the network.

Free me.

She froze and stared at the small body. Free it? No, she still got the sense that the voice was coming through the stone, not from one of the coffins.

Free me.

The words were no louder than they'd been before, so she had no way of knowing if she was closer to her mysterious goal.

"We could take the artifacts, some of them at least," Zakkarat suggested. "Maybe we should take the child's body, Annjacreed."

Annja shook her head. "We don't have the means to do it properly. Everything needs to be recorded and—"

Free me.

Free who? she wanted to shout. Free who? And free you from what? Free the Hoabinhiam spirits? The spirits in the lime?

"Annja, we need to get out of here!" Luartaro gestured behind them. "We need to get out of here right now." The water had risen to cover the edge of the shelf. "This isn't good. The water's moving fast. Not good at all. Come on."

He stepped off the shelf into water up to his thighs. He held the lantern high. "Annja! Zakkarat, we have to move!"

She took a dozen more pictures in rapid succession and reluctantly placed the camera in the plastic. She clutched it tight and jumped into the water.

Zakkarat slogged toward the opposite passage. "Do not thank me for getting us lost, Annjacreed. We could well drown here, and no one will find our bodies. We will be like those ancient corpses."

The water was up to her hips by the time she followed Luartaro and Zakkarat into the next corridor.

She paused in the entry to look back at the coffins, picturing the precious mummies floating away, being sucked under the dark, swirling water. Then she shook herself. She was more worried about the ancient remains than herself and her companions!

As she forced herself to turn away, she whispered, "The loss of history." Her throat went dry. "The terrible, terrible loss."

5

Annja was growing more anxious. She held her camera high over her head as she shoved herself forward in the swirling water. The water was at her armpits now, and the current had picked up speed and strength.

Luartaro sloshed along ahead of her, also straining to move faster in the rising water.

Light from the lantern he carried was both bright and eerie in the enclosed space. The walls were close and the ceiling had dropped from where they had first entered. It was only a few feet above her head.

As the lantern light rippled over them, some of the bats hanging from the ceiling squeaked an agitated protest and some of them flew away.

"We will drown," Zakkarat said. "I was wrong to bring you out here with all this rain. The baht, I wanted the baht. My wife, she will not know. They will find the Jeep, but not our bodies and—"

"I don't need to hear this kind of talk," Luartaro cautioned. "And you don't need to be thinking such things. We are getting out of here, Zakkarat. Just stay quiet and stay near, all right? I'll lead us to safety."

Zakkarat didn't reply, but he did increase his pace.

Annja did, too, peering around their guide to watch Luartaro's inky silhouette. He held the lantern high to illuminate the area directly in front of him.

Roux would like him, she decided. He would like Luartaro's athletic, unwavering ease and his determined voice filled with feigned bravado. And Roux might understand why she so impetuously decided to vacation in Thailand with the Argentine archaeologist.

She wanted to find a way out of this cave and meet up with Roux again and tell him about her inane adventures. And she wanted to see so many other things in this world, including a long list of caves. And so many countries. And many, many digs and many sites, both large and small. Her "bucket list" was endless.

Free me.

She also wanted to find the source of the voice in her head.

The water was to her shoulders. It pulled at her clothes and the backpack and rope over her shoulder and pushed at her knees, making it difficult to stay upright. The growing rush of it competed with the squeaks of the agitated bats and Zakkarat's ragged breath.

"Hurry," she said, half surprised at herself for voicing her concern.

As if the bats didn't want to be outdone by the water, they squeaked louder. They dropped, at first one by one, then in groups, flapping their papery wings just before they touched the water. She felt the air of their passing on her forehead and the tips of her ears.

She put her head down and slogged forward in the

direction Luartaro was leading, looking up from time to time to make sure it was the direction the bats were going.

The river smelled fresh from all the rain, and there was only the slightest fishy scent to it. The rocks had an odor, too, and certainly the bats did. Overall, the scent was neither pleasant nor unpleasant.

The pack she toted smelled of oil and the earth, and she briefly considered abandoning it and her coil of rope so she could move unencumbered.

"A dead end!" Zakkarat spat the words. "We will—"

"It's not a dead end," Luartaro shot back. "C'mon. Up here. There's a way through."

Annja pressed herself against a wall to better see around Zakkarat.

Luartaro was climbing. He paused to shift his feet, then reached up and swung himself up onto a ledge that the water hadn't yet reached. Beyond it was a dark space that looked like the opening to another tunnel.

He balanced on the edge and struggled out of his pack. The fit was so tight he had to drag the pack behind him to slip into the passage.

The coffins had obviously not come in this way. There must have been another passage into the previous chamber and they hadn't noticed it, Annja thought.

Through all his contortions, Luartaro had managed to hold on to the lantern. He swung it in front of him as he disappeared into the opening.

As Luartaro moved away and Zakkarat entered the cleft, the light dimmed.

Annja climbed up the steep, wet wall in near darkness. Her breath came in short, sharp gasps in cadence to her movements up the wall.

Zakkarat's hand filtered down into her line of sight like a barely visible offer of help from the gods.

She gripped it and pushed hard with her feet and slid up into the passage.

She patted Zakkarat's arm in thanks and edged away from the opening. The tunnel angled up steeply.

Free me.

Before she could pause to see if she could determine the direction of the voice, Zakkarat began to fret. "There is no way out of here. We will be—"

"Hush!" Luartaro said.

Annja's heart stuttered, and then hammered at her ribs.

If the tunnel dead-ended, as Zakkarat's words suggested, they would be trapped. They could retrace their steps back to the chamber with the high ceiling and wait for the river level to lower, but they might have to swim underwater part of the way.

She was confident she could do it, almost certainly Luartaro, too, but she didn't know if Zakkarat could manage it. The Thai guide seemed spry, but how long could he hold his breath?

"It can't be a dead end," she said. "The bats get in and out somehow."

Please don't be a dead end, she thought as she dropped to her hands and knees and followed the men up the steep passage. A shard of rock bit into her palm. Her pack slipped from her shoulder, and she twisted so that it was cradled to her stomach.

The air smelled old and foul, and she breathed shallowly.

Boots scraped against the rock. Fabric rustled, tugged by their frantic movements. The lantern clanked as Luartaro tugged it along.

There were no bats in the cramped tunnel, but there was a smattering of fresh guano, a stinky but fortunate sign, she thought. Bats had come this way.

Annja fervently wished she'd taken the lead. She didn't like not being in control. She should have squeezed past the men in the previous passage. It wasn't that she didn't trust Luartaro's capabilities. He was an experienced caver, and she trusted him. But she preferred leading to following. She needed to be in charge of her own destiny.

"Feel it?" Luartaro called back. "The air's moving. We are getting out of here. Stay close!"

With Zakkarat directly in front of her, Annja couldn't feel the air moving, but Zakkarat picked up the pace, crawling as fast as the space allowed.

Moments later, they erupted out onto a flat space.

Luartaro reached down and gave Annja a hand up.

She stood and stretched her back. Her spine, palms and knees were feeling the abuse they'd taken from the rocky climb.

She looked around. They were standing in yet another chamber. This one had a high ceiling and a delicious, faint breeze that stirred her hair.

But after a moment, her sense of relief sank. The air—and rain with it—was coming through a needle-like slit directly overhead. It was high above them and looked too narrow for anyone to easily fit through.

Free me.

She spun around, looking for the source of the words.

"Probably couldn't even get to that opening, let alone squeeze through it," Luartaro said as if he'd caught her thoughts. "The stone is so smooth around it and steeply canted. We have equipment—"

"But not the right kind for something like that," Zakkarat supplied. "I brought only simple caving equipment. We have no pulleys and no harness. Those were in the pack I left behind. Lunch, too. My wife made us pickled cabbage and a little *kaeng hang le*. All of it gone. Lost. I thought—"

"You thought that you were taking us to a different cave," Annja said, still glancing around. "Ping Yah, where we wouldn't need anything overly complicated.

"It's not your fault, Zakkarat. It's pouring outside," she added. "This nonstop rain is only going to make things worse. And I'm the one who talked you into coming out here in the first place."

Free me.

We have to free ourselves first, she thought. Her mind raced. She might be able to get to the slit. She had pitons and could probably make it without pulleys or a harness. She knew how to free-climb and could use the pitons as handholds. And she was the thinnest of them. She could try to force her way through.

Zakkarat was small, but Luartaro wasn't, and without a harness it might be impossible for both of them to get that high. Still, if she managed to get out she could go for help and bring the right equipment, a drill that could widen the opening, some ropes. That might be the best option.

"Worth a try," she told herself.

"Annja, look!" Luartaro pointed to a spot high along a wall. "Are those roots? Am I seeing right?"

"Yes!"

"Then, we're near the surface."

"But we're trapped," Zakkarat said. "I brought you here to see coffins, and now we are trapped in one."

"Stay with him, Lu," Annja said. "I'm going up."

She hurried to the stone directly below the roots and reached into her pack for a piton and hammer.

Just as she drove it into the rock, she heard a great whoosh. She didn't have to look to know what had happened.

The river had forced its way up the tunnel and into the once-dry chamber.

Pack over one shoulder, rope over the other, Annja worked fast. Using the pitons as steps, she climbed. The light was faint, and it shifted as Luartaro sloshed around and inspected the cavern. She was certain he was looking for other passages. She prayed he would find one.

The rush of water was loud, echoing against the stone and mixing with Zakkarat's worried voice and Luartaro's reassuring one.

Her breath came in strong, even bursts, and her heart pounded. The toes of her boots scraped against the rock. The rain pattered down, finding its way through the cavern slit. And through all the sounds, the voice in her head whispered, *Free me.*

The scent of the stone filled her nostrils. She canted her head back to gauge how far she had to go to reach the roots and possibly how much beyond that to make it to the needlelike opening.

Her world went to blackest black. She blinked furiously, but nothing changed. She could see nothing.

She could no longer see the slit overhead, or maybe she was looking right at it but was unable to differentiate it from the deepest of shadows cast by the stone. There was nothing as resolutely dark as a cave. She had a flashlight, but with both hands needed for climbing, she couldn't safely reach for it.

Luartaro must have dropped the lantern in the rush of water, or perhaps it merely gave up the last of its gas, she thought.

She knew he was all right. She could hear him calling for Zakkarat, and could hear the Thai man shouting nervously back.

"Annja!"

"I'm fine, Lu."

"The lantern's gone. We can't see anything."

"I'm still climbing, Lu." She took in a deep breath, then closed her eyes and concentrated. She fought against the blackness to remember the image of the cave wall.

She pictured a section that looked like the spine of some large beast and felt a rocky vertebrae shape in front of her face. She stretched up with her right arm, fingers groping against the stone until they wedged themselves in a crevice. She pushed off the last of the pitons she'd embedded and ascended higher.

No use going for more pitons, she thought. While she could probably do that by feel—find the pitons in her pack, place and hammer them in—she decided instead to spend all of her energy on finding natural handholds.

Free me.

Annja let out the breath she'd been holding and centered herself. She couldn't afford panic. Despite the rising water, the voice in her head and the frantic words of her companions below, she had to stay cool.

Annja could not allow herself the luxury of even a

moment's doubt. Concentrate, she told herself. Remember what the wall looked like.

Falling could mean not only her death, but the deaths of Zakkarat and Luartaro. The whole trip had been her idea, as had her need to go cave exploring, and so she was responsible for them.

She thrust the sounds of the water and the men to the back of her mind and focused on the image of the wall. Slowly, feeling the nubs and cracks in the rock, she pulled herself higher and higher.

She worked slowly and methodically and was rewarded with the smell of earth and wood. She was nearing the section of wall where they'd spotted roots.

She wasn't terribly far from the slit she envisioned herself squirming through. But could she free-climb to it in the absolute dark?

She often amazed herself with her physical feats, but the notion of reaching the slit under the current conditions might be impossible. But what other choice did she have? She had to try!

And she was going to use the stretch of earth to help her. She'd dig handholds there to gain a better position to work from and to hopefully retrieve her flashlight so she could get a look at the ceiling.

Luartaro called to her again, but she ignored him. Mind made up and plan conceived, she couldn't risk dividing her attention at the moment.

Annja felt dirt with the fingertips of her right hand. It was hard packed, but presented a good possibility.

While she couldn't dig through stone with her sword, she could dig through dirt to make some hand- and footholds. Her mind stretched out and wrapped around the pommel of Joan of Arc's ancient weapon.

At the same time, she reached up with her left hand and wrapped her fingers around an exposed root. She let go with her right hand.

In that instant she felt the familiar weapon and gripped hard, driving the powerful blade into the earth.

It went in easier than she'd expected. Do it again, she thought, pulling herself up, withdrawing the blade and plunging it in again a little higher. Her arms burned from the exertion of climbing, but she was in too perilous a situation to pay attention to the sensation.

"Annja!" Luartaro called once more. This time his voice was accompanied by a beam of light angling up from below. It wasn't strong, but it was steady.

The flashlight he'd brought, she realized. He'd found it in the dark and was sweeping it in an arc trying to find her.

"I'm fine," she finally called back. "Don't worry about me." Then she pulled herself higher, tugged the sword free and repeated the motion. This time the blade sunk in even more easily and dirt came free around it, showering her face and stinging her eyes.

The earth wasn't at all hard packed, and when she wiggled the sword free more dirt came loose. "Hollow. It feels hollow," she said.

Annja used the sword for digging. It was awkward but effective.

Clumps of dirt and gravel spewed down, and she closed her eyes as she continued to frantically worry away at the wall. Her eyes were no good here, anyway.

There was more than simply dirt. There was a hollow spot behind it. She couldn't tell how big, though.

Luartaro's light was too dim to be of any help that way. Still, her spirit soared in hope. Maybe the hollow was just big enough for her to climb up into it. She'd be able to give her arms and legs a rest before she attempted to free-climb to the slit. She might even be able to retrieve her flashlight and use it to get a better idea of her bearings and to see how many pitons she had left.

She worked furiously, digging at the soil with the blade. Dirt and rocks pelted her face. Moments later, she sent the sword back to the otherwhere in her mind and hauled herself up into the niche she'd dug out. She crouched on hands and knees and sucked in several deep breaths. The taste of earth and the river and the scent of her own sweat were strong on her tongue.

"Annja! Where are you?"

She maneuvered around so she was facing out toward the cavern, still on her hands and knees.

Far below, Luartaro's flashlight was feeble but it faintly reached her.

Her fingers tested the lip of the niche and she cautiously peered over. She couldn't see him, only the spot of light that was doing little to punch through the darkness.

Carefully, she shrugged out of her backpack and retrieved her flashlight. She turned it on and pointed it down. The beam wasn't as strong as Luartaro's, and she flicked it on and off like a firefly's light. She could use Morse code to send him a message, but she doubted he knew the language.

"I'm okay. I'm in a—" She paused and swung her flashlight behind her. "Tunnel." It wasn't a simple niche that she'd carved; she'd managed to knock away a wall of earth that had concealed another cave tunnel.

"I've found a tunnel, Lu!" she called back with as much voice as she could muster. "I'm going to check it out. I'll be right back. If it's good, I'll lower a rope."

"Hurry!"

The panic in Luartaro's single word spurred her. She spun around and, leaving the pack and coil of rope on the floor, she crawled deeper as fast as she could.

After several yards, she was able to stand.

Flashlight in one hand, she jogged toward what she prayed was a way out. The passage canted up slightly, buoying her hopes. She knew they couldn't be far from the surface because of the tree roots.

Her footsteps echoed against the stone. From somewhere up ahead, she heard the squeak of bats and the patter of rain. Thunder boomed and she felt the vibration through the stone.

Annja knew she wasn't high in the mountains; they'd not traveled upward enough for that. But she was near the surface somewhere, a low spot in the range or perhaps a cleft between peaks.

Thunder sounded again, and she sucked in a great gulp of stone-scented air and plunged ahead faster. The sensation of insects dancing on her skin threatened to send her into a scratching fit.

The tunnel descended again, and just when she worried it might take her back to another water-filled place, she stepped through an opening and into another chamber.

It had a hole in the ceiling that opened to the sky.

Free me.

Rain poured through the hole and the place reminded her a little of a South American cenote because of the pool of water in the center where it collected from the storm. From the amount of rain that had been coming down the past two days, she suspected the pool was deep.

Free me.

The words sounded stronger and even more insistent than they had before.

The gray light filtering through the hole in the ceiling and the pale yellow light of her flashlight revealed the rest of the chamber's contents.

There was a soggy rope ladder dangling down and twisting in the wind that whipped its way inside. The rain blew in at an angle and shimmered in the beam of her flashlight.

Free me.

She swung the beam around.

There were more teak coffins and, off to the side, something that shimmered too much to be made of wood. She took a step forward and focused her light on it.

"Oh my," Annja said. The icy feeling that had gripped her in Tham Lod Cave came back in force and dropped her to her knees.

6

The voice in Annja's head was louder and more demanding, but at the same time it seemed calmer, as if she had finally found its source.

Annja wanted desperately to investigate the chamber that very instant. The mystical voice, the source of her unease, was here. There were also all manner of things that she wanted to study, and preferably without her companions around. But she felt responsible for Luartaro and Zakkarat. They were her first priority.

She raced back down the tunnel, retrieved the men and led them to the rope ladder that would take them to the outside and safety.

For an instant, she'd hoped that they would leave so she could spend time in the chamber alone, but in her heart she knew that wouldn't happen. And she couldn't blame them.

"Annja, this is amazing." Luartaro stood slack-jawed. He'd somehow managed to keep his pack, and it fell with a thunk at his feet. "I...I'm at a loss for words. This is staggering."

"Yes," she agreed. Her own pack rested at the edge of the pool. "It is staggering and amazing and more. I need to get a film crew here for *Chasing History's Monsters*."

"There are no monsters here," Luartaro said, his voice an awed hush. "Just treasure."

"Maybe they'll make up a monster," Annja said. Her producer, Doug Morrell, would do that to get a film crew there. Especially if she told him there was a spirit in the lime.

Zakkarat gasped as he looked around the cavern and muttered to himself.

Luartaro tapped their guide on the shoulder. "See? I said that we would get out of here, and she's found us far more than an escape. She's found a great treasure! So there's no reason we have to leave right away. No reason at all. It's drier in here, anyway."

"She will bring her TV people here?" Zakkarat wondered. "To this lost place?"

Luartaro shrugged. "If she can find a monster."

Zakkarat looked puzzled for only a moment before his curiosity for the treasure took over. Both men fell to examining the objects that lined the walls of the chamber, most of which were stacked on small and large crates that undoubtedly held more valuables.

Luartaro's flashlight beam danced from side to side, up and down, setting gold and gems to sparkling. He spotted a large lantern in front of a crate and lit it. There was a reflector in it that brightened up the cavern.

Annja shared their excitement. A part of her wanted to delight in the discovery and giddily take it all in, run from one niche of the chamber to the next like a character in an Indiana Jones movie. It was a dragon's hoard of wealth.

Instead, she focused on finding the answer to her unsettling feeling. That took precedence, she told herself. She listened for the voice.

"Flash floods are expected this time of year, the beginning of the rainy season," Zakkarat said as he scurried about. "I should not have let your baht lure me out here in the rain, Annjacreed. I got us lost. We all could have drowned, should have drowned, and it would have been my fault. But I am glad I did come out. Most very, very glad! *Chop-mak!* And I am very, very glad I got us lost. You would not have found this great treasure had I taken you to Ping Yah. I must tell my wife about this adventure and the gold."

"We take nothing from this place, understand?" Annja cautioned. "Nothing at the moment but pictures." She tugged her camera from her breast pocket, removed the plastic and started taking shots of the entire chamber, stuffing the flashlight under her arm and using its beam to help illuminate the various objects so the pictures would come out better.

The small cavern reminded her of a museum storehouse or a back room of Sotheby's in New York where all manner of priceless antiques were waiting to be auctioned.

"The answer must be here," she whispered. "Is there something in the treasure that gives me shivers?"

She concentrated on the teak coffins, in which Zakkarat and Luartaro seemed uninterested. At first she thought it odd that Luartaro did not concentrate on the coffins immediately; they were the greater archaeological prize. But the coffins weren't going anywhere, so she was certain he would see to them after the lure of the gold faded.

Where was the voice that had perplexed her, she wondered.

She kept listening, but now there was nothing.

There were five coffins, the largest and most intricately carved of any of those she'd seen so far—and clearly in the best condition. Since the chamber sat higher in the mountains, it had likely not flooded as badly before, so though it was humid, the wood had remained relatively dry. One coffin was easily a dozen feet long, and she recorded images of it from different angles. It was empty, but the wood was stained where at least one body had rested inside, and there were pottery fragments laced with frayed cords where the corpse's head would have been.

Are the spirits of these ancient people trying to reach me? One spirit in particular? she wondered. Should they have taken Zakkarat's suggestion of removing the bodies from the coffins in the previous chamber? Maybe that was what "free me" meant. Maybe earlier cavers had heard the voices, too, and had removed the bodies at the spirits' requests. Maybe she was not the first to hear and react to whatever force was trapped there. Would she have to somehow backtrack through the rising river to retrieve those bodies and find her own peace?

The smallest coffin was filled with intact pieces of ancient pottery that made her heart beat faster. Mixed with the pots were porcelain-like covered bowls that were definitely out of place and certainly not from the same time period or culture as the coffins. No archaeologist had been in this chamber, or the pots would have been whisked off to some museum…perhaps the coffins, too, because of their good condition.

What an amazing find, she thought, easily imagining a film crew recording everything in the chamber for a special on the ancient Hoabinhiam people. And she would find a way to get one here, locally hired or sent from New York after all the proper permission slips and paperwork had been filed with the government—even if she had to fabricate a monster.

But what is it that troubles me? Why is the voice silent now?

Annja was determined not to leave the chamber until she got to the bottom of things, so she worked quickly. When she was finished taking pictures of the coffins, she moved on to the treasure that was stacked against the other walls of the chamber and occupying her companions. Luartaro was still mesmerized by the gold and gems.

The gold gleamed warmly in the beam of her flashlight.

"Maybe it is the treasure," she whispered. "But I'd still swear spirits are involved."

Maybe she was too relaxed, now that their freedom from the mountain presented itself in the form of the rope ladder. Maybe she only heard the voice when she was stressed.

Annja tried to clear her mind and focus on the notion that someone was perhaps trying to communicate with her and that she needed to be more open to it.

In doing so, she brushed the sword again, hovering in the otherwhere, some dimension so easily within her grasp. She caught a glimpse of nothing else but the sword, and the cold feeling persisted and made her uncomfortable.

"What?" she whispered. "What are you trying to tell me? What? What? What? Why won't you talk now?"

The rain continued to drum down, and the wind whistled. Luartaro and Zakkarat chattered, oblivious to her voiced concerns, the latter animatedly talking to himself in Thai.

Luartaro was taking pictures, too, and the flash made the gem-encrusted objects burst with color.

Annja finally roused herself from her musings when she caught a good look at what Zakkarat was doing. He was stuffing his pockets. "I said take nothing!" Annja said sharply.

"I am merely looking, Annjacreed," Zakkarat said. "You are looking! You are taking a good look!"

Indeed, she was looking. It was impossible not to look.

The gold figurines stood out—at least two dozen of Buddha, from the size of a watermelon to one roughly half her height. The smallest had emeralds set in the earlobes and where its belly button would be. The most rotund Buddha was set with rubies and diamonds and its teeth were carved from pearls, and Luartaro stood in front of it, snapping pictures. The flash of his digital camera constantly bounced off the gold.

The thin Buddha came nearly up to Annja's waist and had jewels, including a sapphire necklace draped around its neck that glowed in the beam of her flashlight. The largest gem was the size of a date, as large as any she'd seen in the Smithsonian, and she knew it must be terribly valuable.

The statues had to be heavy, and they weren't carried

down on that skimpy rope ladder. Whoever put them there must have used something sturdier to lower them.

And the statues certainly had nothing to do with the Hoabinhiam people or the coffins. But some of the pieces might be as old or possibly older than the coffins. How had all these antiquities come together?

Between each statue were pieces of ivory, bowls mostly, that were so thin and delicate her light glowed through them. There were pieces of jade and coral, some carved into the shapes of monkeys and birds and fantastical creatures that Annja had no names for. A fist-size jade turtle caught her gaze.

Her eyes flitted from one piece to the next, and she bent close to some as she took more and more pictures.

The lodge where she and Luartaro were staying had suddenly become that proverbial mixed blessing. Though it kept the world at bay with its lack of internet and cell service, it would keep her from sending the pictures to her various contacts.

She would have to take a bus into the nearest town to send them. Mae Hong Son was near the lodge. Chiang Mai was much larger, but farther, though it might be a better choice. She would do that as soon as possible— look for a bus, or talk Zakkarat into driving her there in his rusted Jeep.

Local authorities would have to be notified and the area protected from looters. Annja knew Zakkarat might not be able to keep quiet about the discovery and some of his tribesmen might venture out for a little looting. It was an unfortunate but common occurrence when discoveries such as this were made.

She spotted a pair of jade koi with joined, intertwined tail fins. One was pale green with wide, curious-looking eyes and the other dark with its mouth opened as if to catch an insect. There was a brown patch on the side of the pale one that was not part of the jade. Dirt? Dried blood?

"It could be blood," she whispered. She stared at it for several moments, curious how it got there. Someone cut himself on a sharp edge? Finally, she looked elsewhere. "It could be just dirt," she muttered.

There was a bird with a body that was slightly larger than her hand, which was probably carved from ivory, though it looked bright snow-white rather than the aged yellowish hue ivory often turned. Its wings were spread wide, each individual feather carefully rendered. It was perched on a shiny pedestal that had been carved from a piece of jet-black wood that unfortunately had been marred at the base. She took a few shots of the bird.

The flash illuminated another brown splotch. She was certain it was dried blood. She'd seen enough blood since acquiring the sword. She shuddered, finding the splotch disturbing.

How did this treasure get here? she mused. Who brought it and where did it come from? And what about the blood? Did the treasure have a violent past?

She thought of the temple they'd spotted on their walk to Tham Lod Cave. Some of the objects had a religious significance. Maybe she could show her pictures to someone there.

She took only one shot of a flat wooden box that sat on a tall crate. It was filled with thumb-size fish carved from coral. Annja gingerly moved it aside to find a slightly smaller box underneath that was filled with strings of pearls and gold and silver beads.

"The treasure of a king," she said.

"Of two or three kings, maybe," Luartaro added. "The treasure of an entire kingdom." He'd silently slipped to her side, still taking pictures. "Look at that." He gave out a low, appreciative whistle.

One of the strands alternated pearls with smooth, grape-size rubies. It was short, but there was a long one with smaller stones.

Luartaro bent to touch one, but Annja moved his hand away.

"Don't touch anything," she said in the tone of a museum curator scolding a visitor. "And don't take anything." She paused. "At least, not yet. We shouldn't disturb a single object."

"I'm an archaeologist, too." He shook his head sadly. "You shouldn't have to tell me that. I know better than to touch things. I guess I just got too caught up in all of this."

She instantly chastised herself for moving the box with the coral fish. They were all guilty of becoming too excited by the find.

"I know that things should be studied and documented before they are moved. And you don't have to tell me not to take anything, Annja. But tell that to our guide." Luartaro tipped his head toward Zakkarat.

Annja looked back.

Zakkarat was still stuffing his pockets full of jewelry. He had managed to open one of the smaller crates and was raiding the contents. Inside were gold and silver incense burners, bracelets and candle holders, all padded with straw and wood shavings.

"No!" she shouted. "We take nothing, Zakkarat!"

He ignored her, dipping into the crate and pulling out a handful of bangle bracelets and a pearl necklace.

She rushed at him and grabbed his hands.

A string of chocolate-hued pearls dropped from his fingers, the strand hitting the stone, breaking and sending the beads dancing everywhere.

Annja's grip was firm and her eyes like daggers. "Zakkarat, nothing here is ours. This belongs to history. It must be—"

Zakkarat jerked his hands free. The lines on his face were tight and more pronounced in his ire. "Nothing here is yours! This is my country, Annjacreed. And these things might belong to history, but even you can see that this treasure has nothing to do with the Hoabinhiam hunter-gatherers or their coffins and pieces of pots. Old? Yes, the treasure is that, but it is not the same as the coffins. It does not belong here. See?" He pointed to something on the ground at the base of one of the Buddha statues.

"Annjacreed, I do not think the Hoabinhiam were so foolish as to smoke. Or if they were, they would not have smoked Chinese cigarettes."

A crumpled cigarette pack lay on the ground. Near it was a spent pack of matches, a candy wrapper and behind the crate an empty clipboard.

"Clearly," Annja returned through clenched teeth. "Clearly these things do not belong together."

"Stolen, all this treasure likely is, Annjacreed," Zakkarat continued. He bent and scooped up some of the errant pearls and pocketed them. "So I am stealing only from thieves. How is that wrong? I was not a wealthy man when we started out this morning, Annjacreed. I am not like a famous TV woman with baht to spare."

He paused to examine one of the dark pearls. "But I am rich now. My family will want for nothing, and you will not stop me. You do not have the right to stop me."

Annja fumed. "There might be a finder's fee but for now we take nothing," she said.

"*You* take nothing," he corrected. "Me? I will take what I can carry…which is next to nothing when you look at all of this. What I take is nothing. What I take will not be missed."

He continued to speak, but it was in Thai and she couldn't understand him.

Then he spun away and strode toward Luartaro's dropped backpack. He opened it and dumped the contents, then proceeded to stuff it with bejeweled and ivory trinkets. He tried to put the watermelon-size Buddha in, but couldn't lift the statue.

Luartaro put a hand on Annja's shoulder. "I'm not sure you should stop him, you know," he said quietly.

"The authorities—"

"Yes, we can call the authorities when we get out of here, and we can well report him. Maybe we should. But I don't know." Luartaro took a picture of Zakkarat still trying to lift the gold Buddha.

"We should." Her voice was softer and sad. She sympathized with Zakkarat. Here was an opportunity to live well. If she was in his position, would she do anything differently? "We should report him," she said again.

"We'll have time to talk about it on the walk back to the resort…or the ride if we can find his Jeep. We'll have to go into town, you know, to call people about this."

She nodded. "I…I'm not done here yet, Lu."

"And I wager you'll not get Zakkarat out of here until he is so loaded down he can barely walk." He took several more pictures of Zakkarat, who had finally given up on the Buddha and was taking instead a polished horn with monkey faces carved on it. "And best we take a good long look at as much as we can now in case the authorities don't let us back in. We do have to tell the authorities about this."

"Yes, we do." She returned to examining the treasure, glancing over her shoulder at Zakkarat and deciding that he could stuff as much as would fit in the pack, but he wasn't leaving with it.

She was pleased Luartaro thought as she did—that the Thai authorities had to be told about this place so it could be protected. But she was confident she would be allowed back in. She would be persuasive if she needed to be, and the promise of a television special or documentary always lured people into saying yes.

"Coins!" She heard Zakkarat exclaim. "Old, gold ones."

Everything here is old, she thought, though admittedly some pieces in the treasure belonged to a more recent age than the ancient coffins. But some pieces were also likely older than the coffins.

Was this what had troubled her? The treasure from different times and cultures colliding in this chamber? Had something foreshadowed her finding this place? And Zakkarat stealing? And where was the mysterious voice?

The chill hadn't left her. She retraced her steps

around the chamber, looking past golden Buddhas and into niches that contained still more antiquities and crushed cigarettes and wrappers.

Luartaro followed her. "Annja—"

"What?" The word came out far sharper than she'd intended. "Sorry."

"There is something I saw earlier and wanted to talk to you—"

"Saw what? Where? What did you—"

"Not in here. I didn't see it in here. It was when you were climbing the wall in the cavern, when the river rushed in and I had to use my flashlight because the lantern was lost…. I saw you had a sword, an old one. And you used it to cut through the dirt and—"

So he had gotten a good look at her with the flashlight! It was dark, but he obviously had good eyesight.

She shook her head. "A sword? You were mistaken." Though she considered the lie necessary, it grated on her nonetheless. "I used a piton to cut through the dirt. I didn't have a sword."

It was his turn to shake his head. "What I glimpsed was too long to be a simple piton. It was dark in the cavern, but I know what I saw. Where did you find a sword down here? And where is it now? I couldn't see it well, but it looked old. You scold Zakkarat about taking things and yet—"

"There is no sword, Lu. A sword wouldn't have fit in my pack, and there certainly isn't one here." She spread her hands out to her sides and turned in front of him. "See? No sword."

Once more she touched Joan of Arc's weapon with her mind. She hadn't wanted Luartaro to learn about that part of her life.

"Do you see a sword?" Her tone was light and teasing, hopefully convincing. "A trick of the light and the rain, Lu. It's like I told you. I used a piton to dig through the dirt."

She walked to her pack and brought it near the coffins, not wanting Zakkarat to dump it out and stuff it with treasure.

"No sword," she repeated. Annja unzipped the bag and opened it so he could see it contained only pitons, a small hammer and some other small tools.

He shrugged. "I guess you're right. Sorry. It was really dark, after all. I suppose I could have been seeing things."

"And I'd like to see a few more of these things before we have to leave," she said, glad he had given in to her lie. And before I stop Zakkarat from hauling priceless pieces out of here, she thought. But she wasn't going to squander the minutes to argue with the Thai man at that moment.

Annja turned away from Luartaro and went back to examining the coffins. My answer must be here, she thought. Why can't I see it? Why can't I hear—

Free me.

7

Annja did her best to shut out the sounds around her—the rain coming down and pelting against the pool in the center of the chamber, Zakkarat babbling away in Thai and Luartaro pacing and talking and taking photograph upon photograph.

Annja wanted to leave this place and make sure Zakkarat took nothing—at least nothing of significance or that could bring trouble upon him later. A few trinkets or some gold coins, she truly could not begrudge him that.

"But it's not yet time to leave," she said sternly. "Not just—"

Free me.

She stood in front of the middle coffin and stared at the contents. Her eyes drifted to a particular piece, one of the covered bowls she'd glanced at earlier. This time she felt drawn to it.

"That's it." Annja somehow felt a connection to the bowl, and in realizing it, the chilling sensation that had gripped her vanished and she almost felt a sense of peace.

She'd told the men not to touch anything—not that Zakkarat listened. Now she was going against her own advice, but she had to! The voice wouldn't allow her to wait any longer.

She set the flashlight on the edge of the coffin, angled so it highlighted the bowl. But what is it?

On closer inspection she saw it wasn't really a bowl. She moved some of the other things away from it. The container was a dull white, polished and covered with flowing symbols that might be letters, but it was no language that she recognized.

She took a picture, thinking she knew people on the archaeological networks that might help translate it. She took more pictures from different angles and then returned to it, seeing a thumb-size dark brown splotch.

"More dried blood."

She drew in a deep breath. The air was fresher here than in any other chamber they'd been in, but there were traces of old things in it—the teak and the treasure… and now that she was alert to it, she was sure she could smell blood.

She took another deep breath and picked up the scents of the jungle and the rain.

Finally, she leaned forward, fingers gently folding around the container, chastising herself for doing this without gloves but not able to stop herself.

The moment her fingertips touched the surface, images flashed through her mind. The jungle. Rain coming down. Flowered vines twisting in the wind. The black gaping maw of…of… What? A tomb? Men. White men with green-and-black paint smeared on their cheeks, dirt smeared on their hands, their expressions transforming from joy and excitement to being twisted by fear. Pain. Then eyes closed in death and pale skin flecked with blood.

She shuddered and nearly pulled back, but her need to know what it meant was stronger than her discomfort.

Free me.

"This is it," she said more firmly. "This place in the mountains and this…thing."

Something about the container had led her there, had touched her through the teak coffins and the mountain range when she and Luartaro were at Tham Lod and worried at her enough to pull her through chambers and twisting tunnels filled with the rising river. "But what is it?"

She drew the bowl toward her and held it directly in front of the flashlight. The light played across the surface, and she stumbled. A wave of dizziness washed over her, and she almost dropped the thing in her hands.

The container was a skull.

She closed her eyes for a moment, breathed deeply and evenly, and steadied her hands until she could open her eyes and examine the object.

The top part of a skull had been fashioned into a bowl, the jaw removed. It looked as if it had been polished, then engraved with symbols or letters. Some sort of dye had been applied to make the symbols stand out.

No, not dye. Blood.

The etchings were inlaid with blood like a jeweler might inlay gold or a souvenir maker might inlay cloisonné. The lid was ceramic. It was shaped vaguely like a parasol and had a little nub in the center to grasp to open.

Annja set the container on the floor between her feet, brought the flashlight down and tried to remove the lid. It didn't budge, but the images flashed again, more intensely. Dirty, tired faces transformed by excitement, then fear. The jungle all around them.

She could smell the sickening scent of the thick-petaled flowers. She could feel the tiresome rain that had pattered against the men's faces.

Who were they?

When were they?

She felt their excitement at discovering something, though she couldn't see what it was. She shared their surprise when thunder boomed and felt it turn to fear when it was followed by a *rat-a-tat-tat* that was not part of the storm. And she took their last, dying breaths with them.

She released the breath she hadn't even been aware she was holding and was grateful for the air that filled her lungs. Grateful that she was still alive.

The images of the men's faces swirled around her like the thick morning fog on a riverbank, and then dissipated, leaving her numb.

Free me.

Whatever was inside the skull container wanted out. She could almost feel it thrumming beneath the bone bowl.

But should she let it out? Running her finger around the edge of the lid, she felt a hard waxy substance, like a seal. She wanted to pry at it with her nails. But something held her back.

If she was going to open it, she should take the bowl

with her and open it later when Zakkarat and Luartaro were not around. No use jeopardizing them further.

Free me.

She had witnessed some extraordinary things since she'd come into possession of the sword. She truly didn't know what might happen if she pried open the strange container.

She squatted in front of it and dug her fingernails into the wax, clawing at it even as she told herself she should open it later. The same way she'd told herself she should have come out here by herself.

Maybe Roux would have one more thing to lecture her about. But she wasn't going to wait. She couldn't wait.

Something was demanding she open the bowl *now,* an inner voice that had nothing to do with the one saying, "Free me."

"Now, not later," she told herself. She'd not wormed her way through the tunnels and risked the rising river to wait.

The waxy material broke loose and crumbled in her fingers. She held it in front of the flashlight. It was clay, dried by the years.

The lid shifted. She hesitated for just the barest fraction of a second, and then swiftly plucked it off.

Something threw her backward. Pressure slammed into her chest, like so much compressed air, and shoved. Something she couldn't see.

Images flashed through her mind. The paint-smeared faces beaded with sweat and the rain, visages filled with a mix of wonder and horror and finally relief.

She heard the *rat-a-tat-tat.* Her mind wanted it to be rain, but she knew in her gut it wasn't. There were shouts in a language she couldn't understand, a voice thick with a Southern accent shouting.

"Annja? Annja!"

She blinked. Reality slammed back into her mind, shutting out the voices.

Luartaro was standing over her, holding out his hand. "Are you all right?"

She nodded and picked herself up without his help. "I'm fine. Just slipped." Another lie to Luartaro.

"Find something interesting?"

She looked down at the skull bowl, but she didn't touch it again. "Just this. It has dog tags in it."

"Odd place for dog tags, but then this is an odd place for golden Buddhas and crumpled cigarette packs." He took a few pictures of the bowl, and then one just of her. "I'd like to send some pictures of this to the university where I teach. Never saw anything like it." He took several more pictures of the bowl. "I'd like to get that translated. I don't recognize the script."

When Luartaro turned to take more pictures of the rest of the treasure, Annja gingerly touched the bowl, poised to jerk her hand back if anything happened. The voices were gone, as were the impressions of the men's painted faces. She picked up the bowl, cradling it carefully in her hands.

The dog tags were coated with dried blood, and more dried blood covered the bottom of the bowl. The blood had been at least an inch thick when it was poured in. Her stomach knotted at the sight. She stirred the tags with her finger and read the names. Some of them were difficult to make out, the caked blood so thick. But she flecked it off with her fingernails. Thomsen, Gary A., Baptist; Everett, Timothy J., Catholic; Moore, Gordon

A., Lutheran; Winn, Edgar B., Baptist; Mitchell, Samuel R., Baptist; Farrar, Harold B., Methodist; Collins, Robert B., Catholic; Wallem, Otis H., Methodist; Seger, James A., Jewish; Duncan, Ralph G., Lutheran. There were also blood types and social security numbers on each tag, nothing to indicate rank or home city, and *USA* to stand for United States Army.

Not from World War II. Dog tags then had serial numbers, not social security numbers. Somewhere she had picked up a bit of trivia about dog tags, and it had served her well during a session of Trivial Pursuit. Dog tags had been used by the military since 1906. The ones just prior to and around the early part of World War II listed the first name of the soldier, the middle initial, the surname, serial number, blood type, next of kin and address. From 1941 to 1943 they included immunizations such as tetanus, and the soldier's religion. They dropped the address line in the latter part of the war. In 1959, dog tags switched from their rounded shape to rectangular.

These were rectangular, so definitely post WWII, Annja decided.

And not from the Korean War. If she remembered correctly, it was in 1965 that the dog tags changed again, to use social security numbers rather than serial numbers. So these dog tags were from 1965 to more recent times.

Because of the images of the jungle, she doubted they were from Operation Desert Storm or any other Middle Eastern struggle. And while they could have come from soldiers serving at a base in the jungle recently, she somehow doubted it.

The images had to be soldiers from the Vietnam War.

The jungle and paint from the vision, and their location, made her fairly certain.

She felt a sense of relief and an even greater sense of peace. She'd done whatever it was she was supposed to do simply by taking the lid off the skull bowl. She'd somehow freed the spirits.

Had the soldiers the tags once belonged to been captured? Killed? Were they MIAs?

Annja knew a soldier wore two tags on a chain; if he died one tag was removed and brought back with the men who discovered the body. Often the other was placed in his mouth so he could be identified when his body was returned home.

Could she find records of these men?

"We take nothing," she'd told Luartaro and Zakkarat of the treasure chamber. But she was taking this bowl and the dog tags.

In taking the skull she was taking a nightmare thing, not a glittering relic, and somehow that seemed to make it okay.

Annja retrieved her pack, which Zakkarat was eyeing as if he was about to fill it. She removed the last few pitons, and placed the bowl inside. It wouldn't break, though the ceramic lid might. She had nothing to pad it with, so she cut off one of her pant legs from the knee down and used it to wrap the lid. It would suffice, and she would travel carefully.

She took the dog tags out of the bowl, thinking that she should keep them separate from the skull.

"What is it?" she asked again of the skull. She'd seen hundreds of artifacts through her years as an archaeologist. She was normally less judgmental of antiquities, but this piece seemed sinister. She would get to town—Mae

Hong Son or Chiang Mai—by whatever means available and contact some of her internet resources as soon as possible.

Then she would find a way to come back to this chamber with a camera crew, laptop computer, maybe some local archaeologists to help document everything. She remembered Zakkarat mentioning an archaeological team from Bangkok working in the range by Tham Lod Cave. Surely they would want to come here.

They'd spirit everything off to museums. Document it all.

Everything except the sinister bowl—that was for Annja to study.

She noticed that Zakkarat, Luartaro or both of them working together had opened some of the larger crates. They seemed to be filled with a lot more packing material and more antiquities. Luartaro took a few pictures, nudged Zakkarat back and then resealed one of the crates.

She briefly thought about searching for more skull bowls, but she'd heard no more voices in her head, and the chill that had gripped her earlier was gone.

Instinct told her there were no more such bowls.

She walked around the chamber, surveying the piles of treasure. Pieces stood out—embossments, vessels, jars, axes, rings, earrings. They were made of ceramic, gold, wood, stone and silver. Some things were impossibly smooth, like a river had worn away many of the imperfections and most of the details.

"Whoever put this stuff here will be back for it," Luartaro said. "Maybe they're waiting for buyers, or for a way to transport it. This certainly is not the intended final destination."

"It's all illegal," Annja said. "Whatever is going on here is highly illegal. If this was an honest operation, these antiquities would be in a warehouse or someplace else, protected and dry—not in a damp cavern in the mountains that we found in desperation and by accident. There would be guards and security, maybe sensors and definitely cameras."

"So *we* will find the police or whatever authority polices this mountain," Luartaro said. "We'll get somebody out here, and they'll take care of it."

At least one thing has been taken care of, Annja thought, considering the bowl in her backpack. She suspected Luartaro had seen her take the bowl. Certainly he'd noticed that she was missing part of the leg of her pants. But he hadn't said anything. Maybe he didn't mind that she'd taken a "souvenir," as he didn't seem too upset that Zakkarat had stuffed his pockets.

"You're not taking that pack," Annja told Zakkarat.

"Annjacreed, you have no right to—"

"You heard the lady," Luartaro said. "Your pockets are plenty full." He pointed to the Thai man's chest. A gold chain with a topaz-encrusted fob hung from it. "You've taken more than enough to be a rich man."

With a soft snarl, Zakkarat sat the bag down. "You've no right," he said softly.

"Neither do you, Zakkarat," Annja returned.

Just then a thick bolt of lightning cut across the sky above the hole. The mountain seemed to rock with thunder.

"Man has a lot of dirt that God needs to wash away," Luartaro said.

8

"You're right, Annja. No use waiting out the storm," Luartaro said.

He gave the rope ladder a tug. "It should hold. We need to get back and find out who should be notified about all of this."

And so I can also set the proverbial wheels in motion to find out about the skull bowl, Annja thought.

Zakkarat's gaze traveled from Luartaro and the rope to Annja, and then reluctantly to the bag she'd forced him to leave behind. "No. There is no reason to wait out the storm," he said. He shook his head in disappointment and started climbing up the ladder.

Luartaro held the bottom to steady it.

"This storm might last for days, Annjacreed," their guide said.

"After you, Annja." Luartaro shrugged as if he was also reluctant to leave the wealth.

Annja waited until Zakkarat was all the way up, and then she started, placing the flashlight in her pack, and making sure the bag was secure over her shoulders.

Now that they were leaving, her mind began to race with all that had to be done and her stomach churned.

The authorities needed to be notified.

She wanted to get a film crew here before looters or the authorities could spirit all of it away.

They'd likely leave the coffins, though, she decided. They'd left the coffins in the other caves.

Her crew could film them, and she and Luartaro had hundreds of shots of the treasure to supplement whatever show was put together.

Work had intruded on her precious vacation, after all. And she'd had to summon her sword to break through the earth wall. That part of her life had intruded, too, but fortunately she'd managed to convince Luartaro he hadn't seen a sword.

The hole in the cavern roof was just south of an over-grown and thoroughly muddy trail. Perhaps the cavern had been discovered by accident when someone went off the trail, walked across a thin section of rock and broke through. Maybe that particular someone decided to hide the treasure inside.

As she emerged, Annja spotted a tarp caught on a bush and guessed that it had been used to camouflage the hole, but the storm had blown it loose. The rain beat down on her helmet. It pelted her shoulders, almost painful in its intensity.

The ground she and Zakkarat stood on had turned into a sluicy mixture of mud and gravel. She stared at the trail, which was at best wide enough for a vehicle and more likely had been used for mountain bikes.

"Difficult to get a Jeep up here, Annjacreed," Zak-karat said.

"Inaccessible," she said. "Except to someone who is very determined."

"But people did not carry the Buddhas here in their arms, Annjacreed. And they truly did not manage that…" Zakkarat paused, searching for an English word. "Hoard," he said. "They did not manage to hide that hoard in one trip. Many, many trips, maybe."

He didn't meet her gaze when she looked up; he was clearly still regretting that she'd convinced him to leave the treasure-stuffed pack behind. Annja thought he also looked a little bit ashamed, perhaps because of the looting—even if he was doing it to help his family.

She looked around, trying to get her bearings.

They were in a low spot in the mountains, and the rest of the range rose like the spiny backbone of some prehistoric creature all around them. The highest peaks were to the north.

It was difficult to make out details because the vegetation was so thick and the trees so tall. And all of that was blurred into a miasma of greens and browns by the driving rain.

She canted her head up and squinted through the rain. The clouds were swollen and the color of iron.

Luartaro joined them and tugged the rope ladder up and rolled it. "No use making it easy on whoever has been visiting this spot. Let's get rid of this just in case they come back here before we do."

He worked the ends of the ladder free from clamps that had been hammered into the stone. "Got to find a spot to hide this."

He pointed to a clump of high, thick ferns, the leaves of which were flattened down from the rain. "See? We'll be able to find this place again. A parrot plant. Pretty rare even for this area. Find the parrot plant, find the treasure."

Next to the ferns was a delicate-looking plant that had rosy blossoms in the shapes of parrots hanging upside down. Most of the flowers had been smashed against the ground by the storm.

He bent to stuff the coiled rope ladder under the fern, and then straightened in surprise. "What's this? Annja, it seems this hiding place is already being used."

She slogged toward him and peered around the ferns. "A winch and cable. So that's how they got the treasure into the chamber."

She knelt and examined it. "But it's broken, the motor's burned here and here. They probably discarded it."

"And will have to come back with another one," Luartaro added.

"We should get going." Annja stood and looked to Zakkarat. She had an innate sense of direction and didn't get lost easily, but this section of the mountains—like all of Northern Thailand—was wholly unfamiliar to her. "Can you tell where we are? How far we might be from your Jeep?"

The guide scratched his head. "I am not sure," he said after a moment. He slowly turned, raising and lowering his eyes, and then shrugging. "We cannot be terribly far from anything, Annjacreed. There are many tribes in and around the mountains. More tribes now than there were a few years ago. A few thousand Karen from Myanmar—Burma—settled here not long ago to avoid fighting in their country. Other tribes divide."

"Karen?" Annja asked.

"Yes, but not the long-necked ones the tourists like to

see. So if I cannot find the Jeep, I will find a tribe. I will get home, and you will get to your lodge." He dug the ball of his foot into the muddy path and pointed south. "And this muddy little road must lead somewhere, yes? We will not be lost for long." He started walking without another word.

She gave a last look at the cavern opening, and then plodded forward, passing Zakkarat in a few strides. If he didn't know where they were, she might as well take the lead.

The rain felt good against her skin, neither cold nor warm but more than tolerable on this summer day. It smelled good, it and the trees and mud, chasing out the last trace of mustiness from the cave and all the guano that she'd smelled in the various chambers and knew wasn't good for her.

She nimbly avoided what looked like a deep rut from a tire, filled with water and ringed by small green frogs that made chirping sounds.

They quieted and leaped away when Zakkarat, not walking as carefully, stomped by in his effort to catch up with Annja.

She listened to the slap of his boots against the mud and the jangle of coins and whatever else he'd managed to stuff in his pockets.

It continued to grate on her, the notion that he'd stolen some of the treasure. But she did her best to force her displeasure down…and she decided she would not tell any authorities of his theft.

Let Zakkarat provide well for his family and other Shan members. She couldn't fault a man for wanting to do that, and she'd prevented him from taking out the rest, after all. And she, too, was guilty of removing the skull bowl.

She hitched her pack higher onto her back. The bowl pressed against her spine through the canvas.

Zakkarat poked her shoulder. "Annjacreed, what is this finder's fee you talked about? When will I get this fee? How many baht will it be?"

As if you don't have enough treasure, she thought. "I don't know how many baht. A finder's fee is typically what an agency gives someone for discovering a thing of value or interest. Sometimes it is a percentage of the value of the find, occasionally negotiated. Sometimes museums or universities give them, and sometimes—"

"I should have taken more treasure," he fumed. "And you should not have stopped me." Zakkarat chattered in Thai—profanities, she guessed—waving a hand that had several gold rings on it. She pushed his voice to the back of her mind.

At least the odd, chilling sensation had not returned since she'd discovered the bowl and its contents.

But who put the bowl and the other treasures in the chamber? And why? Where did they come from? And where were they going? What was their ultimate destination?

She shook her head, knowing the answers would not come to her on this trail. First, she needed her computer and her contacts, and that wouldn't happen until they made it back to the lodge and then the nearest city. So she focused on other things, the soggy beauty of the trees and the mountains, the tune Luartaro was humming—something lovely and foreign to her—Zakkarat's boots slapping against the mud, the chirp of an occasional frog, the chitter of an angry, drenched monkey and the soft purr of…an engine.

Her head snapped up just as bullets struck the ground in front of her feet.

"Run!" she shouted to her companions as she dived off the trail.

Feet pounded the ground behind her, and she slowed so that Luartaro could slide past, arm protectively around Zakkarat's shoulders as he shoved him into the brush.

The pommel of her sword formed in her hand. She hadn't even been aware of calling it. She instantly dismissed it.

She didn't want Luartaro to see it again, but more than that, it was useless at a distance and against machine guns.

As she ran, she looked back over her shoulder and caught a glimpse of their attackers.

The men were dark-clad and Asian. She had only had a flash of them as she left the trail, but she knew there were four in the Jeep, and more in a second vehicle that was roaring up the trail. Another man was on a four-wheel ATV. She couldn't make out anything else, as she was moving too quickly in an effort to avoid being shot.

They had machine guns, but she could also hear the firing of pistols. They shouted in what she thought was Vietnamese. There was a loud, long exchange and she could pick up only a few groups of words in the mix. What little Vietnamese she'd learned through the years had been from watching travelogues and foreign action films and visiting one of her favorite New York restaurants. She wasn't entirely sure she was catching the phrases correctly.

She heard the thumps as men abandoned their Jeeps and ran after them.

The men slipped and slid in the mud and over the rain-slick ferns just as she did.

But these men were probably fresh and rested, having ridden in the Jeeps up the mountains, while she and her companions were spent from their ordeals in the caves.

Since they probably couldn't outrun the men, she had to get her companions to a hiding place. Then she would double back with her sword and get some answers.

"Annja!"

"Behind you, Lu!" She was, though she could have easily passed him by. She stayed behind the two men, hoping that she would be the target. And also the first to turn and fight, if she had to.

As she ran, dodging leaves and branches that slapped at her face, trying to stay upright as her boots skated on mud and leaves, her mind worked.

It all fit together, somehow—the treasure, the dog tags and now the men chasing them.

The pounding footfalls behind her sounded like five or six men were in pursuit. The machine-gun fire had stopped, but the wild pistol shots still zipped and zinged over their heads and off into the jungle.

Thank God the ones still firing were lousy shots! How many men were there? And did they all have guns?

Mud and rocks spit up and bit into the backs of her legs. Something slammed into her back. "Move!" she said to Luartaro, though they were already running full out. "Move. Move. Move."

She could stop and stand her ground. Maybe give Lu and Zakkarat time to get away. But the odds were so much against her that she couldn't risk it. But maybe she could draw them away.

"Keep going straight," she hissed at Luartaro's back.

She peeled off away from Zakkarat and Luartaro and slowed just a bit. She slapped the bushes and ferns as she ran, making as much noise as she could to draw the gunmen's attention.

It was a good plan, but it didn't work.

Luartaro, gentleman that he was, hadn't followed her instructions. When she'd veered off, he had, too.

She wheeled around just as one of the pursuers slid to a stop and lifted his machine gun.

"Down!" she shouted.

Tiny pinpoints of fire flashed. Bullets tore into the leaves near Annja's head. Wood splinters exploded from a tree.

She gave Luartaro a shove to get him out of the line of fire and leaped after him, taking cover behind the tree. A big hunk of the tree had been torn away. It smelled wounded and green.

She peeked out just enough to place the source of the gunfire. One of the men had found a good spot to see down the side of the mountain and was firing in an arc. Bullets and mud and pieces of pulverized greenery sprayed everywhere, each arc getting closer to them.

Lightning flashed and the ground seemed to rock in response. It was almost like the impressions she got when she first touched the skull bowl, the storm that had raged in her mind.

The rain poured down, not quite drowning out the shouts of the dark-clad men as they searched the undergrowth. One voice rose above the others, barking orders.

A sudden, shrill whistle cut through the clamor.

"Run, Zak!" Luartaro yelled. "Run for all you're worth!"

Zakkarat tried to obey. He was several yards away from them, and Annja could see him leap to his feet and turn to run.

But as nimble as he was, he was afraid, and he whirled and fell into a tangled mess of vines.

Luartaro slipped and slid over to him and tugged him free. He turned around to make sure Annja was near, and then he wheeled and followed Zakkarat's mad dash down the side of the mountain.

Annja leaped over a low bush and followed, dodging from side to side in case their attackers could still see them.

She struck a low branch, and with a jolt that knocked her breath away, her feet slid out from under her.

She grabbed at a bush, a tree, but everything tore off in her fingers. And suddenly, she was sliding on her back, picking up speed.

She scrabbled for another bush, and for a fraction of a second thought it was going to hold, but then it, too, failed her.

She had time for a gulp of air and a fleeting glance at Luartaro and Zakkarat.

Like her, they had landed on their backs. Like her, they were sliding wildly down the mountainside.

Like big ball bearings in an arcade game, they caromed out of sight.

9

Annja didn't hesitate.

She reached for the sword in her mind. The pommel formed in her hand. Her fingers instinctively closed around it, and she squeezed so hard she imagined that her knuckles had turned white.

She rolled and, at the same time, stabbed out at a clump of bushes. Her shoulder jerked painfully as her mad slide was stopped short. She scrambled to her feet.

With her companions out of sight, though perhaps not safely so, she would confront any who followed. It was their best chance of getting off the mountain alive.

She spun and crouched, ready to meet her pursuers.

She immediately spotted four men, several dozen yards away and closing in. There were more, she knew, but the others might have returned to the Jeeps. She'd worry about them later.

One of the four saw her and swiveled his machine gun up and fired a burst. Bullets chewed into the trunk of an acacia tree near her, and she leaped for the tree to use it as cover. More shots rang out and wood splinters stung her face.

The men shouted and raced toward her.

She pushed off from the tree and darted toward another thick trunk, barely managing to slip around it before more shots plowed into the vegetation.

At least they were concentrating on her. Perhaps Luartaro and Zakkarat were safely away, after all.

She held her breath and listened intently. Rain still pattered onto the leaves, and distant thunder rumbled. The slapping of the men's boots on the ground and another burst of gunfire told her they were close.

She sucked in a deep breath and centered herself.

She could tell the men had split up and were coming at her from two directions. So they were smart and organized, possibly military, definitely with some training.

Annja took off on a straight course, tucking and rolling into a smaller target as bullets struck the ground at her feet and splashed her face with mud.

With a last prayer that Luartaro and Zakkarat were all right, she focused her attention on her fight.

She sprinted for a clump of willowy trees and darted between the trunks. Bullets followed her, but not as many as before.

She risked a quick peek and saw that two of the men had stopped to reload their pistols. She leaped toward them, feet churning over the mud-slick ground.

The other two were a little farther back and to the south.

Even as she homed in on the men, she felt reluctance. She didn't want to kill. All life was sacred to her, even that of villainous souls. And while a man breathed, there remained a chance for redemption.

But she couldn't dare take the chance that these men might redeem themselves at some point in the future. There were too many men, too many guns. She needed to cut their numbers.

She raised the sword above her head. Rain pinged against the blade.

One of the men saw her. He rammed the clip into his pistol and brought it up.

He fired just as she rushed in and swept her sword down, slicing into his collarbone and then through it. He screamed as she pulled the blade free and brought it down again. The scream stopped.

She dropped to her knees, grabbed his gun, brought it up and fired at his companion. It was one smooth, automatic motion, and though she hadn't taken the time to aim, she shot him in the chest.

He didn't even have time to scream. He collapsed.

She dropped the gun. She hated guns.

A phrase flitted through her mind, one she'd heard somewhere before. "It is trying to kill a man that you do not even know well enough to hate…"

Annja allowed herself a few quick breaths before she rose and barreled toward the two men with machine guns. She spotted them through a break in the foliage.

They were both running toward their fallen companions.

She planted herself against a tree, her shoulders against the trunk, her backpack pressing against the small of her back.

She spared a thought for the skull bowl, hoping it

hadn't been damaged by the carnival ride in the mud and all the jumping and running. No time to check now.

She glanced around the tree and yanked her head back.

No sign of the men.

She held her breath. There were no sounds of them, either.

Another few beats passed. She peeked the other way.

One man was easing through a tangle of vines, leading with his machine gun. The second man was behind him.

"Two down, two to go," she whispered. And that was given that no more men from the Jeeps had come down the mountainside after her. They'd probably gone back to the cavern to check on their treasure. In Annja's experience, greed almost always trumped common sense.

The southern third of Thailand was open to the Andaman Sea on the west and the South China Sea on the east. But the northern part was sandwiched between Myanmar, once called Burma, to the west, and Laos and Cambodia. Vietnam was not far away, particularly considering the narrow section of Laos. So the men might have come from Vietnam, through Laos and to these mountains.

But why? Normally Annja reveled in puzzles, but only when she had time to contemplate all the components.

She heard the slide on one of the machine guns snap back. Bullets suddenly whizzed past her.

She dropped down tight against the roots of the tree, hoping to be a smaller target. They weren't giving her time for solving puzzles.

The two men shouted, obviously trying to be heard up the mountainside.

She couldn't hear their words, only the bullets biting into the tree she hid behind.

Then one of the guns quieted, and she heard the metallic ratcheting sound of a magazine being pulled out.

She pushed away from the tree and, somersaulting down the slope, jumped up at the last instant as she reached the safety of another thick trunk.

More shots. More shouting.

Her breath was fast and ragged. Her chest heaved and her thighs burned with the exertion.

"Some vacation," she muttered. "Some wonderful vacation."

She sprang away again, to the southeast, slipping and falling just as bullets cut through the air where her head had been a heartbeat before.

She rolled behind a clump of ferns and crawled toward the men.

Stupid! Stupid! She cursed herself for throwing away the gun.

She hadn't been thinking straight since she got on the plane in Argentina to come here, and certainly not since she went in pursuit of the voice in her head begging for freedom.

The pommel of her sword was so wet from her sweat and the rain she almost dropped it. Everything was so terribly slippery. It was proving to be a slippery vacation.

Why did danger always manage to find her? Why couldn't this vacation have been simply a break away from her other life? Would she ever have a normal life?

Not if she didn't stop her attackers, she admonished herself. Focus!

The men slogged closer, sweeping their weapons in a waist-level arc and firing blindly.

But as long as they were firing so wildly, it meant they didn't know where she was.

She stopped crawling and lay flat. The pack and its skull bowl were heavy against her back. The rain was pattering against everything around her, masking footsteps and words. She strained to hear what the two men were saying. That they were talking meant they were confident in their ability over hers.

She could understand nothing, other than that the words had an edge of anger to them. She didn't have to translate anything to know that the men were intent on separating her from her life.

They passed her, not noticing her among the ferns, and she silently rose up behind them, slipping the pack from her back so she could move more fluidly. One step, two, sword raised over a shoulder and holding her breath.

Lightning flashed. Her blade glittered as it came down and cut through the back of the lagging man's neck.

His head lolled to the side and he staggered forward then fell.

She rushed toward the last man, who had spun to face her.

He'd moved too quickly, however, and lost his footing in the mud. A burst from his machine gun went wild and struck his fallen comrade's body.

She charged him, leading with the pommel of her sword and slamming it hard against his chest. She kicked out and knocked the machine gun from his grasp.

Annja shoved him, and with the ground so slick, he couldn't keep his balance.

He fell back and she dropped on top of him, planting her knees on his chest and hands on his shoulders.

She dismissed the sword and dug her fingers into his flesh.

He struggled to push her off, but she raised him up by his shoulders and slammed the back of his head against the ground. He went limp.

She let out a great sigh of relief. She hadn't been forced to kill all of them.

She straightened and tipped her face up to the rain.

Somewhere she'd lost the helmet that Zakkarat had provided. She supposed he'd be annoyed. She stuck out her tongue and took in drops of cool rain. Her hair was plastered to her skull.

Funny that she'd even worry about losing a helmet, considering all that had happened. Zakkarat would have plenty of money to buy whatever caving equipment he wanted.

She focused until her breath became steady, and at the same time she concentrated, listening for traces of more men coming down the side of the mountain.

Some would surely come in search of their missing comrades, but they would find only bodies and this one unconscious man.

Annja summoned up her strength to break the trigger sear, ruining the machine gun. She tossed it into the brush, then rose and did the same to the dead man's machine gun. She took a holstered pistol from the unconscious one's waist.

It was an unusual model, a Tokyo Marui Colt, manufactured in Japan. It had a gas blowback release and was well maintained, though not a particularly good choice of pistol for any kind of marksman. She tugged free an extra clip and put it in her pocket.

She preferred using her sword, but it was no good at a distance. The Marui would be for just in case…just in case more men came down the side of the mountain. Saving one of the machine guns would have given her a better edge, but in her mind that was not an option. Machine guns were remarkable and simple in their engineering, and the military considered them one of the most important technologies—if not *the* most important—from the past century. They let a single soldier fire hundreds of rounds a minute, laying low an entire enemy company. Too many bullets, as far as Annja was concerned.

Working quickly, Annja retrieved the pistols from the other two men, removed the clips and tossed them away.

Annja slung her pack gently over her shoulders, again feeling the skull bowl rest against her back. Surely if it was broken, it wouldn't feel so solid.

She briefly considered climbing back up to the trail to assess the number of men and take some pictures. But she had Luartaro and Zakkarat to think about.

She started off in search of them.

10

Annja heard men shouting, but their voices were growing fainter as she put more distance between herself and the Jeeps that were higher up on the mountain trail. How long did she have before they discovered the bodies of their fellows and managed to track her? And would she have enough time to find Luartaro and Zakkarat and get them to safety before reinforcements came looking?

Annja knew a good scout would have little trouble tracking her, even given the storm. In her haste she was leaving signs behind. And she also knew that the gunmen couldn't afford to let her and her companions escape—not if they wanted to keep their treasure chamber a secret. In the gunmen's desperation, there was no doubt that they would come looking for her.

It was all a matter of how many minutes she had.

Annja searched for the path that Luartaro and Zakkarat had slipped down. She guessed it was a little to the north, and so she angled that way, moving as fast as possible in the tangle of jungle growth, doing her best not to get caught in the ground plants. The foliage was thick where she traveled, and she had to come to a complete stop a couple of times to squeeze through a tight weave of plants. What was proving to be obstacles could also work to her advantage, she hoped, making her more difficult to be spotted from above.

"Damn!" Annja caught her hair in some low branches and with a vicious yank tugged it free. She pulled at a vine and ripped a length off, using it like a piece of yarn and tying her hair into a ponytail so it wouldn't get in the way. She wanted to holler out to Luartaro and Zakkarat to get an idea where they were and to let them know that she was safe, but that would benefit the gunmen as much as her. So she tried to move as quietly as possible. Branches tore at her clothes and scratched her bare leg and face.

She let out a hissing breath and summoned the sword. Slashing branches might not be as quiet as she wanted, but perhaps they wouldn't hear it over the storm. Lightning continued to flash overhead, sending bright yellow-and-white fingers through the thick iron-colored cloud bank, and thunder reverberated all around her. She started hacking in time with her heartbeat, using the sword like a machete and making a little better headway.

Annja couldn't tell how far she'd traveled since emerging from the treasure chamber, or how far she had to go to reach the bottom; the jungle was so thick that all she saw was a blur of green and brown. Listening provided no clues. She heard nothing but the rain and her thrashing. She didn't hear the men's shouts anymore. The incline was steep one moment, gradual the next, and so she had to watch her footing on top of concentrating on everything else.

The sword was impossibly sharp, and not for the first time she wondered if someone had wielded it before Joan of Arc. Had Joan been able to call it as she did? Had it ever been tucked away in a closet in the heroine's mind? Or had it always been with her? And could Joan see her this very moment and watch how the famous weapon was being used to slice through the Thai jungle?

"Stop it," Annja whispered, forcing herself to focus on moving ever faster and looking for a hint that Luartaro and Zakkarat had passed this way. "Where are you, Lu? Where—"

At the edge of her vision she saw a slick patch of mud and tamped-down grass, evidence that her companions had caromed down it in their accidental mad dash. She'd almost missed it and gone too far north. But she picked her way back to the spot, careful not to step in the gush of muddy water that ran like a stream in a furrow it had created. Following the slick, she spotted broken branches and smashed ferns—more evidence of their passage. The gunmen, if they happened this way, would spot the signs, too.

Annja considered slowing her pace and trying to cover up the evidence, but quickly rejected the notion and instead cautiously increased her speed and tried again to listen for Luartaro. Once more she heard shouting, but it was from above and in a foreign tongue.

"Hurry," she told herself. "Hurry. Hurry. Hurry."

She continued to hack with her sword when she came to a tight weave of plants and a twist of branches that threatened to block her way.

"Annja!"

She recognized Luartaro's voice.

"Annja! You're all right!" His voice rose in excitement

and she cringed, practically running down the slope and releasing the sword when she pitched forward, slipping in the mud. She rolled several yards before crashing into a trunk and getting the wind knocked out of her. She scrambled to her feet, wincing at her sore ribs and glancing furiously around for the backpack that had came loose.

Luartaro grabbed her from behind and held her close, pressing his face into her neck. "Annja, I was afraid they'd shot you. I was—"

"Shhh!" she admonished him as she spun around in his embrace. She tipped her face up and meant to tell him more about the gunmen, but he kissed her hard and held her even tighter. After a moment, she extricated herself.

"There are several men left," she said, keeping her voice low. "And—"

"Left? What did you—"

Annja patted the gun she'd stuck in her waistband. "One of the men fell, Lu." Not a complete lie. "I got his gun, fired and—"

"Killed him? You really are amazing, Annja," Luartaro gushed.

"I had to do something. It was a lucky shot, was all." That was a lie. The lies were coming easier for her, and she hated that.

"I'm so glad you're all right."

Despite his embrace, there was something in his eyes and tone that bothered her, something he wasn't saying but was obviously thinking about.

Was it the gun?

Did it bother him that she'd used one of the men's guns and taken a life?

She'd press him later, now she tugged him into the thicker growth where it would be more difficult to be spotted.

"Where's Zakkarat, Lu?"

Now he tugged her. "At the bottom," he said. "He's hurt a little, twisted his ankle pretty bad when we went for a mud ride. I told him to just sit tight while I went looking for you, and—" Luartaro fell silent and cocked his head. "Do you—"

"Hear them?" Annja's voice was so soft Luartaro had to strain to hear her. "Yes, they're coming down, looking for us. I can't tell how many." She spotted the pack she'd dropped and pulled away from him to retrieve it. The canvas was slick with mud, but she was, too. She slung it over her shoulders, her ribs protesting the motion, and she rejoined him. She wanted to check on the skull bowl, but decided that would wait; its condition was immaterial given the greater concern of the gunmen.

"Too many men," he whispered. "However many there are of those men, there are too many." He moved slower than she would have liked, but he was being careful to pick his way across roots that looked like thick black snakes, so much of the earth around them having washed away. The slower speed gave her a better opportunity to listen for signs of pursuit.

"Hell of a storm, yes?" Luartaro said. They'd reached the bottom of the mountain, and an expanse of water stretched before them. "That little river? It's not as little as before. There—"

On the other side, Zakkarat sat on a flat piece of rock, the umbrella-like leaves of a weeping tree sheltering him from the brunt of the storm.

"It's just wide," Luartaro continued, pointing to the

water. "And fast, but not terribly deep. I got Zak across without too much trouble. Let's go. Let's hurry."

She passed by him, taking the lead and edging out into the water. It tugged her and for an instant she thought about letting herself go with its current. It would be easier than dealing with the gunmen and the storm and whatever else God and Thailand wanted to throw at her. Let the river take her where it wanted. But it was against her nature to simply give up, and so she forged across, leg muscles burning from the day's ordeal.

The water swirled around her hips, and she reached a hand to her waistband, pulling out the mud-caked gun and holding it up with one hand, taking the camera out of her breast pocket and holding it high with the other. She didn't want to risk the river ruining either. She especially didn't want to lose the camera, with all of its pictures of the coffins and the treasure. Annja heard Luartaro sloshing behind her. He was talking softly, but his words were lost in the water and the rain.

The water was up to her shoulders in the middle of the river, the current more insistent there. But Annja was determined and reached the other side, climbing out and plodding to Zakkarat and then looking over her shoulder to spot Luartaro doing the same.

"The treasure would not have mattered, Annjacreed," Zakkarat said, his sad eyes locking on to hers. "The pack I filled would not have made it down the mountain with me."

"But at least *you* made it down," she returned, kneeling by him and looking out across the river for signs of the gunmen. She glanced at his foot. He'd taken his left boot off, and the ankle was terribly swollen and discolored. She suspected it was broken, rather than sprained, and she knew he would not be able to get the boot back on. "I know you should rest. We all could do with a little rest. But we have to keep going, Zakkarat. Those men—"

"Will be after us because of what we saw," he finished. "I know."

"Can you—"

"Walk, Annjacreed?" He made a tsk-tsking sound. "I will have to, won't I?"

"And I will help you," Luartaro said. "Come on. Let's get away from the river. They might be able to see us here." He helped Zakkarat up, pulling the Thai man's arm across his shoulders and taking the weight off his left leg. "Any idea who they are, Zak? Did you recognize any of them?"

Zakkarat shook his head. "Some very bad men, I know that. Very rich and very bad men. And they are not Thai."

Luartaro raised an eyebrow.

"They are Vietnamese," Zakkarat explained. "Or maybe Laotian. They are not Burmese. I have Burmese friends."

Annja struck out perpendicular to the river, eyes downcast, and choosing a path across springy ground cover that might not reveal their boot prints. She tried to avoid stretches of mud where it could be easier to spot their tracks.

Maybe the gunmen had given up and were concentrating on their treasure, she hoped. Maybe because of the storm and the swollen river and the treacherous terrain they had decided to let her and her companions go and spend their time loading up the Jeeps with gold.

A shot rang out, followed by a burst of machine-gun fire, ending her wishful thinking.

11

Annja preferred to avoid physical confrontations. She didn't worry that she would get hurt. Rather, she worried that she would hurt someone else. Violence against another person rankled her. Years past or maybe even long months past, she would have preferred to run rather than fight for that reason alone. That hadn't been her attitude recently, though. Lately she'd tended to confront things head-on and settle matters because she'd almost come to accept the various villainous factors that were constantly crossing her path. And while it bothered her that she'd killed the men on the mountainside—and knew it would continue to bother her for quite some time—she also knew they hadn't really given her any other choice.

She wondered if she should go after the second batch of men who had chased them across the river.

"Maybe I should," she mused. "They're not far away."

But there was still Luartaro and Zakkarat to consider...as well as the automatic weapons that she really had little defense against save for the stolen Japanese pistol that looked so old it might have been manufactured during World War II. So running was her best approach—at the moment.

"Buy some time and distance," she snarled softly. "Find them a safe place." More loudly, she said, "Zakkarat, any idea where we are? Any place close to that trail that leads to Tham Lod Cave or our resort?" She thought she could eventually find her own way back to the resort, but it would take extra time. Directions would help a lot. Even a faded sign advertising the bird show would improve the situation.

"Not too close to that cave, I think, Annjacreed." He spat something out of his mouth and swatted at a fly. "We got twisted and turned around inside that mountain. Hard to tell just where we are. But I do know that we are east of the river. East of the river and somewhere north of your resort. And so we are still lost. I would tell you to follow the river south, but I am not sure that is a good idea right now."

"Too easy to be seen," she said, picking her way in a southeastern direction and increasing her pace, forcing Luartaro to struggle along faster with the injured Thai guide. She knew Zakkarat was in pain, but making him go faster was brutally necessary. "You said there are villages around here."

"Plenty of villages by the river and all around the mountains," he said, out of breath. "We could hide in one. I would not think those men would follow us into a hill tribe village. Too many eyes and too many questions, yes? They would want to avoid the villages."

"Then let's find one of those villages. And let's find it in a hurry," Annja said.

Certainly someone in a village would have a Jeep or ATV or some form of transportation they could use, she thought. And if nothing else, she could leave Zakkarat there to be looked after by Luartaro while she doubled back and dealt with the gunmen, picked them off one by one. No more running.

More gunfire erupted, letting her know the men were persistent. But it did not sound so close this time. Maybe the men had not yet picked up their trail and were firing blindly, or maybe they had found something else to shoot.

"This has been one crazy vacation," she heard Luartaro mutter. "Why did I ever talk you into going to that spirit cave, Annja? Why couldn't I have settled for an elephant ride or visiting the long-necked women? Or why didn't we just stay in?"

She smiled in spite of their dire situation and forced their pace faster still.

Questions continued to dance in her mind. If the men were Vietnamese or Laotian, how did they get into Thailand with all of those weapons? Help from the locals? Through a place where there were no border posts? She also wondered what all the treasure was about, and at what lengths the gunmen would go to find her and her companions to keep word of the treasure silenced. And why put it there, in a cavern in the northern Thailand mountains?

Why put the treasure there?

She would never have discovered it if she hadn't wanted to pursue the voice in her head, if Luartaro hadn't first suggested going to a spirit cave and if she hadn't met him while filming in Argentina and on a whim decided to travel halfway around the world on a vacation with him. If she—

Annja caught sight of a trail to the south, doing a double take to make sure that's what it was. Then she cut a path toward it, pulling at vines and bending branches to squeeze through here and there, and looking over her shoulder to make sure Luartaro and Zakkarat were reasonably close behind. She'd not heard any gunshots in the past few minutes, but she wasn't allowing herself to relax. Annja would not let her guard down until she was certain her companions were safe and she had notified the authorities about all of this.

And get a film crew, she thought.

The trail was narrow and well traveled, as evidenced by the utter lack of vegetation on it. But it was also slick with mud, and the still-pounding rain had created a gully stretching roughly down the center of it. The depression was caused by a vehicle, she decided after a quick look, most likely a motorcycle—and that meant the possibility of fast transportation. With a fifty-fifty chance on picking the right direction, Annja chose to follow the trail east, away from the main river and the gunmen. The insects were thick and formed a cloud around her head; she gave up on batting them away.

If the gunmen found this trail, they would also see her tracks, as she had little choice but to slog through the mud if she wanted to follow it. The trees and bushes that grew along the sides were too thick to walk through, and so it was either the trail or look for another route entirely. She hoped that if the gunmen did find this trail, they would be so many minutes behind her that it would not matter, that she and Zakkarat and Luartaro would be safely ensconced in a village.

Annja looked at her watch, curious how much time they'd spent in the mountain. But the crystal had cracked and it was water filled. It had stopped at 11:10 a.m. She paused and turned to ask Luartaro if his watch had fared better, instead deciding that just like the lyrics to an old Chicago song, it didn't really matter what time it was. She knew it wasn't yet evening; despite the dark gray clouds, there was too much light for that.

"You all right, Annja?"

"Fine, Lu," she answered after a moment, and resumed her slogging trek, straddling the gulley as she went. She was fine, but she was also tired and her muscles burned from the day's ordeal, and so she knew her companions were not faring any better. "I'm fine."

It didn't take them long to reach the end of the trail, which opened onto a small village. The trio breathed a collective sigh of relief. The village consisted mostly of bamboo and thatch-woven buildings, with a few made of sheet-metal panels. Most of them were small with open doorways. But two of the structures were long and shaped like shoe boxes, as if they might serve as a community meeting house and a school. These two had several windows, all with shutters closed against the still-driving rain.

Benches and stools stretched along the outer walls and near some of the muddy paths that wound around the buildings and rain-battered flower and herb gardens. There were no signs of modern amenities, such as power lines or electric lights or—to Annja's dismay—vehicles. Still, to Annja's eyes the village seemed beautiful— primitive and peaceful, almost magical, as if such a village might have looked just like this a thousand years ago. It was as if time had stood still in this part of the

Thailand jungle, and the residents had happily allowed the world to advance elsewhere.

She wished she had come here under different circumstances so she could enjoy it.

She saw several villagers crowded on a bench beneath the awning of one of the large buildings. Under another overhang, children played with a small white dog. She watched as a few youths darted out into the rain in a game of tag. Near them, a boy floated a wooden toy boat in a big puddle.

The people wore simple clothes—sleeveless shirts and straight pants without pockets. The colors were mostly green and pink pastels, with a smattering of khaki. The children were dressed mostly in robin's-egg blue, a few of them with bright red shorts that stood out.

Annja tugged her shirt out of her waistband and covered the gun stuck there. As she brushed aside a large fern leaf and edged into the village, the people saw her and came out from under their shelters to meet them, a dozen voices chattering all at once, not a single word of which she could make out.

"We need help for Zakkarat," Annja said, hoping someone understood English. From the expression on the villagers' faces, there was no comprehension. She gestured behind her to Luartaro, who was still propping up Zakkarat, and she repeated the statement in French, then Spanish. Still nothing. Zakkarat tried, too.

After a moment two men moved forward, one of them waving to the closest long building and taking Zakkarat's other side and nudging him in that direction. If they hadn't understood the words, they understood from Zakkarat's appearance that he was hurt.

Inside, it was dry and cozy—and loud, with rain pelting the roof mixed with the chatter of villagers who had followed them. A few windows were opened to let in a little light, though most of the place remained in shadows. Annja did not see any lamps or candles to improve the situation. She slipped off her backpack and sat it inside the doorway and contemplated taking off her soggy boots to give her feet a chance to dry. She decided not to allow herself that luxury—at least not yet. She needed to look for the gunmen as soon as Zakkarat and Luartaro were settled.

She tried a few other languages, but nothing clicked with the villagers. Zakkarat tried again and finally nodded to one man with a sun-weathered face and a thick shock of inky hair. He said something in return.

"They are Thins, Annjacreed." Zakkarat grimaced when Luartaro and one of the villagers helped him up onto a table at the back of the single large room.

It had the looks of a classroom, with rows of benches and narrow tables that could serve as desks, a table and chair at the front of the room and a bank of shelves stuffed to overflowing with books and papers.

She raised an eyebrow. "Thins?"

"Yes. That man, Rangsan, said they are Thins. There are maybe a half dozen main hill tribes in this region—the Karen, Lahu, Lisu, Hmong, Mien and Lawa. There are smaller tribes that came from them, such as the Thins, and each has its own language. Thins have lived in Thailand for a long, long time, maybe more than a thousand years, and some members of the main hill tribes have joined them."

He grimaced when they stretched out his legs, and he leaned back on his elbows. "Thins have preserved their way of life, making little changes since they migrated here from China. There are said to be less than thirty thousand of them in this country. Most of their villages are in the Nan Province, but some are farther north near the mountains, like this one. The Thins build with bamboo, as you can see. Lots of bamboo."

Annja had noted that nearly all of the buildings were either made of bamboo stalks tied together or woven into thatch panels. Even the floor of the building was bamboo.

"The Thins are—" Zakkarat frowned as one of the villagers examined his sore ankle "—practitioners of swidden agriculture, my father taught me. They farm glutinous rice. Some are Buddhists, but many are just considered animists."

"Their language…" Annja started. She tried to keep her frustration in check; she enjoyed the local history lesson, but now was not the time for it. She needed to be on her way—to find the gunmen if possible, and to find the authorities. She watched as one of the villagers brought in a wooden bowl filled with water and gently cleaned Zakkarat's ankle. Another villager stood by with a strip of cloth, ready to wrap it. "Their language, Zakkarat…what do they speak? It doesn't sound quite like Thai. Can you make them understand—"

Zakkarat shrugged. "Thins, I guess. They speak Thins. Like I said, most of the tribes in Thailand have their own languages, Annjacreed. But this man here—" He nodded toward the one with the bowl. "Rangsan. He seems to understand me well enough."

Annja's words came fast now and breathy with urgency. "Tell Rangsan about the men with the guns who chased us down the mountain," she said. "These people need to know about the guns."

Zakkarat was not as quick with his speech, repeating a few of the words so that the villager could better understand and talking longer than Annja would have liked. "They do not need to know about the treasure," he said softly. "They do not need to go into the mountain looking for gold and finding trouble."

"Ask them…ask Rangsan about transportation, a Jeep, a motorcycle. What is the name of this village? Do you know where we are, Zakkarat? Are we anywhere near your Jeep? Can one of them draw us a map?"

"This place has no name, Annjacreed." He shrugged his shoulders at the rest of her questions and translated.

"It goes without saying there would be no cell phone or satellite phone," Annja continued, talking to herself as much as to Zakkarat and Luartaro. "But transportation. And directions. If they have a map or can draw a map, give us a better reference to Tham Lod and our resort, the river. Anything. Otherwise, I'm about half a heartbeat from heading off on my own." She refused to lose the urgency of the situation.

Zakkarat kept speaking slowly, again repeating words.

Annja gestured for him to speed up, but he shook his head and kept at it.

"How far are we from the resort? From a town?" she asked. Annja paced in a tight circle and listened for the answers. She also listened to the rain, which hadn't let up in its intensity, and the soft chatter of the villagers. "Hurry, Zakkarat."

"Hurry? You do not understand tribal life, Ann-jacreed," Zakkarat said. "These villages are ancient and remote. You cannot do things quickly here. And you cannot go too slowly because time is not measured in hours, or maybe even days. I doubt anyone here owns a watch." Annja noted that Zakkarat's own watch had been broken, too. "Time is measured in seasons and years. And distance? It is not a measure of kilometers or miles, but in time, how long it takes to get from one place to the next…and that depends entirely on the method of transportation or how long your legs are. So, Annja-creed, some of your questions cannot be answered."

She paced in a wider circle, the villagers stepping back to give her room. "I appreciate their way of life. I envy it a little. But, Zakkarat—"

"Annjacreed, a man named Erawan—someone already went to get him—has an old motorcycle. They also have a few bicycles and a good cart and an ox. Another man has gone in search of a doctor who lives nearby."

A burst of laughter came from just outside the doorway. Children were crowded around it under an overhang, one of them parroting Annja's pacing and facial expressions.

"A bicycle will do little good in all this mud. And I don't need an ox, Zakkarat. I can walk faster than an ox. The motorcycle would be good, though. But I'll settle for a map. Ask someone if they can draw—"

"I already asked that. One of them is drawing you a map, the teacher at the front of the room." Zakkarat cleared his throat. "Annjacreed, I have been thinking a lot about that treasure. Maybe those men came to the cave because they were worried about all the rain. Maybe they wanted to move as much treasure as possible before that cave flooded. Maybe I should go back with the ox and cart and take whatever they could not haul away. I could find the place again, I know that. The men will be gone by the time I get back there. I could take…*we* could take whatever they—"

Annja made a hissing sound like a kettle left too long on a burner. She balled her fist and calmed herself before replying. "Zakkarat, you can't take the chance that the men will be gone. If they are still up there, they will kill you. And the treasure will do you no good if you're dead. Your life is worth more than all of that gold."

One of the children in the doorway balled her fist and hissed like Annja. More laughter followed, and the little white dog yapped happily. The children scattered when a broad-shouldered young man in khaki pants and a pale rose-colored T-shirt entered. He exchanged several words with Rangsan, who in turn spoke to Zakkarat. After a moment, Zakkarat translated for Annja.

"This is Erawan, the man with the motorcycle. He says you can borrow his—"

"We will pay him to borrow his motorcycle." This came from Luartaro, who had been silent since entering the building.

Zakkarat wagged a finger. "You have only to promise that you will bring it back when you can. He doesn't care about baht beyond using it to buy gasoline."

"I promise," Annja said, facing Erawan. "I promise to bring it back as soon as possible—and give him baht for gas. Please thank him for me. And please remember to tell all of these people about the men and the guns and—"

The wind gusted, bringing a shower of rain inside

the building. Thunder boomed and beyond the doorway fingers of lightning flickered. The dog yapped shrilly.

A single burst of gunfire sounded. A heartbeat later another followed. From somewhere outside a woman screamed and a child wailed.

Annja rushed past Erawan, reaching under her shirt and drawing the pistol, stopping just outside the doorway and taking everything in.

The children who had been playing streamed into the other large building across a mud-slick clearing, shooed by a gangly woman in a sleeveless pink shift. Others looked out from windows and doorways, eyes fixed on the body of the small white dog that one of the gunmen had shot.

Annja looked around the corner and saw four men, shoulder to shoulder, machine guns raised at waist height. They were some of the dark-clad men who had come from the Jeeps on the mountain. Annja recognized their hard faces. One stepped forward, fired another burst into the dog's carcass and hollered something she couldn't understand. A moment later he repeated it in English.

"The foreigners…the strangers. Surrender them now or everyone dies."

With another burst of gunfire, they advanced into the village.

12

Annja whirled in the opposite direction from the gunmen, hugging the building and darting past a bench, then slipping around the far end of the school, leading with the pistol in the event more men had come in from another direction.

No one else had—at least that she could see. Apparently, there were just the four. And they hadn't seen her yet. She heard the frightened voices of the villagers inside the school, the wails of children across the way, the continued shouts of the gunmen and the rain striking everything.

"Surrender the strangers," one of the gunmen repeated, punctuating the demand with another burst of gunfire. "The white woman and two men. Surrender them now."

The villagers don't understand what you're saying, she thought. They don't understand English or Vietnamese, and only one of them seems to speak Thai. But they understand that you killed a little dog and could just as easily kill them. They understand that you're dangerous. And I understand that you need to be dealt with now.

More children cried, and a woman leaning out a window shouted something Annja couldn't make out.

"Surrender, or we will kill you one by one!"

"I give up!" This came from Luartaro. There was more wailing and chatter and he shouted to be heard over it. "Don't shoot anyone. Leave these people alone. It's me you want."

"No," Annja growled. She slipped around the next corner, intending to come up from the other side, where the men still would not be able to see her. "No. No. No, Luartaro."

"The woman's not here," Luartaro continued. "I lost her in the jungle. Who knows what happened to her. It's just me. Take me and leave this village alone."

There was a quick exchange in which she could pick up only a few groups of words.

"Surrender to us."

The phrase was repeated several times and made Annja furious. The villagers had done nothing to provoke this; she and Luartaro and Zakkarat had simply been at the proverbial wrong place at the wrong time, and seen piles of treasure that the smugglers wanted no one else to know about.

She peeked around the next corner, spotting the four men and immediately drawing her head back. They'd advanced a little farther into the village. Another look, and she couldn't see them anymore; they'd passed out of her line of sight. But she heard Luartaro, again calling for the men to leave the villagers alone.

"On your knees!" shouted the man who could speak English.

Annja crept around the next corner of the building.

"Where is the woman? You lie! She is not in the jungle. She is here. Send her out."

"Here!" Annja hollered as she spun around the last edge, brought the pistol up and fired at the closest man. "I'm right here." She struck him in the hand, her intended target, and he dropped the machine gun and fell to his knees, clutching his bloody fingers and cursing in Vietnamese. The next two charged her, firing, the fourth staying put, crouching to make himself a small target and shooting at something she couldn't see.

I should have gone after them, she thought. Should have left Luartaro and Zakkarat on the trail and gone after the men. Shouldn't have risked them finding us. Shouldn't have risked drawing them to the village.

Then she shoved her second thoughts to the back of her mind and managed to squeeze off two more shots before the pistol jammed. One of the two men pitched forward, grabbing at his chest, where she'd hit him. The other grinned wildly and ran at her, sweeping his gun in a tight arc and firing. Bullets chewed into the corner of the building, splintering the bamboo. Annja ducked back around, tossed the pistol and called for the sword. Before it had fully formed the man fired at her again, ripping up more of the building. Someone inside screamed, and needle-fine pieces of bamboo flew into Annja's arms and legs. She gripped the sword and raised it back over her shoulder and whipped it to the side as he fired again.

She felt blood running down her arm, hotter and thicker than the rain. The wind gusted at that moment, rustling the leaves and rattling the building and providing just enough distraction. The man squinted in the

force of the rain that was coming sideways at him. Annja
closed in, and as he fired again she brought the sword
down, aiming for the machine gun and striking it and his
right forearm. He screamed in agony, blood spurting and
bone protruding. She reached out and grabbed the gun
as it fell, tossing it wide and bringing up her leg, kicking him in the gut and sending him on his back, muddy
water splashing up around him. He writhed, grabbing at
his arm as she raced past him and rounded the corner
of the building to face the fourth gunman.

"Dear God, no!" Annja's throat constricted as she
spotted Luartaro facedown in the mud, the final gunman
standing over him, head canted back and yelling to the
villagers. The one whose hand she'd shot was struggling
to his feet and reaching for a small holster at his side.
She knocked him over, kicking him in the jaw as she
headed toward the last man standing with a gun.

"It's me you want!" she spat. "Me, you thief! Mur-
derer!"

He fired as he turned, and she dropped and somersaulted as she closed the distance. Annja was slick with
mud, globs of it flying off her as she rose and brought
the sword around with as much strength as she could
summon.

Who had Joan of Arc fought with it?

How much blood had she drawn?

And how many lives had she ended before she met
her own end in a pyre remembered for all time?

Had someone wielded the sword before Joan?

And who would have it after Annja was dust?

The tip of blade caught the end of the machine gun
and turned it, bullets still spitting and striking the

school building again and chewing into an empty bench out front.

Annja pulled the blade back again and brought it down and around, powered by the fading strength in her burning arms. The impossibly sharp edge struck the machine gun once more and the gunman's fingers, slicing a few of them off. He didn't holler in pain as she'd expected. Instead, he screamed in anger and tried to bring the gun up again, pulling the trigger with his thumb.

Annja was furious with herself that she'd not gone after these men earlier, thinking they might not follow them to this village…furious that he and his fellows would jeopardize all these innocent people…and livid to the point that heat surged up her neck into her face, burning her like a fever.

Her arms felt on fire as she swept the sword forward, rain pinging off the blade. She'd intended to strike his arm, maiming him and ending the threat of the machine gun. But he moved at the last instant and slipped in the muck. The sword struck higher, slicing into his chest and ripping through his dark clothes and padded vest. The gun went off as he went down. Bullets spit into the mud and into Annja's leg. She sucked in her lower lip to keep from crying out, took two steps toward the man she'd just killed, then fell forward into a puddle.

ANNJA AWOKE ON THE SAME table Zakkarat had occupied, a coarse blanket draped over her, another folded blanket serving as a pillow. Her head pounded, her right arm ached terribly and her right leg felt…nothing. She propped herself up on her elbows.

"Hello, there." A man well into his middle years

tended her numb leg. "I expected you to be out for quite some time longer, Miss—"

"Creed," she replied. Her tongue felt thick and unwieldy. She opened her mouth to speak again, but one of the villagers held a ladle up to her lips and encouraged her to drink. The mixture was a pulpy, fruity nectar that tasted sweet and went down her throat slowly.

"Well, Miss Creed."

"Annja. Call me Annja." She nodded her thanks to the villager. "And you are?"

She had other questions on her mind...where was Luartaro's body, where was Zakkarat, what about the gunmen...where were the two thugs she'd left alive? How long had she been out? It was still raining; she could hear it rhythmically strike the roof. It didn't sound quite so hard as earlier.

Someone had brought a lantern or two into the schoolroom, the glow filled with gnats and illuminating the concerned faces of the villagers and the craggy visage of the doctor. She remembered Zakkarat saying someone had gone to get a doctor who lived nearby. A white man, though well tanned. He was clearly not Thai.

"Nigel Willingson...or Doc as the Thins call me."

British or Australian from the sound of his accent. She could better pinpoint it when he talked more. "Thank you for taking care of me, Dr. Willingson. Where are—"

"Nigel will do, or just Doc. Nothing formal for me anymore. Doc, actually—I prefer that."

Definitely British, Annja decided.

He glanced over his shoulder at a broad-shouldered woman with a careworn face and spoke quickly in what

Annja assumed was the Thins language. "They want
to know why the men came after you. What you did
to make those men so angry they would shoot you…
and kill little Kiet's dog. They want to know where you
came from and when you will be leaving. These are a
peaceful people, Miss Creed."

"Annja," she said. "Nothing so formal for me,
either."

He smiled, revealing crooked teeth stained yellow
by smoking. "We can deal with their questions later…
Annja. Right now I need to deal with your wounds.
I've already plucked three bullets out of your calf. I
have one left to go. They tore into your muscle and did
some damage, but nothing you can't recover from. It
certainly could have been much worse. You could have
lost the leg. And I want to get those bamboo splinters
out of your arm. Give you a tetanus shot just in case…
or have you had one recently? There's a good risk of
infection, all the mud and muck you were rolling in.
Have you had a tetanus shot?" He didn't wait for her
answer, sticking a needle into her leg. "Then I need to
see to your friend."

"My—"

"Mr. Larto." He butchered Luartaro's name.

Her heart leaped. "He's not dead? Lu is—"

"Ah, Lu…much easier to pronounce. I like that, Lu.
No, he's not dead. But he does have a concussion. He's
on another table, er, desk. You can't see him for all the
Thins. Nearly half the village has managed to fit in here.
Curious, they are. Your Lu said one of those bad men
hit him hard on the top of his head with a machine-gun
stock. I have him resting. You're my immediate concern." He spoke more to the broad-shouldered Thins

woman, punctuating his speech with a clacking sound that a few others nearby echoed. "Yes, we'll deal with their questions shortly, Annja. I want to finish patching you up and make sure you're cleaned up properly and are strong enough to travel. We need to get you to a real clinic."

Annja realized most of the mud she'd been wearing had been washed away. She lifted the blanket and dropped it back down. She was naked. Looking over the edge of the table, she saw a wooden bowl filled with muddy water and her pile of mud-caked clothes.

"That would be Som's work, Annja. I asked her to clean you up a bit. You must have been wearing ten pounds of jungle mud. Som will find you something else to wear." He paused and leaned close. "You should be in a hospital, actually. A clinic doesn't have near the facilities. You and Lu and two of those disagreeable fellows— who you took out with a sword, Som tells me—should all be in a hospital. But there are few roads, and they are all flooded, and it's still raining and dark as pitch outside, so you'll have to settle for my ministrations at the moment. But we'll put you and Lu in an ox cart in the morning when hopefully the weather lets up a little bit and we'll get you to a proper place where people far more skilled than I can look after you. Don't know what we'll do with the two disagreeable fellows. The ox cart won't hold all of you."

"Listen, Doc, I—" A wave of dizziness washed over her and she slumped back flat onto the table.

"No, you listen. You're my patient. Much as I'd rather you not be. Much as I'd rather none of you folks were injured in this village. I'm not a medical doctor, Annja. I'm a veterinarian, a retired one at that. Retired to this beautiful country to be left alone and not to be bothered by people shooting at one another."

"A veterinarian? Retired? I don't—" Annja finally succumbed to the sedative he'd given her.

13

Annja's head was pounding when she awoke the next morning, feeling the sun stream in on her face. She wasn't on the table in the school any longer. She was on a thick sleeping pallet in one of the villagers' homes. Luartaro sat next to her, propped against the wall, eyes closed and head wrapped in a pale pink bandage that had a bloodstain on the side. It took her only a moment to realize he was sleeping, his breathing deep and regular. He was wearing different clothes—a pale green tank top over baggy trousers that had cargo pockets down the sides. He'd stuffed the pockets with something so that they looked like the jowls of a chipmunk that had been foraging. The trousers looked several inches too short for his tall frame, the green tank a size too small. She smiled; the latter made his muscles stand out. He was barefoot, his mud-caked boots sitting nearby.

Her arms ached, though not as much as they did the night before, and she felt a dull pain in her right leg, the numbness having worn off. All in all, however, she pronounced herself in more than reasonable condition given what she'd been through. Her stomach rumbled; Annja tended to eat a lot because she was active, and she hadn't had anything since very early yesterday morning. She needed food to help her recover.

"Gotta find something to eat," she said. She made a move to get up and realized she was still naked under the blanket. "Where are my clothes?" she muttered.

Doc poked his head in the door. "Being washed, though I'm not sure they're fit for anything more than rags, what with all the bullet holes and rips. Som is finding something that might fit you well enough. Give her a few moments. She was going to tend to that last night, but got distracted. Things tend not to be immediate here."

He came in and stretched, and Annja saw that the circles were dark under his eyes, as if he hadn't been to sleep at all during the night. He was wearing the same shirt and jeans he'd had on yesterday, all of it spotted with blood and mud, the sweat stains deep under his arms.

"Lovely morning," he went on. "It quit raining about an hour ago. About damn time, eh? Sometimes it rains so much here I expect to see Noah pulling up with his ark." He came to her side, stooped over and reached for her hand, taking her pulse and looking at his watch.

"You heal quickly, Annja. Quite a remarkable young lady, you. I'd like to say it's my medical skill responsible, but I don't think so. I thought for certain the lot of you would need a hospital." He nodded toward Luartaro. "He's faring all right, too. But he will probably sleep away a chunk of the morning—in fact, he should. He insisted on being in here with you last night. Quite the fellow you have not to leave your side."

He dropped her hand and shook his head. "I couldn't save one of them, you know. The fellow with the broken arm bled out on me last night. Internal injuries, too, judging by all the bruising on his chest. From what the Thins tell me, you hit him pretty hard with a sword and kicked him for good measure." He paused. "Not that he didn't have it coming."

Annja didn't say anything. She just waited for him to continue, which he eventually did.

"The fellow with the maimed hand, he'll be all right. Missing all but the thumb, though. Couldn't find the pieces in the mud to even try to reattach them. Sleeping now—I sedated him pretty good. I'm limited in what I have to work with, you understand. I used some tranquilizers that work on oxen on the fellow, on Lu, as well. Used up most of my medicines and supplies on the lot of you, and I'll probably have the devil of a time replacing them. Retired and all. And not licensed here anymore. Just never bothered to get it renewed."

He gave a shrug of his shoulders and rubbed his lower lip. "Couldn't be helped, though, I suppose, using my supplies. I just couldn't let you all lie there untended."

"Thank you," she said, "for taking care of me and Lu."

He gave another shrug. He was a thin man wearing an overlarge shirt. "Don't expect things like this to happen in the jungle. Violence is city stuff. That's why I retired here, for the peace. Used to work in Chiang Mai, you know. It's the largest city in the north. Some years back I came here on a holiday to see the temples and decided to stay, settled in Chiang Mai. The wife had passed. I converted to Buddhism when I fell in with some monks. Learned to speak Thai—not the easiest language to master, don't you know. And then just learning one dialect won't do. There's Lanna, or lower Thai. And the people in Northern Thailand have their own dialect called Kham Muang, though most of them understand regular Thai. Then you have the hill tribes, of course, which all have their own languages, like these Thins. Took me more than a little while to master 'Thinspeak,' as I call it. Still don't know all of it, but enough to get me by. Anyway, I eventually quit my practice in London, shipped some stuff over and started a limited practice up in Chiang Mai. Didn't make near so much the money, but the climate suited me better." He tugged up the blanket and checked her leg, blotting it with a rag dipped in peroxide.

"Did some work in Chaing Rai also, which is where Thailand kisses Laos and Myanmar, and in Mai Sai, Nan—which is surrounded by mountains, such a pretty place Nan is. Spent a month or so in Pai, then in Phit-sanulok, which is between Bangkok and Chiang Mai, a gate to the Sukhothai Park it's called, which you should see while you're here. I even hung out my shingle in Mae Hong Son for a brief time, though it is a spit of a place. Tiny, but with a beautiful vista. It's where the tourists go who intend to do some trekking to the various hill tribes. Did some trekking myself, and that's how I decided to settle out here in the middle of nowhere. The Thins helped me build a house about a year back. Have two rooms, that's quite the thing, don't you know, two rooms."

He checked her arms next. The right one had a strip of gauze wrapped just above her elbow; it had taken the brunt of the bamboo splinters when one of the men had shot the building.

"You're lucky they found me at home, Annja. I still travel…to Chiang Dao, Chiang Khong, Thaton for the boat rides, Mae Salong and the national parks. As I said, the climate here agrees with me and I can still get around pretty well. Might as well hike, eh? At least while my legs can still carry me. No TV reception out here. Northern Thailand is considerably cooler than the rest of the country, and I like that it is a virtual melting pot of cultures—folks from Myanmar and Yunnan… China."

Annja enjoyed listening to him, liking the sound of his accent, which was still thickly British despite the years he'd obviously spent away from the country.

"You know, for quite a long time most of Northern Thailand was considered off-limits to anyone but the natives. There were lots of Communist insurgencies that made it not so safe. Couple that with drug issues from Myanmar—Burma—and all the little civil wars that spilled over the borders. There still are some tiffs from Myanmar that vex these hill tribes and the backpackers, but it's not near the problem it used to be. Drug trafficking has been seriously cut. Still, one has to be a little cautious when traveling near the border, especially if you're in Tak or Mae Hong Son." He rocked back on his heels and looked to the doorway. "But I do babble, don't you know. Wonder what's keeping Som? Shouldn't take her that long to find something suitable for—"

As if his words had been a gentle summons, the broad-shouldered woman entered, holding some folded garments in front of her. She smiled warmly and handed them to Doc, bowed, said something Annja couldn't decipher and left with a few backward glances over her shoulder.

He held the clothes out to Annja.

"I've been talking up a storm," he said. "I shouldn't let my tongue wag so. It's not polite. How about you do a little talking for a change? How about you answer some of the Thins' questions…like what you did to get those men so angry, and what brought you three out here to the middle of nowhere in the first place."

"It would only be polite," Annja said. She let out a deep breath, the air whistling between her teeth. "All right. Sure. I am an archaeologist, Lu, too." She proceeded to tell him about their trip to Tham Lod and then hiring Zakkarat to take them on a little more adventurous caving expedition, and about her plans to do a special for *Chasing History's Monsters* on the teak coffins and the remains. She left out the part about the voice in her head and finding the skull bowl and the dog tags, but she did mention the treasure and the need to tell the authorities about it and the gunmen.

"I think they were Vietnamese, all the men with the guns, though they might have been Laotian, I suppose." She didn't tell him about the ones she'd killed on the mountainside, or that there might be more of them with the treasure.

"And so the men were shooting at you because they didn't want witnesses to report their ill-gotten gold," Doc finished. "Or who might come back and steal it. Not such a lovely vacation for the two of you, eh? Relic traffickers you ran into, no doubt, come from Myanmar or Laos, going to Myanmar or Laos or China and using the cave as a stopping point while arranging for buyers. It sounds like the same operation some folks used to follow for drug trafficking. And poor, beautiful Thailand is once again caught in the middle. And the unfortunate Thins were the victims yesterday." He folded his arms. "Two villagers were killed during the ruckus. Two young men shot dead, leaving their families to grieve."

14

Annja's eyes grew wide. She hadn't seen any villagers get shot, but after a moment she realized what had happened. "In the school. The bullets went through the wall."

Doc nodded. "Two boys…well, two young men. Boon-mee and Tau were their names. I know most of the villagers here, and I'd gone fishing with Boon-mee on more than one occasion. Friendly chaps. I'd put them in their late teens. They don't really keep track of age around here, so I can't say exactly. Too young to die in any event. They will be buried later today. Good boys, they were." He leaned forward, fingers gripping the edge of her pallet. "And the saddest thing is, Annja, the Thins couldn't give a whit for treasure. They couldn't care less. They live simply, want for little and wouldn't pay the proverbial rat's ass for whatever those men were smuggling. They're not interested in Lu's wealth or your celebrity."

He turned his back to her. "I'll leave you to dress, and then I'll meet you across the way. If you're going to the authorities, you'll want to talk to the man with the maimed hand to get some information. He speaks a little English...was mumbling it while I worked on him. I've got something left that'll bring him around."

Annja watched him leave, looked at Luartaro, who was still sleeping soundly, and then rose and got dressed. The clothes she'd been given had belonged to a boy, she guessed from the cut of them. She wondered if they were from one of the two who had died. The gray pants fit snugly and hit her just above the ankles, and the shirt, made of coarse green broadcloth, rubbed a little uncomfortably against her skin. There were no pockets she could put her hands in. She couldn't complain, though. These people had showed her compassion in spite of what she'd brought into their village, and she doubted they had a lot of clothes to spare.

She blamed herself for the two boys' deaths and for Luartaro being injured. Had she done things differently, she could have confronted the gunmen in the jungle.

"Maybe I could have," she said. "Hindsight is always perfect."

She wondered about Zakkarat. She'd check on him, too, and ask Doc if his ankle was sprained or broken. But first she'd see to the remaining gunman. Doc was right; she wanted some information from him. She'd also want to borrow that old motorcycle she'd been offered yesterday, and retrieve the map someone had been drawing. She slipped on a pair of sandals that fit her surprisingly well. They were made of woven reeds with a strip of ox hide for a sole.

Taking a last look at Luartaro, she left the hut, nodding to Som on her way out. The broad-shouldered woman hovered nearby, talking to another woman and cocking her head back to no doubt indicate Annja and Luartaro. Annja headed to the building she'd been brought to the previous night. Several villagers were out, all of them pausing to watch her before they went about various tasks. Children were seated on the benches, none of them playing this morning. One pointed at Annja and talked animatedly to her companions.

Annja smelled something cooking. She couldn't tell what it was, but it smelled wonderful and her stomach rumbled again to remind her she was famished. Thirsty, too. Her mouth was dry and her tongue felt a little swollen.

"Doc?" Annja peered inside the doorway, seeing the Brit hovering over the remaining gunman. He was on the same table she'd been put on yesterday, and she saw that the top of it was stained from the blood. The windows were open, letting in the scents of jungle flowers, whatever was cooking and the almost overpowering odor of the moist loam. Light streamed in from all directions, giving the large room a much different appearance from her previous visit. At the end opposite from Doc and his patient was a slate board across part of the wall. Artfully rendered letters about six inches high stretched across it. She thought their alphabet much more beautiful than English or some of the other languages she was familiar with. It looked more like art than words.

There was a globe on a stand next to the teacher's table, and there were other accoutrements any classroom would have: rulers, mugs filled with pencils and paintbrushes, a skeleton hanging from a pole—plastic from the look of it—and jars filled with grass and insects. The details had been obscured yesterday by the storm and all the people gathered inside. In addition to the student tables and benches, there were a few plastic chairs like someone might find in a department store's garden department. There were also a collection of toys in the far corner—a dump truck, a Raggedy Ann doll, a few brightly colored pails and shovels, a faded basketball and three Barbie dolls with badly shorn hair.

"Doc?" she repeated.

He nodded and said something to himself. He rubbed a cotton swab under the man's nose, and the eyelids fluttered. Annja came close and heard the floor creak behind her; Som and the woman she'd been talking to hovered curiously just inside.

"His name is Ba An Dung, according to the papers in his pocket." Doc pointed to a wallet next to the prone man. "So definitely Vietnamese. From South Vietnam, maybe, if he is the second child."

"I don't understand," Annja said. She stood opposite Doc, looking down at the man, who had yet to regain consciousness.

"In the southern part of the country, the second-born son is given the name *Ba,* which means 'third'…the third member of the family. But in the north, *Ba* is given to the third child. *Ca* goes to the oldest, *Hai* the second. Just a bit of trivia for you. *An Dung* means 'peaceful hero,' but I wager this fellow is neither peaceful nor a hero." He scratched at his nose. "I spent a year in Vietnam, right after my wife died. She was Vietnamese. We'd always talked about going to visit her sisters. Just never got around to it while she was alive."

"You're an interesting man, Doc," Annja said.

"Not near so interesting as you, Annja. An archaeologist you said. And a TV personality? A treasure finder and the target of a Vietnamese army."

"I'd hardly consider them an army," Annja said.

"They had the firepower of one, eh? Ah, here he comes. He definitely could benefit from a hospital, and your friend Lu should be checked out there, as well, I suppose, or at least a clinic. I dare say you're mending well enough on your own that you won't need one." He wagged a finger at her. "I want none of you suing me now because I'm not a real medical doctor. I did the best I could." He took several steps back from the table to not interfere with whatever she planned for the man.

"You did great, Doc. Really great."

Annja leaned over the man. He stared up at her, a snarl forming on his lips. Still, he made no move to menace her or to get up.

"Ba An Dung," she began. "Tell me all about the treasure in the mountain." Annja asked him plenty of other questions. How many men were involved in the smuggling operation, what he thought the remainder might be doing now, would any more be coming after her and her companions, where did the gold come from and where was it ultimately headed?

He gave her nothing, just a string of curses and threats that were clearly intended to frighten her. The fingers of his good hand clenched and unclenched, and veins stood out along his neck and temples.

"What about the skull bowl?" she asked, her eyes daggers aimed at him. "And the American dog tags?"

This interested Doc, who took a step closer.

She saw no spark of recognition on the man's face, and so she described the bowl, thinking perhaps he did not know it was made from a human skull. He didn't react but he showed recognition when she mentioned the golden Buddhas, however. Annja growled from deep in her throat and pushed away from the table.

"Nothing," she said.

"I'm not surprised," Doc said. "Violent men are not terribly cooperative. I've no sodium thiopental or sodium pentothal—truth serum as it's called. Ethanol, scopolamine, a handful of barbiturates, temazepam—some of those might work. They're all sedatives and block cognitive function and interfere with judgment. Don't have any of those, either. As I said, I used up just about everything on the lot of you." He tapped a finger on the edge of the table. "Japanese torture squads used to have something called cisatracurium, and some agencies in England thought cannabis because of its THC component would work as a truth drug…. I'm well-read, don't you know."

"Apparently."

"You could just beat it out of him, I suppose."

Annja made a face.

"'Going all Jack Bauer' is the expression I heard when I was living where there were TVs and DVDs."

"Or I could let the authorities deal with him," she said, the resignation thick in her voice. Annja had considered calling her sword and holding the blade to the man's neck to force some information out of him. But not with Doc and Som and the other woman watching…along with the villagers who were peering in the windows. And she'd had enough violence for a while. She was more interested in finding out about the skull bowl. "Definitely let the authorities deal with him."

She stuck her hands under her armpits and felt the skin pull on her right arm. Annja healed fast, but she wasn't a hundred percent yet.

"Hungry, Annja?" Doc pointed to the doorway. A young Thins man came in with a tray and two bowls and a jar of water on it. "I've already eaten. Fixed myself a double serving of instant oatmeal a little while ago. I have a nice stock of it. Cinnamon-raisin." He paused. "And it's one of the few things I don't share." He gestured to the tray. The young man carried it to a desk and put it down, bowed and stood against a wall.

"Yes," Annja said. "I'm very hungry."

"Thai food, even from these hill tribes, is a tad spicy for my palate," Doc said. He rose on his toes so he could see into the bowls. "That's *johk,* in the bowls. It's a rice soup, on the thick side, sort of like porridge, sometimes with pork in it if they catch a wild pig…but it doesn't look like it this morning. Seems they put an egg in it for you. That would cost you an extra five baht or so if you bought *johk* in a marketplace. It's a bit like *khao tom,* if you've had that before. But it's spicier. See? They put shredded ginger in it just for you. Grown locally, and quite a treat, the ginger." He wrinkled his nose. "You can have my bowl, too, if you'd like."

Annja sat and tipped the first bowl to her mouth. There were no spoons. The mixture was warm and not as spicy as she'd expected, and it was as thick as porridge. She found it pleasant and filling and hoped Luartaro would be served some when he woke up. The second bowl quickly followed the first, and she drank the water in one long pull. She could have eaten at least one more bowl, but she stopped herself from asking for more.

"Thank you," she said to the young man.

Doc translated for her.

The young man smiled, bowed again and retreated outside with the tray and empty bowls.

Annja stared at the doorway. She remembered taking off her pack yesterday and setting it just inside. It wasn't there now. "Doc, my bag. I put it there—right there—yesterday."

His gaze followed her finger. "I wouldn't know anything about that. I was paying all my attention to you and Lu…and him." He pointed to the Vietnamese man, who was trying unsuccessfully to get up. "His muscles won't be cooperating for a little while. The stuff I gave him is made to subdue an ox, don't you know."

"My bag." Annja felt her throat tighten. It had the skull bowl in it, the only real treasure she was interested in, and it had all the dog tags, as well. "Maybe one of the villagers moved it, to clean it. You said they were washing my clothes. And my boots. Where are my boots?"

Doc spoke to Som and the other woman, making a clacking sound with his tongue against his teeth. After a moment, he translated the reply. "Som's sister has washed what is left of your clothes, and they are drying on a tree. Your boots are there as well, soaking to get the mud out. As for your pack, they did not touch it. Som thinks your other fellow—"

"Zakkarat."

"Ah, yes, I remember him telling me his name last night. Zakkarat Tak-sin. Som thinks Zakkarat took your pack. A nice enough chap. I put a tight bandage on his ankle and told him he should have it x-rayed. Might be broken, don't you know. Had a helluva time trying to put on his boots, couldn't get the one over the swelling, and so he traded them to Anuman for a good pair of sandals."

Annja turned. "Where is Zakkarat?"

Doc shrugged. "He left last night, the rain still coming down hard. Borrowed Erawan's motorcycle and took off. Good thing the headlight was working. Don't know how far he managed to get, though, all the rain and the mud. The trails are basically streams. I hope he brings Erawan's motorcycle back. It's the only one in the village."

Annja felt herself go pale. "My skull bowl."

"Pardon?"

"Something very important to me was in that bag. Did she see which way Zakkarat went?"

There was another exchange in the Thins language.

"Som said he went west, back into the jungle the way the three of you had come."

Annja spun and dashed past the two women, sandaled feet slapping over the still-muddy ground. "Lu!" she hollered. "Trouble!"

15

She raced to the small building, nearly bowling over a hunchbacked man who was trundling by with a bundle of soggy reeds.

"Lu!"

He was snoring gently, still propped up against the wall, a thin line of drool spilling over his lower lip and ending in a half-dollar-size wet spot on his borrowed shirt.

"Lu." She knelt by him, gently jostling him. "Lu, wake up. Enough tranquilizer to take out an ox, huh? Wonderful."

He mumbled something and kept snoring.

"Do you have my camera?" She'd just thought of it, praying that it hadn't been washed in her clothes. Plastic bag or no, it would be ruined, and all the pictures of the caves, treasure and skull bowl would be lost. She patted the bulging pockets of his trousers, finding it on the second try by its boxy shape. She unsnapped the pocket and pulled it out. "Thank God." It was still in the plastic bag and looked dry. She patted at more of his pockets, finding his camera and some extra batteries, the latter of which she palmed. Her own borrowed clothes did not have pockets, and so she would have to find some sort of pack or bag. She'd ask Doc to borrow something, and maybe get someone to pack her a lunch, too.

"Lu." She patted down all his pockets, though she couldn't say why she did this. Then she opened one, and then another, cursing when she discovered ancient gold coins and necklaces, one of which had a large sapphire dangling from it and that she remembered had hung around the neck of a Buddha statue. She rocked back on her heels, replaced the treasures in his pockets and snapped them closed. "Damn it, Lu. That's stealing. You're an archaeologist. A good one, I thought."

She shook her head, so disappointed with this man she thought she might eventually fall in love with. When had he taken these things? A fortune! He was the last to climb the rope ladder out of the cavern, and so he could have grabbed the treasures while she and Zakkarat were climbing. She'd been so preoccupied with the skull bowl and the teak coffins that he could have conducted his little raid then, stuffed things in the pockets of his pants and jacket, and transferred them to his borrowed clothes while she was unconscious.

So that's what Doc meant when he said of the Thins, "They're not interested in Lu's wealth or your celebrity." She felt a flush of anger rising in her face. But did she have a right to be upset? Annja stood and paced. The treasures had been stolen from somewhere, and certainly a good portion of them were being whisked away from the cavern now…if they hadn't already been carted off in the backs of the Jeeps. Luartaro had kept these few valuable pieces out of the thieves' hands. But this made him no better than a thief.

"Yet I took the skull bowl," she whispered. The line was so often blurred between good and evil, right and wrong. There'd been so much treasure…maybe it was just too tempting to Luartaro. It certainly had been too tempting for Zakkarat. Maybe Luartaro had never done such a thing before, snared antiquities for his personal gain, but she suddenly doubted that. He didn't seem at a loss for funds…not when she'd met him, and not when he agreed to this vacation and exchanged a stack of his money for Thai baht at the airport.

"Damn it, Lu." She stood ramrod straight and stared down at him, finding it difficult to hold on to her ire. "I took the skull bowl." And she meant to find Zakkarat and get it back. But if she couldn't, at least she had the digital camera and the pictures and could download the shots. Cradling the camera and batteries to her chest, she spun and headed to the door.

"Annja?"

She stopped and looked over her shoulder.

A groggy Luartaro looked up at her. He made a move to rise, but gave up on it, like a drunk whose muscles wouldn't cooperate.

"Annja? You all right?"

"Fine," she said, coming back to him. "Mending, anyway."

He blinked and twisted his head from side to side, the gesture looking comical. "You heal fast." He worked his lips and tongue. "You are remarkable, Annja. I'd been so worried, I—" He started to doze again.

She wanted to talk about the treasure he'd taken, but stayed silent on the matter.

"Lu?"

His eyes fluttered open and a loopy grin splayed across his face. He might as well have been drunk for all the motor coordination he had. Another line of drool spilled down.

She talked fast, wanting to get all the information out before he fell back asleep, and praying he could retain some of it. She explained about the two dead boys, about the one surviving gunman and about Zakkarat leaving last night on the motorcycle. As much as she wanted to go to the authorities right this very moment, her more immediate concern was Zakkarat…and after that the skull bowl.

"The authorities after I find Zakkarat," she said. "If I can find him. But maybe if you're feeling better, you could—"

"Get to a city?" His words were thick and slightly slurred. "I would do that, Annja. And I will meet you back at our cabin."

"Yes. Fine."

"About that sword…"

Her eyes went wide.

"I saw you with the sword again. On the side of the mountain, before we crossed the river. It had blood on it, and you used it to cut through vines. You obviously did not know I saw you with it. A beautiful, old sword. European?"

"You're mistaken—" she tried.

"I saw it again when you killed one of the gunmen yesterday. It was yesterday, was it not? Things are blurry." He blinked and tried to wipe away his drool. "A beautiful, old sword, though not so beautiful as you. Disappeared into thin air, I saw it. An invisible sword.

A woman who heals amazingly fast and who carries an invisible sword. A magical woman."

Her shoulders slumped. "Listen, Lu. Yes, there is magic in the world. I suppose you could call it that. I heal quickly. I'm blessed." There was no other explanation for her ability to mend so rapidly. "There are just some things beyond the realm of normalcy. Yes, there is a sword. I can't explain it." I won't explain it, she thought. "Maybe later."

He nodded groggily. "Some things defy explanation, beautiful Annja. Your secret, whatever it is, tell me later. I will keep it."

"We've all seen things on digs that defy explanation," she said. "You have secrets. We all have secrets."

She backed toward the door, reluctant to leave him in this condition. "You're safe, Lu," she told herself. "Zakkarat isn't."

"You go find Zakkarat, my remarkable, beautiful Annja with the invisible sword." The loopy grin got wider. "I think I will have me a little more sleep. Just a few more minutes. Then I will go to the city and find the police and tell them all about the machine guns and the gold. I will—"

He was snoring again, a gentle, sonorous sound that Annja found pleasing.

"A little more sleep for you," she said. "And a lot more speed for me." She hurried to find Doc, who loaned her a net sling bag for her camera…and told her the bag was just like a few Zakkarat had borrowed the previous evening.

Doc had securely tied the gunman to the table.

"That foul man is not going anywhere," he told Annja. "And if he wiggles too much, I've got two or three more doses of tranquilizer left that I can give him. He'll stay put until your friend Lu brings the authorities—whatever authorities police this part of Thailand. I've got some stuff to rouse Lu and get him moving." He tipped his head. "I've never run afoul of the law, Annja, so I don't know much about such things, getting the police and all, don't you know."

"My boots, Doc. Do you know where they are?"

"Washed, I said. Where?" He shrugged. "I don't know about such things, either. Sorry. I was taking care of my patients. Not their belongings."

Annja thanked him and raced down the path that she'd taken into the village, thinking perhaps the retired veterinarian didn't at all mind administering ox tranquilizers to people. Had he dosed her with it, too?

It wasn't difficult to find the motorcycle tracks. It obviously had still been raining when Zakkarat left, but it hadn't been raining quite enough to obliterate the wheel marks. The depression was filled with water, but the edges of the tracks were drying under the warm sun. The tracks were narrow, hinting at an older dirt-bike model rather than anything recent.

"We will be known forever by the tracks we leave," she mused. It was one of the Native American proverbs she'd committed to memory. Another favorite came to mind. "We do not inherit the land from our ancestors, we borrow it from our children." The Thins were taking good care of the land for their children, she thought, keeping it the same as they'd found it, perhaps keeping it nearly the same as it had been a thousand years ago. But she couldn't say the same for a lot of other people who lived in Thailand and some of the tourists who visited. They all but obliterated the cave paintings in Tham Lod, for example.

What sort of tracks am I leaving behind? she wondered.

Annja loved running—when she was running *to* something and not being chased. She loved the feel of the gentle burn in her arm and leg muscles, her increased heart rate and the heat in her chest. She waited for the flush to find her face, the first sign of welcome exertion. She could have run a little faster, perhaps, in her boots, though they were thick-soled and a tad clunky. The sandals slipped and were probably birthing blisters, but they were serving well enough and she hadn't been willing to spend any more time in the village searching for her things. She listened to the regular slap-slap the sandals made against the still-damp ground and the swish her left arm made against the foliage along the side of the trail. It was music to her. While there was pain in her calf, she was able to cope with it.

She drew the humid air deep into her lungs, finding the earthy scent of the ground and the myriad flowers almost intoxicating; it made her think of groggy Lu. Annja quickly brushed thoughts of him away, as she didn't need that distraction.

The motorcycle, no matter how old, would have made better time than her running, and he had quite a head start on her. But the motorcycle couldn't have carried Zakkarat across the river. She expected to find the bike ditched there. He would have swum across to the base of the mountain, climbed and searched for the cavern, marked by the rare flower. And he might well be back in his own village by now—if he found the cavern quickly and managed to cart away enough relics to suit him. Or perhaps he was in the nearest city selling whatever he gained. This trip could well be futile; she might not find him. But she had to give it a try, both to recover the skull bowl and to make certain Zakkarat stayed safe and did not run afoul of any more smugglers.

She guessed she'd passed about two miles when she noticed traces of the gunmen who'd come this way yesterday. There was a crumpled cigarette packet and broken branches, and several deep boot prints that had filled with water. They were obvious signs, and she suspected she would have found more if she'd been actively looking. She could tell where the gunmen had come upon the trail.

The trail of Zakkarat's borrowed bike kept going west, and so she continued to follow it.

She came upon the motorcycle several miles later, just as the swollen river loomed in sight. It was a faded red Bridgestone 65cc two-cycle dirt bike, vintage from the 1960s and with very little rust. It was canted on its side in a swath of mud, clumps of earth drying on the tires, and the front fender dented. The bike had been clumsily discarded, and she would have to return it to the Thins village later. Annja scowled; Zakkarat was not taking care of the earth for his children, and he was not leaving the best tracks in his wake in this world.

There was no wading this time. She had to swim. She took off her sandals and stuffed them inside her shirt to keep them from being washed away. She wanted to take her camera with her. Wrapping the plastic tighter around it, and then twisting the net bag around that, she held it in one hand and swam with her arm out of the water. It was awkward, but she managed. The current was strong and pushed her downriver, and so she emerged quite some distance from the motorcycle.

Her arms and legs ached from the river's buffeting, and she felt as if she'd been ten rounds in the ring by the time she emerged several minutes later, the sun directly overhead to signal noon.

Annja found Zakkarat on the rise just past the opposite bank, on a narrow game trail leading up the mountain. He'd been dead for at least a few hours, she could tell with a practiced glance, his legs riddled with bullets and a knife stuck in the middle of his chest.

16

It was an older military knife, the leather-wrapped handle cracked from age and stained with oil. Annja stared at it, anger and sadness welling up.

"A senseless death."

She said a silent prayer and allowed herself only a few moments to grieve for Zakkarat and wonder how to find his family and deliver the news. The lodge, she decided, from which he gave tours, would be a good place to start. Someone there would know how to contact his wife. She tugged off his shirt, tried futilely to shoo away the flies with it and laid it across his chest and face. The pockets of it had been ripped, as had his pants pockets. The pieces of jewelry that he'd looped around his neck and stuck on his fingers were gone, too. It looked as if a few of his fingers had been broken in the process of recovering some of the pieces.

So the thieves took back their gains and left Zakkarat's body to rot. He'd had no weapons. They could have regained the gold without killing him. He was no threat, save for knowing the location of their treasure cavern.

Three empty net bags were strewn a few yards away—what Zakkarat had intended to put more treasure in. She didn't see the pack she'd put the skull bowl in and that he'd supposedly taken. So the thieves had probably grabbed that, too. She searched for it, though, combing through ferns and looking along the riverbank before finally giving up…and deciding to pursue the men who'd killed Zakkarat.

Annja would have gone after them regardless of whether they'd left behind the bowl. Partly a need for revenge, she recognized, but it was more of a need to stop them from killing anyone else who might chance to get in their way. She took a last look at Zakkarat's corpse, trying to memorize its location so she could direct the authorities to it. To help, she took one of his net bags and tied it to a tree branch that overhung his body.

Then she started up the mountainside, her feet slipping in the sandals and occasionally getting stuck in pockets of mud. The tracks the men left were easy to follow—their heavy boot prints distinct despite all the rain, and they'd been careless with the foliage, breaking branches and smashing flowering plants in their wake. Even someone without tracking skills could have followed the path they made.

Although Annja knew she might have had difficulty locating the cavern on her own, the terrain being too unfamiliar to her, the men were making it easy. She hoped Luartaro had recovered enough to go in search of the appropriate authorities, that he could either accompany them or give them good enough directions, and that they might be on their way there soon.

Her feet pressed spent bullet shells into the ground as she climbed. She found the whole thing odd. A gun—the one she'd taken from one of the men and briefly used—was decades old, and an old-style military knife had been used on Zakkarat. She'd thought that men with so much treasure could have afforded more modern and expensive weapons. Perhaps they just favored things from the past.

Her mind touched the sword, and she called it into her hand before she had traveled very far up the side of the mountain. She heard or saw no evidence of the men being nearby, and therefore she had no immediate need for a weapon. But the sword's pommel felt good against her palm, and she wrapped her fingers tight around it as she drew her lips into a thin line.

"I might not have found the cavern again on my own," she said aloud. "At least not without quite a bit of searching. But you vile men are showing me the way. Might as well have put up a road sign, as clumsy as you idiots are. Please, still be there." She very much wanted to confront them—and despite her distaste of violence, she planned to make them pay.

She climbed slower than she would have liked, but she was still fatigued from yesterday's rigorous ordeal. The stitches in her leg from where the retired veterinarian had cut out the bullets pulled. She guessed it was about an hour of steady climbing when she spotted the roof of a truck in a gap in the branches of a pair of acacia trees. The men indeed had not left. In fact, they'd managed to bring a truck up the narrow trail. They probably needed it because the Jeeps they'd had yesterday were not sufficient to haul away all of the treasure. She edged closer, staying low so she could get a good look at what was going on.

The truck seemed to have more rust showing than paint, and it had a high, boxy back. Its tires were thick and mud-crusted, and from the height of the axels it looked like a four-wheel-drive setup—no doubt necessary in this terrain. The truck was narrow, but barely fit on the overgrown trail, and it appeared to be a Howo design. Annja had seen several trucks made by the company during a trip to China. This model had quite some age to it, and she suspected it would haul a good bit of the treasure. There was a Jeep, too, several yards behind the truck and lower on the trail. No one was in either vehicle.

She waited, resting the sword flat against the ground and resisting the urge to brush away the gnats that were dancing around her face. Within minutes, two black-clad men passed by her hiding spot and loaded a crate onto the back of the truck, struggling under its weight. The men she'd seen yesterday had also been dressed in black. They weren't wearing uniforms, however, as it didn't look as if any of the shirts and pants matched. One man had on jet-black jeans, the other work trousers; one wore a T-shirt, and the other a short-sleeved shirt with a patch on the pocket and beige buttons. The shoes ranged from tennis shoes to heavy boots, to loafers on the third man who appeared, all caked with mud.

She watched for several more minutes, trying to gauge just how many men were involved. She only saw the three, but that didn't mean there weren't more in the cavern helping to bring up the goods. She heard a whirring, chugging sound, and smelled something acrid.

They were using a gas-powered winch. She shifted her position and saw that they'd brought a cumbersome contraption to replace the broken one she'd spotted yesterday. It wheezed and belched a small cloud of exhaust. So there was at least one more man down below attaching things to the cable.

Had they been loading treasure all night? Had the torrential rain slowed them? How much had already been carted away? Annja would find out soon enough, and she would try to keep them from taking away any more. She left her camera in the bushes and crept toward the Jeep, crouching low and hunkering behind it. The men were around the truck and didn't see her.

Stay quiet! she admonished herself as she carefully thrust the tip of her sword between the threads of the right rear tire. The rubber was thick, and it took some worrying at it, but she finally pierced it. She made two more holes in it and stretched her hand forward, feeling the air slowly escaping. Then she worked on the other rear tire. The truck would not be able to easily get around the Jeep…without pushing it out of the way, and the Jeep could not get far on only its front tires. For good measure, she punctured the spare that was affixed to the back.

Annja listened as she worked, hearing the men load another crate and groaning under its weight. None of them spoke English, or any other language she knew, and she promised herself that she would learn a few phrases of Vietnamese. She heard one of the men strike a match as another continued talking. Her eyes widened when she picked up the words *Chiang Mai.*

Peeking around the rear of the Jeep, she caught a good profile of one of the men. He was short, no more than five feet five inches, and he stood straight, shoulders back in seeming military posture. He brought his head forward when he sucked on his cigarette. She memorized his face. She couldn't get a good look at the other two; they kept their heads down and they wore caps, one with an extralong brim. The one farthest away turned and walked out of sight; she shifted her position and watched him climb down into the treasure cavern.

Like a shadow, she slipped around the other side of the Jeep, edging to its front and poking her head up only briefly to see that the two men were still standing and talking at the back of the truck. It was half-filled with crates, and she saw the dark outline of a Buddha statue. Likely they hadn't cleaned out the entire cavern before now because there'd simply been so many relics in it. Hauling away that much stuff required time and multiple vehicles, and no doubt multiple trips. The men were taking care with the goods and not hurrying.

She calculated how to take the pair out without killing them—she didn't need their deaths to meet her revenge. She just needed to catch them.

A part of her knew this was something the Thai authorities should handle. But they weren't here, and she worried that the men might not tarry long enough for the authorities to arrive...though her stopping the Jeep would help that matter. Stopping the truck would cement the deal.

Annja weighed the options and decided the authorities could deal with her prisoners. She would explain that the smuggling operation was being packed up and moved because she, Luartaro and Zakkarat accidentally stumbled across it, and so she had to act.

She crept closer and tightened the grip on her sword.

The shorter man dropped his cigarette and ground it out with the ball of his foot. He was looking down, studying a turtle that had crawled out of the tall grass, and Annja chose that moment to strike. She sprang forward, sword pulled back, and she cleared the distance to the closest man in a heartbeat.

The shorter man looked up just as Annja rapped the pommel of her sword against the back of the other man's head. He crumpled just as the shorter man drew the pistol from a holster at his side, brought it up and shouted.

It was a warning of some kind, she was certain, as she spun to her right when his first shot went off. The gun looked similar to the one she'd briefly used, and she counted herself fortunate that in his haste he was a bad aim. She closed the distance and brought the pommel down like a hammer on his hand. The gun dropped and he shouted again.

He fumbled for a knife at his waist and tried to back away from her, but the ground was still damp and he lost his balance. She brought her leg up and caught him hard in the thigh, then kicked him a second time.

As he dropped to his knees she thumped the pommel against the top of his head, cringing when she heard a cracking sound and praying she'd only knocked him out. No time to check, she vaulted over his body and whipped around the side of the truck, feet churning over the ground and heading toward the hole the winch sat in front of. A man was emerging from it, awkward in his climbing because he had a gun in his hand.

He fired it without aiming, and he struck a front tire of the truck. Annja smiled at that.

"Now shoot out the other one," she said as she charged him.

He managed to climb all the way out by the time she reached him, and he squeezed off two more shots, one grazing her arm. It felt like fire, and she ground her teeth together. She swept the sword around, turning it so the flat of her blade would hit his side, but he was too fast for her. He leaped backward, across the hole, hollering to whoever was still inside.

"I definitely need to learn Vietnamese," she said. She skirted the hole as shots were fired upward through it, spit rapid-fire from a machine gun. Then she whirled as the man up top fired again, this time at least one of the bullets striking the blade of the sword.

"No!" she hollered. The sword had been in pieces when it had come into her possession, and she could well imagine it breaking into pieces again.

She led with the sword again, darting toward him and spinning, making herself a difficult target. This time she let the edge of the blade cut through the air, fairly whistling as it cleaved the distance between her and the gunman. The blade bit into his arm, and he dropped the pistol.

He hollered in pain and shouted a string of words she couldn't comprehend. Then she brought the sword around again, striking his arm a second time. Annja hadn't wanted to maim another one of them, but she needed to take this one out of commission so she could deal with whoever was still below with the machine gun. She stepped to the side so she could keep an eye on the hole and the rope ladder.

"Down!" she barked at the injured man. He bent forward, cradling his sliced arm, blood flowing over his hand and his face etched with an expression of pain. "I…said…down!" She gestured with her free hand and he got the idea, gingerly getting to his knees. The rope ladder moved, and Annja clocked the wounded man on the side of his head with an elbow to knock him out.

Moving fast, she dismissed the sword so she could have both hands free, ran back to the hole and pulled at the ladder, ducking back just as more bullets came from below. Someone was climbing up it, but they backed off and she yanked the ladder up, stranding them.

"You can stay down there!" she shouted. Annja doubted they could leave the cavern via the way she'd come into it yesterday. All the rain would have thoroughly flooded the passageways, and there hadn't been time for the water to recede. She knelt and tried to get a good look into the cavern. "Trapped like the rats you more than certainly are." She allowed a rare smugness to creep into her voice.

An idea formed in her head; she could use the rope from the ladder to tie up the three unconscious men. Then she would wait for whatever authorities would be arriving. She'd use one of the dropped pistols, if necessary, to keep the men in the cavern under control.

"Oh, Luartaro, I hope you've contacted someone by now. I don't want to sit up here all day. I hope—"

"Annja Creed. Put your hands to your sides and stand up." The voice sounded brittle and hard, like ice shattering.

She glanced over her shoulder, seeing another black-clad man holding a machine gun pointed at her. He must have been in the back of the truck, hidden by the shadows, or maybe off to the side of the trail attending to something personal. Her lost backpack was slung over his shoulder.

"You took that from Zakkarat." She pointed at the bag.

"I only took back what is mine. I assure you that I am a good shot, Annja Creed. And if you do not surrender now, I will kill you."

Annja had no choice but to comply.

17

"You wonder how I know your name," the man said.

Vietnamese or Laotian, Annja placed him in his early forties. He had a cruel look about him, with fleshy pock-marked cheeks, as if he'd suffered a disease in earlier years. He had intense, unblinking eyes that were hard like river stones.

"No," she said. "I do not wonder. You tortured Zakkarat. He gave you my name."

A thin smile cracked his face. "Zakkarat Tak-sin did not deal well with pain. He called you 'Annjacreed,' a name that meant nothing to me until he said you and your companion, Lou Ardo, were archaeologists who wanted to explore some caves. He had a handful of baht in his pocket that you'd given him. He said you wanted to bring a film crew back with you later and put the caves on television. I deduced that you must be *the* Annja Creed, the famous archaeologist who chases history's monsters." His laugh was forced. "Even in my country your silly, worthless program airs."

"And what country is that?"

"Actually, I have two. America and Vietnam. Educated in the first, I have embraced the latter. Vietnam is home now. I have no use for Americans."

It was Annja's turn to smile, having gained a measure of information. It explained why he was so fluent in English, and his accent sounded far more East Coast than Vietnamese. Boston, perhaps?

"Is Lou Ardo with you? Hiding in the bushes?" He stared into the foliage. "Come out, Lou Ardo, or I will kill Annja Creed."

Lou Ardo? If she got out of this, she would tell Lu how badly the villain butchered his name.

"And you are?"

"My name is of no consequence to someone who will die soon…and who will die forever and never find heaven or hell." He dropped his shoulder and the bag slid down, the straps catching against his forearm. "The old one taught me how to capture souls." He balanced the machine gun against his hip with one hand and used the other to place the bag at his feet. "I will kill you, Annja Creed, and I will cause your soul to rot for eternity."

A shiver raced down her spine at the notion.

"Then kill me, you thief," she taunted, trying to get him to act in anger. She readied to spring into the tall grass. "Kill me and be done with this. Come on, get it over with."

His fingers played against the machine-gun stock. "I've no reason to hate you. So quickly, yes, I will kill you, and likely without too much pain. Not as much pain as Zakkarat felt, I can assure you. Quickly…if you will cooperate first."

"Cooperate? And if I don't?"

"Then your death will be agonizing and very, very

slow." He grinned wider, showing uneven ivory-colored teeth, one of them with a gold edge. "The manner of your demise matters not to me, Annja Creed. Your slow death would amuse me."

"Cooperate? So I can more quickly rot for eternity?"

In the silence that stretched between them Annja measured him. His hands were calloused and dirt was thick under his fingernails. That gave him the look of a laborer, though she suspected he wasn't. He acted more like a thug who had dirtied himself hauling treasure— that was how he gained all the calluses, from his skin rubbing against the crates. Only a hint of stubble on his face, his hair was short and styled, though it was greasy from not being washed recently. Perhaps he was a businessman who worked in an office…when he wasn't smuggling. Like the others he wore dark clothes, but his were green, so deep that at a distance they had appeared black. His shoes looked expensive.

She listened to his breathing, which was loud and had a slight rattle to it. A smoker? The one who'd left behind the crumpled cigarette packs? She heard movement in the cavern behind and below her.

"Yes, cooperate, the famous Annja Creed. Perhaps I will only let your soul rot for a decade or two." Again the forced laugh. It sounded like nails dragging against a blackboard.

She took a step back, her heel bumping up against one of the stakes that held the rope ladder.

"I want to know where you went, Annja Creed, after you left my trove and ran down the mountain yesterday. Where did you go? And who did you tell about my… acquisitions? And where is Lou Ardo?"

"He is where you won't find him," she answered.

"I am a resourceful man."

"Resourceful enough to stash your ill-gotten wealth in a mountain," she said. "And resourceful enough to get some vehicles here fast to retrieve it." She paused. "Since you intend to kill me, anyway, why not tell me what this is all about. Where did all of the gold come from?"

"And where is it going?" he said.

She nodded.

"I told you I was educated in America. I grew up on James Bond films." He shifted his weight to the balls of his feet. "All the villains revealed their plans, lording it over James Bond, who was trussed up to some torture device. He always escaped."

"You worry that I'll escape?" She gave him a petulant expression. "You've got a gun on me."

"I am not a James Bond villain. I am not a villain at all—just a businessman, an opportunist, who made fortunate alliances so he could make a fortune. I do not need to explain my plans to an archaeologist who stars in a silly television program." He steadied the stock of the gun against his stomach. "And no, I do not worry that you will escape. Now tell me, Annja Creed, where did you go yesterday? Who did you talk to?" He made an exaggerated motion of laying his finger farther across the trigger. "Where is Lou Ardo?"

"He's beyond your reach." She took another step back and dropped into the opening, knees bent and hands forward at waist height, calling for the sword and feeling its pommel form against her palms before her feet hit the stone. Bullets sprayed the air where she'd stood a moment ago. The impact on her sandaled feet was jarring, as if she'd jammed her heels against red-hot thumbtacks. She clamped her mouth shut to keep from crying out and whirled, sword leading and slicing into a man who'd been darting forward, pistol raised.

The flat of the blade hit his hand, sending the gun careering off a crate.

"Drop it!" Annja barked at a second man she spotted. She leaped out from under the opening in the ceiling, worried that she'd be as good as a sitting duck for the man up top.

The second man reluctantly lowered his machine gun, his gaze darting between her and his companion. Bullets rained down through the opening, and Annja edged farther into the chamber, all the while keeping her eyes on the two men. They stank so strongly of sweat and cigarettes that she nearly gagged. The light was better than on her previous visit—a tall battery-operated lamp was responsible, casting a fluorescent glow everywhere and making the beads of sweat on the men's faces glisten.

"Drop it now!" she repeated. "Drop...the...machine gun...now."

The man—the younger of the two—made a move to do just that. But it was a feint. As more bullets came down from above, he instead raised his machine gun, firing straight ahead and missing Annja by inches, but only because she'd sprung toward the cenotelike pool in the center.

"Idiot," she growled as she circled around behind him, quick as a cat. She raised the sword high and brought it down, biting into his shoulder with enough strength behind it to break his collarbone. A second slash ended his scream and sent the other man to his knees, arms up in surrender.

"Annja Creed!" came a shout from above. "Show yourself!"

"So you can shoot me?" Annja laughed.

He muttered a string of expletives in English and Vietnamese.

"Where is Lou Ardo? Who have you told about this place?" He shuffled around the opening, poking his head down and cussing again when he was unable to see her because Annja had moved behind a stack of crates. "I'll let you live if you cooperate, Annja Creed. I'll lower this ladder and you can climb out."

"You think I believe that?" she called back. "You probably have a bridge somewhere you want to sell me, too."

The man who'd surrendered hollered something that Annja couldn't understand. He shuffled on his knees toward the opening, and she guessed that he'd asked his boss to be let up. He hollered again.

"Shut up," Annja told him. "And stay put."

He seemed not to understand her and called up once more. Annja dismissed the sword, slipped out from behind the crate and reached for the dropped machine gun. She cocked it, and the man stopped shuffling.

"You might not understand my language," she said. "But you understand this well enough." She swung the machine gun to the left, as a gesture that he should move away from the opening.

He shook his head, spittle flying from his lips and his eyes wide with uncertainty. She gestured again, and he complied, though he kept looking up.

"Annja Creed," the man up top said. "I could torture

the information out of you. But torture is rather messy. Why not just tell me who you talked to? This is your last warning."

Silence was her response.

"I don't need to shoot you," he continued. "You can starve down there. You can die of exposure at night when the temperature drops. No one comes up to this part of the mountain. No one will find you. Just tell me what I want to know."

Again, she said nothing.

His venomous string of expletives echoed down through the opening. He fired another burst, rock fragments from the stone lip showering down and biting into the man who'd surrendered. He scooted farther away from the opening. Then it was quiet.

Annja heard a bird cry. A moment later a monkey screeched. But there was nothing else from the man above. An engine started, the sound faint because of the distance and the intervening rock.

"The Jeep," she said. "He's starting the Jeep." But why not leave in the truck? It was filled with crates of treasure. She'd ruined the back two tires of the Jeep. The truck was probably big enough to bull its way past the Jeep, knock it out of the way and down the mountain. Maybe he was just moving the Jeep to make things easier. "Unless he doesn't have the keys to the truck. And doesn't know how to hot-wire it."

She looked to the surrendered man and the body of the man she'd killed. On the latter's belt was a clip with several keys.

"Your boss isn't going to get far in that Jeep," Annja said. From the blank look on his face she knew he couldn't understand her. "But you understand the gun.

Thugs always understand guns." She pointed the muzzle at him, then at a crate and then to a spot beneath the opening. "Move!"

He looked puzzled for only an instant, and then he clambered to his feet and stepped around the body of his dead companion, eyes lingering on the blood.

"Move!" Annja figured the other man would be back soon when he gave up on the Jeep. "Hurry!"

If he didn't understand the words, he understood her intent. The crate was roughly a meter cubed, and he strained to push it under the opening. He looked to the dozen crates remaining and picked a smaller one to set on top.

There had been five or six times the number of crates when Annja was there before. They'd worked at a steady pace to move the goods. But move them where? At the far side of the cavern the teak coffins stood undisturbed. Fortunately, they'd not cared about those treasures, which Annja considered every bit as valuable as the gold Buddhas—more valuable in an archaeological sense.

He had a hard time lifting the crate and looked to her for help.

She shook her head. "I'm not dropping the gun," she told him. Again, a blank look met her steady stare. "Try again. You can do it."

While he struggled with it, she bent and retrieved the keys from the dead man's belt, and then patted his pockets, pulling out a few business cards and a folded piece of paper. She stuck these inside her shirt, intending to look at them later when she was out of here. His other pocket was empty. No wallet or ID or any sort of a passport that would facilitate traveling across borders.

The man grunted as he arranged the second crate

so it could serve as a ladder. Annja gestured for him to step back.

"What to do with you...what to do." She sucked in her lower lip. "If I let you go up first, you might try to kick me or do something else to cause problems. You might holler and bring your boss back. If I go first, you might grab my leg." She slipped close to him and lifted the gun. He closed his eyes and gritted his teeth just as she brought the stock down against the side of his head.

Annja didn't want to kill another one of them. She wanted them alive for the authorities to question. Eyes flitting around the chamber, she spotted a length of rope around a crate. She dropped the machine gun and unfastened the rope, and then used a length of it to tie up her prisoner. Adept at knots, she felt certain he wouldn't be getting out of this anytime soon.

She checked his pockets, finding no ID, but pulling out a few business cards and a pack of cigarettes. The latter she dropped with disgust. Spotting the pistol, she snapped it up and thrust it in her waistband.

"Can't afford to leave you a weapon," she said. Then she struggled to prop him up against a wall near the lamp, and took a moment to examine the head wound she'd given him. His chest rose and fell regularly.

"I think you'll be all right," she pronounced. "Fit enough to serve a prison sentence." A last look around the chamber and a moment more to disable the machine gun, then she started toward the coffins, wanting to see if the pottery was still inside them, but she heard the engine again. She climbed up the crates. Her legs ached, the right one still sore from where Doc had removed the bullets. She felt the stitches pull. The impact of jumping into the cavern hadn't helped, and she wished she had taken the time to locate her boots before she'd left the Thins village.

She pulled herself halfway out of the hole and grabbed at the rope ladder bunched up at the top. "Lovely."

The man who'd taken off in the Jeep had returned on foot, his machine gun again pointed at her.

18

He didn't bother to ask questions this time, no doubt realizing she wasn't about to give up Lu or any other information. He aimed the machine gun, snarled at her and pulled the trigger.

She dipped her head below the rim, feeling the bits of earth and rock pelt the top of her head from where the bullets chewed up the ground. One end of the rope ladder came loose, shot through, and she hung on the other side as it swayed precariously. The firing continued, the bullets ripping into the ground furiously, as if they were as angry as the man who fired them.

When they stopped, Annja didn't pause. Quick as lightning she lifted herself up over the lip again and rolled toward him, seeing that he was jamming in another magazine. Vaulting to her feet, she put her head down and barreled into him.

Annja drew her right hand back into a fist and punched him in the face. Blood spurted from his nose as he fell back.

She followed, knees on his chest, left hand reaching

for the pistol she'd stuffed in her waistband, drawing it and shoving the barrel under his chin.

He made a move to shove her off, and she clocked him again with her fist.

"You're the one who needs to cooperate now…if you want to live." She pushed the gun against his throat. Annja didn't intend to kill him—despite everything he'd done, including admitting to torturing and killing Zakkarat. But she didn't need him to know that. She dug her knees in harder, inadvertently cracking at least one of his ribs. She almost apologized.

"Tell me what this is about—the treasure…the trucks." Some part of her realized that she didn't need the information. She'd stopped the relic smuggling and captured the villains, salvaging a happy ending amid the tragedy of her Thai guide's murder and the deaths of two Thins villagers. She could leave the questioning to the Thai authorities—let them track the treasure already hauled away. It was their country and their problem. Let them interrogate this foul man.

But another part of Annja needed to know. That part wanted everything tied up with a neat little ribbon.

"I…said…talk."

He groaned when she dug her knee into his side and pushed the gun against him with more force. She eased up only a little so he could speak.

"You are more than a television archaeologist, it seems." His words were strained from her weight and his broken ribs. He coughed and grimaced.

"Talk."

"I'm only a part of this, Annja Creed." He smiled then, the malevolent expression sending a shiver through her. "A sizable part, yes, but only a part. You have cut the tail off the snake, not its head."

He said nothing else, despite her repeated questions and jabs with the gun.

"The skull bowl. Tell me about that."

He shook his head and grinned wider.

"Damn it!" Annja pushed herself off him, further injuring his ribs, and again forced back an apology. She waved the gun at him, but he made no move to get up.

Bending over him, gun still threatening, she tugged a pistol from a holster at his side and flung it with such anger that it arced out of sight down the slope. Next, she rifled through his pockets.

No wallet. No ID. Nothing.

"Who are you?"

He kept smiling, blood from his broken nose spilling over his lip. He stuck the tip of his tongue out and licked at the blood.

She fumed and dug the ball of her foot into the ground, ran her free hand through her hair and got a good whiff of herself. God, but she stank, from the mud and the river and from the sweat. She needed a long, hot bath.

Had Luartaro reached the authorities? Were they on their way? Should she wait for them?

"No," she said out loud.

He looked at her quizzically.

"I can't wait."

Maybe Luartaro was still groggy from the ox tranquilizer the retired veterinarian had used on him. Maybe he hadn't reached the authorities yet.

She would take that task on herself, just to be sure.

Annja gestured with the pistol, and the man got to

his feet slowly. She gestured toward the hole. He showed no emotion, but he kept his eyes on her.

"The authorities are on their way," she told him.

Still no reaction on his face. Could he tell she was bluffing?

The authorities will be on their way if they aren't already, she told herself. A quick glance at the truck showed that the front tire that had been shot had not gone flat, and with luck it wouldn't.

"Sit."

After a moment, he complied.

She pulled up the rope ladder and practically co-cooned him in it, tying him up. She made sure the knots were tight; he wouldn't be freeing himself. She used the cable from the winch to secure the men up top she'd subdued earlier. One of them was groggy, but a quick tap to the side of his head sent him unconscious again.

"Let's get some mug shots," she said, going to the side of the trail where she'd dropped the net bag containing her digital camera. She came back to the cocooned man and wiped the blood away from his nose. "Say cheese."

Annja unwrapped it from the plastic. "Nuts." She hadn't noticed it earlier, but the camera had been ruined sometime during her mad dash yesterday. A bullet was lodged near the lens, spiderweb cracks radiating from it. She tried to thumb it on, just in case. "Nuts. Nuts. Nuts."

She made a move to heave it down the mountainside, but stopped herself. The memory card might be all right, meaning all the pictures she took yesterday could be saved, or maybe someone could fix the camera. She wrapped the camera in the plastic and the net bag again.

Then she leaned over the hole, taking another look at the crates and craning her neck so she could see her captive. Testing the cable and rope on the men up top, she pronounced them as secure as she could make them.

She climbed up to the truck, pleased to see her backpack sitting on the passenger seat. Opening the door took a bit of muscle, as it was dented and did not fit properly. It took two yanks before it whined and relented. So the man had driven the Jeep out of the truck's way and had come back to take the truck, dropping her pack in it. But he hadn't possessed the keys—or else she suspected he would have roared away and left her in the cavern. Annja jangled the keys she'd taken from the man in the cavern and on her first guess found the one that fit in the ignition. Despite the rust and the age of the vehicle, the engine purred.

"On second thought—" She left it running and slipped out, leaving the door open and marching straight to the man cocooned in the rope ladder. Her muscles grew sore as she tugged him to his feet and shuffled him to the back of the truck. Opening the tailgate and lifting him inside was almost impossible, but Annja was nothing if not determined and finally heaved him in. Then she latched the tailgate and climbed back into the cab.

Annja practiced with the clutch, gas and brake pedals, which were stiff. She had to move the seat forward and adjust the rearview and side mirrors, all of which were covered with a dirty film. The stink of cigarettes permeated the cab, but her own bad odor overpowered it. She fought the bile rising in her throat and stuck her head out the window to suck down some better air.

"Let's get out of here. But first, let's see where here is." In her net bag was the map one of the villagers had drawn for her. Though pretty and well rendered, it wasn't terribly useful. She leaned over and thumbed the glove box. "That's better." Several maps were stuffed inside, and she got lucky with the first one. It even had a faint blue circle drawn on it that she guessed approximated the location of the treasure cavern. "The lodge would be here." She tapped her finger at a spot that didn't look terribly far away. That's where she intended to go first.

She would see if Luartaro had made it back and then head to the nearest city to contact the authorities…likely the city she and Luartaro had taken the bus from to reach the lodge. Annja nudged her pack to the side and spread the map on the passenger seat and studied it.

She reached for the backpack, unfastened it and dipped inside. Her fingers found the dog tags immediately. The lid she'd padded with a piece of her pant leg was intact. But the skull itself was in four pieces. Her heart sank.

19

Annja carefully backed down the trail. The truck was too wide to fit on it for most of the way, and so she took it over bushes and ferns, scraping against trees and trying to retrace the path it had taken to limit the damage to the foliage. In places, she followed deep ruts the truck had made when it came up when the ground was muddier.

She was confident the skull bowl could be repaired. Many artifacts in museums and collections had been reconstructed from fragments. Pottery and clay figurines were often painstakingly reassembled because they were found in pieces, though sometimes just the pieces were displayed. The skull bowl had been sturdy, and so she hadn't thought to pad it. But then she hadn't expected to take it on a wild slipping-and-sliding ride down the side of the mountain when she was first running from the gunmen. Her fingers occasionally continued to rustle through the bag and over the skull segments, finding a bullet. Maybe the bowl had stopped a bullet that would otherwise have found her.

The bowl could be repaired, but should it be? Though she'd seen many grisly archaeological finds through the years, this one particularly disturbed her. Maybe it was better off shattered.

She punched the brake on a steep incline and felt the truck shimmy and slip and heard the cargo in the back shift. She wondered if her prisoner was being squished by crates and was mildly disappointed with herself for not stopping to check on him when the slope became gradual.

Annja did, however, stop to look at the map. It was shiny with a thick, slick lamination and rendered in a combination of pleasing pale and bright colors. It was the sort of map bookstores displayed in their travel sections, not something a driver would pick up at a gas station or in a way stop. It included the topography of Northern Thailand, listing the elevations of different sections of the mountain ranges, and the borders were dotted with pictures and interesting snippets of information about islands, beaches, temples and the larger cities. Names and numbers at the bottom on the opposite side were probably towns and cities and their populations. The print was too small to read in this light. The reverse side also showed street maps of Chiang Mai and Bangkok—the latter looking formidable because of its size. She flipped it back over to the side showing Northern Thailand and the mountains.

She'd save the map for Luartaro; he'd like it and might find something marked on it he'd like to see.

"But no more spirit caves."

She touched her index finger to the tiny silhouette of an airplane. Mae Hong Son's airport was the one they came in at and took the bus from, and Mae Hong

Son was the closest city to her current location in the mountains. She noted all the streams and rivers in the area, many of which she suspected would have flooded their banks. To the north and south the waterfalls were marked—Pha Sua and Pha Pawng; she remembered seeing them coming in on the plane. Beautiful from the air. Plenty of roads were marked on the map, but there were no names that she could spot. One stretched up to Huay Pha, a town or large village. That road cut around a hill and to Doi Pai Kit, another village. She recalled seeing a brochure for the area at the lodge. So if she found the road and made it through those villages, she'd find the lodge and could use the phone in the office to contact the authorities. She'd also look for Luartaro.

Next would be Mae Hong Son and Chiang Mai. Outside of a thread-fine line that may or may not have been a road, the map didn't show a direct route from Mae Hong Son to the larger city. But there were several routes that twisted and turned through the mountains and would eventually get her there—taking the scenic route, so to speak. She'd heard the men mention Chiang Mai, and one of the business cards listed Chiang Mai. Annja's desire to finish the puzzle would lead her there.

"And maybe lead to a nap first." She stifled a yawn and rotated her shoulders against the seat back. God, but she was exhausted and achy. A brief nap would put her in a better mood and make her more alert. A bath was on her list, too. She didn't want Luartaro to get a whiff of her right now.

The mountain trail she backed down wasn't on the map, nor was the thin gravel road she found at the bottom. It wasn't really a road, either, she decided after half a mile. It was a mountain bike path, and she saw deep ruts from the truck's tires and maybe the Jeeps before it, and a few small trees with badly scraped bark.

The truck bounced along on it, able to turn around in an area of tall grass so she was pointed south, in the direction she was heading. The seat was uncomfortable, the springs in it shot, and she had to stretch to reach the pedals. Although Annja was tall, she couldn't move the seat forward quite far enough; the mechanism was rusted. She figured the tall man she'd taken out first had been the driver. The steering wheel was caked with a dirty film, and the gearshift was likewise filthy. She noted it all, but it didn't bother her; she was as dirty as the truck.

CLOUDS WERE INCREASING and the light was fading by the time she found a proper road, one with a sign that indicated Tham Pla National Park, Tham Pla Cave and—to her relief—Mae Hong Son.

She reached the resort on the outskirts of town before sunset and parked the truck in front of the office. There was no trail wide enough leading to the cabins and she wasn't about to ruin the manicured gardens for her convenience. She made a quick check on her prisoner, who looked the worse for wear but in no danger of dying, then she headed inside, relayed the bad news about Zakkarat, made sure someone would contact his family, and then she asked about Luartaro. Yes, he'd returned, but he'd gone out again after using the telephone. Yes, she could use the telephone, too.

Annja retold the story three times before she was convinced they'd put her through to a police official who believed her and who was fluent in English. She was on the phone for the better part of an hour, answering questions and providing directions to the mountain treasure chamber as best she could. She told them about Zakkarat, the men she'd tied up and the truck filled with crates. And she agreed to wait for police to meet her at the resort; they would accompany her and the truck to Chiang Mai, where the department had a headquarters. Annja wanted to go there, anyway. She made one more phone call, this a quick one.

Since she knew it would be several minutes before anyone arrived, she dashed to her cabin and into the shower, thankful they'd spent the extra baht for accommodations with a private bath. She let the warm water sluice over her as she peeled off the loaned Thins garments. When had Luartaro returned? How had he got here? Had he found a ride somewhere? A motorcycle to borrow? Was he all right? He must be all right, she realized, if he'd gone back out again.

She turned the knob as far as it would go so the water pounded wonderfully against her, and she stood there longer than she had intended. Finally—and reluctantly—she ended it when the water started to get cold. She wrapped a towel around her, and didn't bother to dry her hair. The other towel was only faintly damp… Luartaro had been there a while ago.

Annja padded around the room, seeing Luartaro's borrowed Thins garments folded next to a chair, his suitcase opened and the clothes in it rumpled, as if he'd searched through it looking for something clean to wear.

She turned to her own suitcase. There was a note on top of it from Luartaro. He was taking the bus to Mae Hong Son to find the authorities and report everything.

Annja wondered if he'd already met any of the people she'd repeated her story to on the phone. Couldn't the police have told her someone had already reported this and saved her the time? She decided it didn't matter; she'd had to call, anyway, just to be sure…and she had the truck and its contents to hand over, along with her prisoner.

Luartaro had written that he intended to "stuff his face" while he was in town and would see about buying a puppy to replace the dog that the gunmen had killed in the Thins village. She smiled at that line.

Annja was still upset that Luartaro had taken some of the treasure from the cave—and intended to tell him to turn it over—but he partially redeemed himself with the line about the puppy.

"See you soon," he wrote. "Love, Lu."

She swallowed hard.

Love, Lu.

Did she love him? Could she love him after finding his pockets filled with pilfered jewelry? Was it true that some women were just attracted to "bad boys"?

She didn't want to love him. Her life didn't have room for such frivolities at the moment.

To get her mind off him, she looked through the business cards she'd found in the smugglers' pockets. They were all for antiques dealers—in Chiang Mai in Thailand, Luang Prabang and Vientiane in Laos, and Hue, Dien Bien Phu and Hanoi in Vietnam. There were phone numbers scrawled on the backs, and initials and numbers that had no meaning to her. But the phone numbers might prove useful.

Annja dressed quickly in comfortable jeans, a maroon polo shirt she'd worn only once before and running shoes that made her feel as if her sore feet were in heaven. She brushed out her hair, which dripped down her back, then she strapped her fanny pack around her waist, made sure her wallet and passport were in it and that there would be enough room for her ruined camera. She thrust the antiques-dealer cards in her back pocket, and then she headed outside to wait for the police.

Two cars were already there waiting for *her*. Both had their emergency lights flashing, and one officer had a gun pointed straight at her.

Annja felt for her sword hovering in the otherwhere.

20

"That was my fault, really, that Sergeant Ratsami held a gun on you." The police officer looked as if he'd just graduated from high school, as he sat in the passenger seat of the rusty truck. He let Annja drive, saying that way he'd have his hands free to take notes.

One of the police cars was in front, emergency lights turned off, leading the way to Chiang Mai. The other was behind her.

"I've lived here half my life," he continued. He'd introduced himself as Andrew Steven Johnson, born to American diplomats and now a permanent Thai resident by choice, his parents retired back on a ranch in Fort Worth, Texas. "And I know Thai and quite a few of the tribal dialects, but I mispronounce a few things from time to time, and Wiset and Ratsami thought you were some kind of smuggler—not the one who captured a smuggler. Sorry about that."

Annja smiled good-naturedly. "No harm done," she said. Then she frowned. "The smuggler in the back admitted to killing our guide, Zakkarat Tak-sin, after torturing him."

"It'll make things easy if he also admits it to us," Johnson said.

Annja could help persuade him, if necessary, she thought.

"We have a few men going up the mountain now," Johnson told her. He tapped the clipboard on his lap and pulled out a pen. "If they can find the place in the dark. And those men you said you tied up, they'll get taken into custody."

Twilight had taken a firm hold on the resort area, and with no streetlights, it was a world of shadows with charcoal-like slashes of trees looming up on both sides of the truck. The truck's lights weren't very bright, perhaps by design. Annja fixed her tired gaze on the taillights of the police car ahead of her. The windows rolled all the way down, she tried to take in the pleasant sounds of the evening, the birdlike chirping of hundreds of frogs, the cry of some night bird and the gentle rustle of the leaves in the breeze.

Annja had set the backpack with the skull fragments and dog tags in it behind the driver's seat. To her, it was not considered part of the treasure she was detailing to Officer Johnson. As far as she was concerned, the police didn't need to know about it…at least, not yet.

"Mae Hong Son doesn't have the resources of Chiang Mai," Johnson explained. He continued to banter, ruining nature's music, but his chatter helped to keep her awake. How long had it been since she'd rested?

"That's why we're going there, to Chiang Mai. There's a big department there, called the TNPD…the Thailand National Police Department. I figure I'll apply someday and work in Chiang Mai or Bangkok. More excitement there. The TNPD is a division of the Ministry of the Interior, and it was set up to handle police duties throughout the whole country. Some folks think it's even more influential than the Thai army."

Annja listened, mildly interested, and mildly amused that he'd told her he wanted to ask her questions.

"The TNPD does more than just police the streets and pick people up for breaking the laws. They go after insurgents. Those are people who—"

"I know what insurgents are," Annja cut in.

"From Burma—Myanmar—mostly. And from what I understand, if there's a war, or a really big force moved in from Myanmar or Laos or wherever, the TNPD would come under the control of the Ministry of Defense and in effect become a second army." He paused and rested his head against the seat and softly tapped his clipboard rhythmically, as if he were listening to a song in his head.

"How long has it been around, the TNPD?" Annja didn't really care to know, but she was drifting off and wanted him to keep her awake. She'd briefly toyed with the idea of having him drive so she could nap, but she liked to be in control. "Is this a relatively new police organization?"

He sat up straight and adjusted his seat belt. "No, Miss Creed. It's got quite a few decades under its belt. See, from what I studied…I knew I wanted to be in law enforcement ever since I was a kid, so I read a lot about it."

And how old are you now? she wanted to ask. He couldn't be more than twenty.

"The TNPD was modeled after Japan's national

police force—pre–World War II, of course. It was reorganized a few times as new ideas were introduced and the need for specialized training came up what with international terrorism and such. The United States sent some people over to help with training and equipment. That was back in the fifties. It's quite the organization. It's all centered in Bangkok, where the big headquarters building is. From there, technical support is provided for law enforcement throughout the whole country. They help the provincial police, the BPP—that's Border Patrol Police—small local agencies and the Metropolitan Police."

"I wish you luck joining it."

He nodded, his head bobbing so vigorously it reminded her of those little mechanical birds in bars that constantly dip their beaks into glasses of water.

"Don't need much luck, Miss Creed. Me being so fluent in English and originally from the States, I'd be welcomed, able to help with tourist matters and such. I just need to make sure I can find a nice, affordable apartment in Bangkok or Chiang Mai, in a good neighborhood with a movie theater nearby. I'll probably do that come the winter."

When he became silent again, Annja tried to turn on the radio, but the knob broke off in her hand, and no amount of fiddling would get it to work. She gave up on it and watched the road as they passed through two small villages and then entered Mae Hong Son.

Johnson started talking again. "You're here as a tourist, right? Did you get to see much of Mae Hong Son?"

Annja shook her head and worked a kink out of her

neck. She was thankful he was going to start babbling again.

"We're a little less than a thousand kilometers from Bangkok here, in Mae Hong Son. This is a big city, and it should have a bigger police force, I think. Someday it will. There's seven districts, and the Muang district, where I live, has a little less than fifty thousand people. We've got all the mountain ranges surrounding us, plenty of forests and the mists. You've probably heard that they call it the City of Three Mists." He waited for her to nod.

"It's big on tourism. Wasn't really that way when I was a kid, though. More a recent thing. Lots of ecotourism. It's an interesting place, lots of ethnic groups, including a few American families in my district who work for some tourism company. There are some Shan."

Like Zakkarat, she thought sadly.

"And some hill tribe villages are close enough to hit with a tossed stone—the Karen, Lahu, Lisu, Hmong, Lawa. The tourists love them, and the villagers coax the tourists out to see their crafts and watch the dances."

She followed the lead police car as it turned off onto a wider road.

"If we were going to Chiang Mai as tourists, we would be taking Route 1095 by way of Pai. It's less than three hundred kilometers. We're taking 108 by way of Mae Sariang. They're doing that for your benefit, Miss Creed. It's not near as scenic, but it's an easier drive."

"How long will it take?"

"To get to Chiang Mai? About five or six hours. Split the difference and call it five and a half." He tapped the clipboard again. "Now, about those questions I wanted to ask." He reached up and turned on the dome light and tilted it so it lit up his paper. "Let's start with how one woman was able to overpower three smugglers?"

"I think there were five. No, six, counting the one in the back." And that wasn't counting the men she'd dealt with the day before.

"Would've put him all comfortable in the back of one of the police cars if he wasn't so filthy and bloody," Johnson murmured. "And if you hadn't managed to truss him up so well. Now…six men, you said. That's quite remarkable for one female television archaeologist." He paused. "We get your program in my district, but it's dubbed. Your voice is a lot prettier than the woman who speaks in your place here. I saw the episodes you did on ancient Egyptian mummies being found in Australia and that goat-sucker creature in Mexico."

Annja gripped the steering wheel tighter. She'd already handed over the pistol she'd taken from one of the men. She hadn't shot any of them with it, and ballistics would show that. Still, she didn't want to have to give too many details about what had happened over the past two days.

"So, six men, with just one pistol, and no shots fired from it that we could see. Tell me how you did that." The skepticism was thick in his voice.

He was finally asking her pertinent questions. Annja took a deep breath and started to recount pretty much everything, including finding Zakkarat's body. She left out the sword, of course, and she didn't mention that she'd killed one of the smugglers. That would come out later, and she'd deal with it then. No doubt the fact that she'd killed other thugs in the Thins village would also surface. She'd dealt with such issues in the past, always scrutinized and never formally charged. But the grisly little details about the deaths yesterday and today didn't need to go into Johnson's notes right now.

His questions ended an hour later, leaving her four-and-a-half hours to herself. Annja chewed on the inside of her cheek, the slight pain keeping her awake. She ran the events and discoveries over and over in her mind, trying to put the pieces of the puzzle into place and meeting with little success.

21

They came into Chiang Mai from the south in the middle of the night, and that's where Annja stopped following the police car and took her own route.

"Hey, what are you doing?" Johnson was surprised and flustered.

"Taking a precaution," she answered as she stepped on the gas. "Covering my bases. Just in case." Just in case the questioning turned ugly when they discovered the slain smugglers. She wasn't guilty of any wrongdoing…but this wasn't her country and from experience she knew it was better to play it safe.

She took a left onto Charoen Prathet Road and sped up. On her right was the Mae Nam Ping, a wide dark strip of river that sparkled with the reflection of streetlights. She turned on Tha Phae Road and wove around a double-parked truck that was unloading boxes at a nightclub. She leaned forward and looked at the street signs, finding Tud-mai Road and swerving onto it, and ignoring the protests of Johnson, who tried to grab the wheel.

She slapped at his hand and squealed onto a side street, heading east now. The police car that had been following her turned on its lights and siren.

"Please let me have gotten these directions right. Please, please, please," she mumbled.

"Where are we—"

"Going?" She picked up speed as she turned onto Wichayanond Road. "To number 387," she said, spotting the series of buildings she was looking for and honking madly, driving through as the gates were opened. The trailing police car stopped on the street and turned off its siren.

The second phone call Annja had made in the lodge office was to the U.S. Consulate General in Chiang Mai. They'd provided a little advice—come to them as soon as possible—and they gave good directions. They said glowing things about Thai police, but cautioned that coming to the consulate first would be the best tactic.

She knew that this was the only United States consular presence outside of Bangkok. It had originally been a traditional consulate, but was upgraded to a consulate general more than two decades ago.

"Just in case," she repeated, turning off the engine, reaching for her bag and sliding out.

Johnson smiled and gave her a tip of his hat. "Well played, Miss Creed."

The consulate was the base for Department of State employees, some members of the U.S. Air Force, DEA officers and Peace Corps officials.

Pete Schwartz, aid to the consular chief, met her at the front door. Annja gestured that Johnson was welcome to join her.

They turned her captive over to the police officer

on the street and promised to also give them the crates later.

The entry smelled wonderful, of oiled, polished wood and flowers that filled a massive crystal vase.

Consulate officials—and, with her permission, Johnson—occupied her for an hour, scanning the map from the truck glove box and the marks Annja had made on it. She sat in a padded straight-backed chair, declining the more comfortable-looking couch on which she suspected she would quickly nod off. Schwartz and the others rattled off one question after the next and took copious notes as she once more related everything that had happened in the past few days and described some of the treasures. Three men from the consulate hovered during the interview, one recording the proceedings.

"We have pictures—mug shots, in the American vernacular—and we'd really like you to come into the department and go through them," Johnson said.

She got him to back off on that count until sometime later—when she could have a representative from the consulate with her.

"Hopefully, we'll have those men in custody by then," Johnson said. "The ones you said you tied up in the mountains."

"You've sent someone up there, right?" Annja had been concerned about the ones she'd left in the cavern. "You told me on the ride over here that—"

"They are on their way…were on their way around the time we left your lodge, following the directions you provided. Slower going in the mountains at night, but I'm sure they made it some time ago if the directions are true."

Finished with their questions—at least for the moment—Annja requested some time alone. She had a lot of things to do. They let her use a secretary's desk in a small reception area on the first floor. The desk was polished oak, pitted in places and with rounded corners from being bumped through the years. The chair was much newer, an ergonomic chrome-and-leather design that Annja settled comfortably into.

I could sleep in this chair, she thought. And she would fall asleep if she didn't concentrate on the task at hand. How long had it been since she'd gotten a little rest? She resisted the urge to look at a clock. Her broken wristwatch was in a trash can back at the lodge. She waited for a promised laptop and focused on the items on the desk. A coffee mug was stuffed with mechanical pencils, pens and fine-line markers. A black plastic-framed photograph showed a young man and a woman sitting on a bench—the secretary and her significant other, perhaps. A flat-panel monitor wasn't hooked to anything—Pete had mentioned the computer being out for repair. A resin figurine of a pug dog with a shiny black nose gazed happily at her. Annja leaned back in the chair and closed her eyes.

Just for a minute, she told herself. I'll just close them for a minute and maybe this headache will go away. Her temples throbbed, and her legs ached, but the pain wasn't so bad that it prevented her from drifting off. She was roused by the harsh click of shoes against the tile floor.

"Miss Creed?" Peter Schwartz said.

She sat up straight.

"Here's a computer you can use. We're wireless here. The battery should have enough charge, but if you have any problems, just give me a holler and I'll find the plug and an extension cord. I'll be in my office." Pete pointed to the open door behind her.

"Thanks, Pete. I'll make a copy of everything for you. Provided there's something salvageable to make a copy of." She knew they'd access the computer when she was done, anyway, and retrieve whatever she sent and received. She didn't care; she wasn't doing anything illegal or questionable. She had no secrets surrounding this. They were probably watching her, too. A place like this would have cameras scattered throughout. And she could probably spot the cameras…if she cared.

"I'm interested in seeing pictures of this treasure you talked about." He gave her a tired smile. "I suppose lots of people will be interested in that. Coffee? I've put a pot on."

"Coffee? Definitely." She nudged the only empty cup she spotted toward him. Annja opened up the laptop, a Toshiba with a good-size screen. Well used, the letters *J, F, T* and *H* were worn off. She was a touch typist and didn't need them.

"You needn't worry about all of this, Miss Creed. From what we can tell, you were the hero. Probably wouldn't have had a problem going straight to the police department. But you were wise to take our advice and stop here first."

"Just in case," she said.

Pete grabbed the cup and walked away as the floor overhead creaked; people were walking around. Music filtered down the stairwell, a jazzy instrumental piece. After a moment she recognized Maynard Ferguson's jazz-infused version of "Summertime." She gingerly took her digital camera out of her pocket. Definitely ruined. Too much water, too much jostling around, and the bullet it had stopped had finished it for good.

She released a shallow breath, opened the catch and carefully extracted the memory card. "Please be good," she said. She held it up to the light. It didn't look damaged. "Here goes." The card fit snugly in the appropriate laptop slot. Nothing happened for a moment, and she slumped forward and rested her chin in her hand. Then the screen blinked and a square appeared, asking if she wanted to download all the images, and if she wanted to delete them from the source when she was finished.

Yes to the first question, she clicked. No to the second.

The screen filled with postage-stamp-size images of her Thailand trip. The first were of the sky-blue bus she and Luartaro took to the lodge, then outside shots of their cabin and one of him picking at a local dish that room service had brought. She needed to call him—as soon as she sent some images of the skull bowl to the archaeology world. The next pictures were of the cave Zakkarat had taken them to, some dim because the lighting was so low and the shadows so deep. But several pictures of the teak coffins turned out remarkably well, showing the intricacies of the carving. Later pictures showed the ancient remains and the intact pots. Finally came the pictures of the treasure. Because the lighting was much brighter in that cavern, all of the shots looked good, though a few had hot spots where the flash bounced off the shiny gold.

"Summertime" ended and a new track began— "Conquistador," a hard-driving, slightly shrieking piece that Ferguson had cowritten. Annja had a few of his CDs at her apartment in New York and was particularly fond of "Conquistador." She had to concentrate on the pictures to keep herself from humming along.

"Buddha, Buddha, Buddha, crate, jewelry, Luartaro, skull bowl," she said. She'd taken seven shots of the bowl from various angles, and these she enlarged and saved to a separate folder she created and dubbed "macabre bowl." She intended to take more pictures of the skull-bowl shards when she acquired a new camera. But these pictures were more than adequate for what she needed to do right now.

Annja logged on to one of her favorite archaeology newsgroups. Several of the members had helped her ferret out information on this topic or that relic through the past few years. She suspected someone on her list would help with the skull bowl, too. But how soon that help would come was a proverbial crapshoot.

Minutes, maybe, if someone was online this very moment. Hours, or even a few days, if they were busily engaged in their own interests. She attached the photographs, along with a brief description of where they were found. Annja did not mention the golden treasure that had been found with it, but just before she hit Send, she added the dog tags—but not the names of the soldiers—and mentioned all the dried blood.

"Macabre bowl, indeed," she said.

"Here's that coffee."

She'd been so intent on typing that she hadn't heard Pete approach.

"No cream, sorry. None in my office. I usually take it black. But I have a few of these fake-cream packets." He sat the mug to her side and scattered the packets near it. "Rose keeps sweetener in one of her drawers. Is that some of the treasure? A little misshapen, isn't it?" He looked over her shoulder at the image of the skull bowl that took up most of the screen. "Ivory?"

"It was with the treasure," she said. "But I don't think it's really part of it. Everything else was gold or bejeweled, or carved from jade or coral or ivory. This is part of a human skull."

He wrinkled his nose and pointed back at his office. "You better make a couple of copies of all of that."

"Just in case," Annja repeated, slugging down the coffee and pushing the cup forward for a refill. "Do you have anything handy to eat?" Her stomach rumbled so loudly she suspected Pete heard it.

"I could poke through the kitchen. I'm sure I could find cream there, too. Or I have a box of Twinkies in my desk."

"Twinkies would do nicely." Annja salivated at the thought of sugar and empty calories. "And another cup or two or three of coffee."

22

It's not Vietnamese or Laotian, Benjamin Vaughan wrote. Or Thai, Chinese, Nipponese, Burmese. It's not Asian at all.

Vaughan was a junior college history teacher from Baton Rouge who frequented the archaeology blogs and chat lists on the weekends and in the summer months, calling himself a "lurker," but often contributing useful tidbits. He'd helped Annja in the past, but she hadn't heard from him personally in more than a year. He must have been on the internet cruising through the chat lists when she'd sent the images and description of the skull bowl.

Lucky for her, she thought. She remembered Vaughan's past information being reliable, though rambling.

It's American, he continued in his private post to her. That container you found is American, most likely. At least, I'm pretty sure it is—American by way of

Africa. From New Orleans, to be precise. But don't
quote me on that until I can take a hands-on look.

Surprised and intrigued, Annja read on, leaning close
to the screen as if she might absorb the words better by
a nearer proximity.

I saw something like your device—your container—two winter breaks ago in a museum in
Florida, down by Orlando. They had a collection of shrunken heads, too, but the curators
were going to put the heads in storage because
a group of locals were picketing and had gotten
the newspaper involved. They were up in arms
about human remains being on public display.
The Field Museum hid away its shrunken heads
about the same time. Anyway, I found out that
several months later the head curator in Florida
packed up the heads and sent them to the
Ripley's Believe It or Not museum that had just
opened in New York City, down by Times Square,
where they're a major attraction to this day.
The museum claims to have one of the largest
collections of shrunken heads in America. The
heads are the last thing you see when you leave
the building. One of the folks at the museum
said it was so visitors would have a lasting
impression of the place. I was at the Ripley's
museum, too, and saw them. That was just a few
months ago when I was attending a conference
in Manhattan for spring break. I don't otherwise
have an interest in shrunken heads. Couldn't tell
you how shrunken heads were made. Don't es-

pecially want to know. I couldn't care less about shrunken heads actually.

"You're rambling, Benjamin." Annja yawned and sipped at her coffee. It was a strong brew, but she wished it was even stronger and had a little more of an acrid bite to it. She really needed help staying awake.

Anyway, I was at the Florida museum two winter breaks past because of their Voodoo display, not because of the shrunken heads—which it was silly of the locals to protest against in the first place. You know that Voodoo is a special interest of mine. I have a cousin—a second cousin, actually—on my mother's side of the family who considers herself a mambo, a Voodoo priestess. That's not why I'm interested in Voodoo, though. I'm just interested.

He capitalized *voodoo*, giving it respect. Many of the literary sources she'd read through the years capitalized it, too—just like Baptist, Catholic and Lutheran were capitalized.

Annja skimmed through the next few paragraphs, marveling at how fast Vaughan must be able to type and post. Then she got through his ramblings and to the real attention-grabbing material.

Your container looks just like the one that the Florida museum displayed. The spitting image of it, in fact. I remember because it left one of those lasting impressions on me. I found it particularly grisly that they'd lumped it in with the Voodoo display. The skull's not exactly Voodoo. Not true Voodoo, in any event.

Grisly was the term Annja had used when she'd come upon the skull bowl, as there was something unsettling about the thing. She'd been raised in an orphanage in New Orleans, where voodoo was both a tourist concern and a religion. She'd learned quite a bit about voodoo and hoodoo, and had some friends who'd thoroughly embraced them.

Voodoo meant "God Creator" or "Great Spirit," and could trace its roots back perhaps ten thousand years on the African continent. Those who really knew about it considered the sensationalized tales of human sacrifices and devil worship laughable and the stuff of bad movies. Practitioners believed voodoo was life affirming and spiritual, and she recalled reading that there were millions who practice it around the world today, though most notably in Africa, South America, Central America, the Caribbean islands and parts of the United States. Undeniably ancient, it had been labeled the "Cult of Ancestors," and was tied closely to animistic spirits. She remembered Zakkarat mentioning that some of Northern Thailand's hill tribes were animistic.

Annja had attended more than a few voodoo ceremonies in New Orleans, during her unescorted youthful adventures away from the orphanage. In the back of her mind she relived the music and colorful clothes. In one outing a tall woman went into a trance to communicate with the spirits of her dead relatives. In New Orleans Catholicism was mixed in with some of the voodoo ceremonies, and healing the mind and body was a central message.

Historically, voodoo spread from Africa in the 1500s as the slave trade blossomed. Tribesmen abducted into slavery from Africa's west coast, now Gambia and Senegal all the way to the Congo, brought their religious beliefs with them. In the Caribbean islands, where they were forced to work on the plantations and their owners tried to turn them into Christians, they kept their faith and continued performing the ancient rituals in secret. The term *voodoo,* or *vodou* at the time, came from the African Dahomey tribe.

Annja knew that even in the present day voodoo practitioners believed in one supreme being that ruled over men's and women's families, love matters, justice, health, wealth, happiness, work and their ability to provide food for their children. Offerings were made as requests for help in a particular area, such as to improve hunting or harvesting. The practitioners' ancestors were sought for protection and guidance through trances and spells, and more than half of the rites involved health or healing.

When slaves in the New World were threatened with death if they continued the old rites, they found a parallel in Catholicism and outwardly adopted that religion. Catholics prayed to saints, as voodoo believers sought the spirits of their ancestors—all to intercede in their favor to the supreme being, or one God.

But in all the time she'd been in New Orleans, she'd never come across something like the skull bowl.

New Orleans was perfect for voodoo to spread because of its mix of cultures—French, Spanish and Indian. Haitian immigrants were added to the meld of Africans who were brought to Louisiana via the slave trade.

The New Orleans rituals Annja had observed involved healing, pacifying the spirits of ancestors, reading dreams, creating potions, casting spells for protection and initiating new priests and priestesses. She'd been to more than she could remember, finding it all fascinating and far more interesting than schoolwork and chores.

Vaughan covered some of the history in his ramblings, unaware that Annja was well versed on the subject, and oblivious to her New Orleans roots.

On one of her forays away from the orphanage she had hopped on a Haunted Tour of New Orleans and visited Marie Laveau's tomb. Annja performed the traditional wish spell, turning around three times in front of the voodoo queen's grave and knocking three times on the tomb. She had wished to be adopted the next day by a nice family, and she left a hair ornament as an offering. The wish didn't come true, and Annja had thought her offering not good enough. In later years Annja realized the wish spell was only a hook for tourists.

New Orleans was often referred to as the birthplace of Voodoo in America, Annja. Louisiana gained slaves from the French colonies of Martinique, Santa Domingo and Guadeloupe—which were considered thick with Voodoo. Haitians fled to New Orleans to add their beliefs. As it evolved, New Orleans Voodoo began to differ from practices in Africa and the Caribbean because it tended to put more emphasis on magic than religion, incorporating live snakes and thriving, as Voodoo was not suppressed in the States. Magical charms were prevalent, including gris-gris bags and Voodoo dolls," he wrote.

The last time Annja visited New Orleans, an old friend told her that a little less than twenty percent of the population embraced voodoo and new churches had sprung up. Annja's friend was involved with hoodoo, which incorporated spells and superstitions and included elements of the occult and witchcraft.

Your skull container might be Hoodoo, not Voodoo, Vaughan continued.

Now Annja stopped skimming and focused on each word. She took a gulp of coffee and held it in her mouth as she kept reading.

Or, more likely, it might be from some subgroup that became disenfranchised with Voodoo and created a dark offshoot as a way to punish their persecutors. It is dark, Annja, that thing you found...just like the one in the Florida museum. Those symbols on the outside, they're a corruption of a traditional, ancient Voodoo spell. They incorporate the symbols for Kalfu, Papa Ghede and Legba.

Annja was familiar with the names. Papa Ghede was the *lwa* of death and resurrection; Legba was the keeper of the gate between the worlds of life and death, and he was considered the origin of life and regeneration; and Kalfu was Legba's counterpart, the birther of darkness, and a dangerous *lwa*, or *loa*—a voodoo spirit.

The largest symbol on your container is a melding of the sun, the moon and a cross, the symbols of Legba, Kalfu and Papa Ghede, respectively. That's why I think it came from New

Orleans, because a few Voodoo-related cults that sprang up there in the late 1700s were known for corrupting traditional symbols and values. The cults were subsequently put down by the real Voodoo practitioners who considered their rivals malevolent and dangerous. I'd set your container at two hundred and twenty to two hundred and forty years old. Best guess without studying it firsthand. The container in the Florida museum was suspected to be that old.

She remembered that Papa Ghede was supposedly the first man who ever died in the world and that now he waited at the crossroads to escort the dying to the afterlife, a favorable counterpart to the striking and ominous Baron Samedi.

I want to study the symbols a little longer and do a little reading, but I believe the intent of the spell on your container is to trap the soul of a person, keeping it hidden from Kalfu, Legba and Papa Ghede. The person ensorcelled in effect never reaches the crossroads and dies for all eternity, experiencing the moment of his or her death over and over and never able to go beyond it. A horrendous torture…if such magical things are to be believed. Something intimate of the person—a finger, maybe, or a hank of hair—would have to be sealed inside. Very black magic.

Dog tags and blood would be intimate to a soldier, Annja thought.

I found the skull bowl in the mountains in Northern

Thailand, Annja had written, believing it to be an Asian relic…not in her wildest imaginings to be something from New Orleans.

Amazing that such a thing got all the way over to a remote part of Thailand, Vaughan wrote in a second message. But then how do people get from one spot to the next—planes, trains, automobiles and ships. Maybe someone bought it at a flea market and sold it on eBay to a collector in Bangkok. Who knows? Are you going to bring it back to the States with you? I'd like to take a closer look. We could meet somewhere.

Annja didn't reply to that last question, though she did email him an effusive thank-you note and told him the container had been broken and that she would stay in touch with him if she learned more about it.

The Ferguson CD ended and a classical piece started, a piano concerto that she guessed was Brahms. Annja groaned. She didn't mind classical music, but at the moment she would have preferred something shrieking or at least livelier.

She looked at the business cards of the antiques dealers that she'd taken from the smugglers. Maybe the skull container had come to one of them. Maybe quite a bit of the treasure in the cavern had come through one or more of the antiques shops.

There were phone numbers on the back, different than the ones listed on the front with the business name and address. Annja downed the rest of the coffee and reached for two of the Twinkies Pete had dropped off. She ate them quickly, barely registering the taste and craving more. Then she stretched forward for the telephone.

But the next call wasn't to one of the dealers, or to Luartaro. She glanced at the wall clock. It was 4:00 a.m., too early to disturb Luartaro or whoever was on duty at the lodge front desk. She dialed Doug Morrell and left a message on his voice mail.

"They're called spirit caves," she said. "They're amazing, and I found one undisturbed, with real remains. None of the coffins previously discovered had any bodies in them."

Annja took a deep breath, adopted her most persuasive voice and continued. "As for the monster rumored to be involved, I think you'll be surprised at just how… grisly…it all is."

She intended to start in on the antiques stores, calling the one in Chiang Mai first. But her body had other ideas. With the exception of the brief time she'd dozed after Doc had mended her leg, she'd been up for forty-eight hours. Annja slumped forward on the desk and fell asleep.

23

Someone nudged her gently. "Rose is here for work. And she'd, uh, like to use her desk."

Annja got up with a start, her neck making a popping sound and a lengthy list of curse words stopping in her throat. She'd had so much to do! She hadn't time for the luxury of a nap.

But she had to admit the sleep was necessary. She glanced at the clock—eight-thirty. She'd slept for four-and-a-half hours. No wonder she felt better, but at the same time stiff. Her shoulders cracked when she rotated them. She hadn't chosen the most comfortable position for a snooze. Feeling her forehead, she detected a line across it, a mark left by the edge of the desk.

Pete shoved another cup of coffee under her nose. "With real cream. The kitchen's open. Join me for breakfast?"

That was an invitation Annja was quick to accept.

A short, stocky young woman in a three-piece suit nodded curtly to Annja and took her place behind the desk.

"Rose Walters, meet Annja Creed," Pete said. "Annja, Rose."

The women gave each other polite smiles.

Annja's stomach growled noticeably.

"Our cook used to work at O'Malley's downtown."

"An Irish restaurant?"

"The best in my opinion," Pete said with a grin.

Shortly after she settled at the table and was brought a steaming plate of food, Annja thought it was the best she'd eaten in quite some time. As Pete, who had changed into a suit and tie sometime while Annja was sleeping, explained about his dealings with the Chiang Mai police, she wolfed down a perfectly seasoned rib-eye steak, three eggs scrambled with peppers, country potato cubes, mushrooms, toast and jam, fried tomatoes and baked beans.

"So you're not a suspect in anything," he finished as she upended her second glass of orange juice. "You're a hero, stopping a smuggling operation that has probably plagued this part of the world for quite some time. I got a call shortly after you, uh, took a nap. It was Officer Johnson. He seems quite taken with you, by the way. He said that fellow you had trussed up in the truck was quite talkative. Maybe all that bouncing around."

"Or maybe somebody went all Jack Bauer on him," Annja said as she reached for more potatoes.

Pete cocked his head, not understanding the expression.

"Maybe the Thai police are persuasive," she said.

He picked at his own breakfast, then reached across the table for the coffeepot and poured her another cup.

Annja thought she might float away from as much

as she'd been drinking. She looked around for the restroom.

"Phillip came in two hours ago and went over to the station with that rust bucket of a truck you drove here. He called a little while ago on his cell—"

Annja gripped the edge of the table. Luartaro had a cell phone, but she didn't know the number. She needed to call him…after a visit to the restroom. She downed the rest of the coffee.

"Phillip got a look at some of the stuff, and someone in the station told him one piece dated back several centuries and had been reported stolen last year. Probably quite a bit of it does date back a long way. Old, old stuff you found. A real hero, Miss Creed."

She pushed herself away from the table.

"There's been a problem for some time, people smuggling relics from ancient Asian temples and museums. It happens all over. Central and South America had tons of trouble with treasure hunters raiding the ruins. It was in the news," Pete said.

Annja well knew about artifact theft and the resulting cultural loss.

"This gang you broke up trafficked particularly in gold."

She could have told them that, based on what she'd seen in the treasure cavern. In fact, she had told Johnson that during the ride to Chiang Mai. And she'd probably tell the authorities again and again when they questioned her.

"Wonder if they still need to talk to me."

Pete nodded and stirred his eggs. "Phillip said they expect you down at the station sometime this afternoon. Just for questions. Like I said, you're not a suspect.

You're a hero. The local paper will probably want to do a piece."

Standing over the table, all the wonderful scents of the kitchen assailed her. The spiced eggs and potatoes were especially strong, and she almost sat back down and asked for thirds. For some reason, she never seemed to gain weight no matter how much she shoveled in.

"Restroom?" she asked.

He pointed to a door over his shoulder.

"And you'll get me a ride to the police station?"

He'd finally taken a forkful of eggs and was eating it, the words coming out muffled. "Driffmyself." He swallowed. "I'll be happy to drive you myself."

She shook her head. "You look exhausted. On second thought, I'll take a cab. I insist."

She had a stop in mind before the station. After freshening up she returned to Rose's desk and picked up the antiques-dealer cards she'd left there and the bag with the broken skull bowl.

"Mind if I borrow your phone?" she asked.

Rose waggled her fingers at it. She was busily typing away on the laptop Annja had been using. But this time it was plugged in so the battery could recharge. Annja took the phone a few feet away from the desk, as far as the cord allowed.

It took several minutes for the man at the lodge's front desk to summon a sleepy and somewhat incoherent Luartaro.

"I have been worried about you!" He added that he had not yet panicked, however, as the resort reported that she had come and gone yesterday evening, and that he spoke with one of the policemen who'd remained behind after Annja left for Chiang Mai.

Annja gave him a rapid-fire account of finding Zakkarat's body and dealing with the smugglers at the cavern, and told him she would return to the resort as soon as possible.

"I have to talk to more police today. Just routine." Indeed, she figured it would be. There were always reports to fill out. "And there's an antiques store here in the city I want to—"

"You think someone there's involved with this." Luartaro's tone was matter-of-fact. "I think I know you well, Annja. You are curious, and you cannot quit on a mystery. My sister would like you."

Annja had no reply for that. "I have to go," she said.

"Take care of yourself, Annja. I don't want to lose you."

The cabdriver took her for a tourist, and when she asked him a few questions about the city, he broke into a clearly memorized speech in fluent English.

"This city, it was the capital of all the Lanna Kingdom after it was founded almost eight hundred years ago. It was also the land's cultural center, and the center of Buddhism in Northern Thailand. Many, many temples were built by King Mengrai. We will drive by one of them."

Annja had passed him the address she wanted to go to.

"It was a little more than four hundred years ago that King Mengrai's dynasty ended and Burma occupied this land. To this day you can see the Burmese influence on the city's architecture. There and there." He pointed to a pair of squat, ornately decorated buildings, one of which looked to be an art gallery.

"It was in the late eighteenth century that King Taksin—"

Annja thought sadly about Zakkarat Tak-sin and wondered if his wife had been notified. She would call Luartaro later to make sure, and she would send flowers or whatever was appropriate.

"—defeated the Burmese forces and took back this land." He turned and looked over his shoulder, grinning broadly. "In the 1930s Chiang Mai grew to be more important when the last remnants of the Lanna Kingdom dissolved."

She saw a man in a three-piece suit riding a bicycle and balancing a briefcase on the handlebars. Two blocks later she spotted more bike riders in business attire. Traffic had been light when they left the consulate, but it was becoming heavier now, and the driver wove in and out of the lane close to the sidewalk. The sky had been a brilliant blue, although it was full of clouds over the consulate. The farther south they traveled the more gray the sky became.

"It is going to rain again," the cabdriver said.

"I wonder if all this rain hurts tourism." It was an idle thought, and she'd voiced it to be conversational.

"Tourism is very good to Thailand. And Chaing Mai is important to tourists like you. Very scenic, this province, because of mountains, valleys, flowers. Good weather." He paused. "But we are in the rainy season now. So many things to do—mountain biking, elephant shows, trips to hill tribe villages. There are many places you should visit. Chiang Mai Zoo has more than two hundred Asian and African animals. And Doi Suthep-Doi Pui National Park—"

"I don't have much time for sightseeing," Annja said

politely. She slid to the other side of the backseat and looked out the window at a temple that was being renovated. Workers scurried over it, accompanied by music from a large boom box on the sidewalk.

"But you have time for shopping, yes? There is Walking Street that you must visit. A big market opens there on Sundays with handicrafts, all displayed and very colorful and very nice. Good prices. Silks, embroidery, umbrellas—hand-painted by the hill tribes. *Sa* paper, silverware, celadon, souvenirs."

Annja tapped his shoulder. "On my next trip to Thailand. I'll act like a proper tourist then." She would come back, to see more of the caves and have a proper vacation, maybe with Luartaro. Definitely to see the long-necked women.

"It is too bad you do not have time for seeing sights this trip. There are many caves in this part of the country."

Annja's thoughts were suddenly thrown back to Tham Lod Cave and the caverns Zakkarat got them lost in the following day, and to the teak coffins with the precious and remarkable remains in them.

"You do have time for a little shopping, yes? The Night Bazaar, three blocks long, is good for tourists. Many goods there. Many restaurants."

She sighed and bobbed her head. She smiled wistfully when the first few raindrops hit the windshield. "I will try to visit the Night Bazaar before I leave." She had no intention of doing so, but she thought it would placate him.

"My brother has a restaurant there. Café Duan. Very good food. Good prices."

He pointed out a few interesting buildings as he drove

south on Suthep Road, one a massive white structure with ornate steps and roof sections.

"This was outside the city until the city grew," he said. "Wat Suan Dok. Legend says that King Ku Na favored the pious monk Sumana Thera, and lured him and his teachings of Buddhism here from Sri Lanka. King Ku Na gave the monk his royal flower garden as a place to build a temple upon, and so Wat Suan Dok was built in 1371. Half of a very holy relic is housed inside. The other half is in Wat Phrathat Doi Suthep."

"It is beautiful."

"Part of the Maha Chulalongkorn Buddhist University of the Mahanikai sect is inside. The *wat* is open to tourists."

"On my next trip," she said.

The driver turned west at the following intersection and slowed. "So you will do a little shopping." He stopped in front of an antiques store. *Chanarong's Antiquities* were the English words displayed beneath the much larger, flowing Thai script.

"Wait for you?" he asked.

"No, thank you. I might be a while."

"If you need another ride, you ask for me." He passed her his card—Thai on one side, English on the other—as she handed over several more baht than the fare called for.

"I will do that. Thank you." She slung the backpack over her shoulders, the broken pieces of skull clinking.

He drove away and she turned to scrutinize the business. The drizzle was turning into a steady, soft rain. Nearby, a restaurant which hadn't yet opened for the day advertised lunch specials. The antiques shop was on the corner, an alley too narrow to drive down, to its left. It was an older building, three stories, made of dark red bricks that had been painted a few times, the current color dark green. The upper two floors looked to be apartments, one with a window air conditioner, one with a box fan, all of them with mismatched curtains. The antiques store had lighter green paint around its windows, and red chipped paint on the door trim. All of the windows were streaked with the grime of the city, but she could see vases, bowls and wooden knickknacks through the smears. She also spotted a small closed sign propped up against the bottom corner.

"Wonderful." Annja had thought about calling the store before she came over, but didn't want to tip anyone off. She'd decided just to stop by, as it should be open according to the hours printed on the card.

She stepped close to the door, which had a small window set in it, and she peered inside. The overhang kept her dry, rain pattering against it in a steady rhythm. It was dark in the shop, but she noticed shadowy shelves filled with all manner of objects, and larger pieces— chairs, tall urns and statues lining the walls—all of it too dark to make out much detail. It was not a large store, and everything looked cramped—a curiosity-seeker's paradise.

A faint glow came from the back, and at first Annja thought it was a security light. But it flickered, as if someone was walking past it inside the shop, and she realized there was a doorway in the rear behind the sales counter, and the light was coming from a back room.

Annja didn't hesitate; she headed down the narrow alley, tipping her head up to the rain and seeing a fat orange tabby cat resting against the screen of a second-floor window. The police might already have been here; she'd given them the name of the place last night…or was it early this morning she'd done that? Maybe that was why it was closed; the owners were being questioned. She'd kept the business card, though, and the other cards—all tucked away in her fanny pack. She slowed at the end of the alley, out of force of habit, and took a quick peek around the corner.

The back of the shop was up against another alley, one that was wide enough to drive delivery trucks down and cut through by the back doors of other businesses. Trash cans lined the alley, several of them tipped over and spewing their contents onto the gravel. It reminded her of alleys she'd been down in New York. The smell was just as bad—smog from the city mixed with the garbage, the predominant odor being spoiled food tossed out by the restaurant, all of it picking up an even stronger scent in the rain. As she slipped around the corner, an oversize rat scurried out of her way and disappeared several yards away in a mound of wilted vegetables.

Only one vehicle was in this section of the alley, and Annja crept toward it. An older model Jeep, it was parked directly behind the antiques shop, and its tires were caked thick with mud. The top was off the Jeep, and rain pattered against the worn seats.

Annja put her ear to the back door, which was painted the same red as the front and peeling in equal amounts. She heard voices, but they were muffled by the wood and the rain, and she didn't understand the language, though it clearly had an Asian sound. Music was playing to complicate matters, from something that had poor speakers. It was fuzzy-sounding and crackled with static.

She tested the knob. It wasn't locked.

Annja almost didn't go inside. The police should deal with these people—if they were involved in the smuggling. And they most definitely were involved somehow, she knew; the Jeep was evidence of that. It was no doubt one that had been in the mountains when she, Luartaro and Zakkarat had emerged from the treasure cavern. But the police might have already been here and found nothing concrete, or they might already have arrested people. However, it was equally possible that they might not have checked out this lead yet.

Annja slowly opened the door, the hinges creaking, but not loud enough to be heard over the static-laced music. She had to go inside; her curiosity had won out, coupled with a desire to see the puzzle through. She glided through the door and hugged the shadows thrown by a tall shelf. The light was in the forward part of the room, near the door to the shop. It spilled from a wrought-iron pole lamp that probably was an antique; a fluted bowl covered with a dusty film shielded the bulb, and the bowl part of it was definitely an antique. It threw a pale yellow light over a man who was scratching at something on a desk, maybe writing in a ledger. Another man, one in his sixties judging by the gray-speckled hair, stooped shoulders and overly thin frame, hovered over him. Between the men and Annja was a high countertop that had two crates and packing material on it. They looked similar to the ones that had been in the cavern, but crates were crates. She started toward the counter to get a better look, her mind touching the sword…just in case there was trouble.

And there would be trouble. Except for a few days

spent in the cabin, this vacation had been nothing but trouble.

Annja didn't see a weapon on either man, but then she was only getting back views. The radio was on a shelf above the desk; the music stopped playing and was replaced by a commentary she couldn't understand. She held her breath and edged forward, listening for the third man, the larger shape she'd earlier seen walk in front of the door and blot out the light. She picked up a rustling sound from somewhere in the shop; the third man was still out there.

Scattered in the packing mix were brass figurines the size of lemons—small Buddhas, gazelles, apes and pigs, some with other metals inlaid in them and all of them looking old.

Annja took another step, preparing to hunker down behind the countertop. One more step, and then pain consumed her as something heavy crashed down on her head. Darkness reached up and swallowed her.

24

Annja knew she was dreaming, but she couldn't wake up—didn't want to, as this was thoroughly pleasant. She was floating, or at least treading so lightly on her feet that she couldn't feel what she was certain was marshy ground under her. However, she could feel—or imagined that she could—the soft brush of fern leaves across the backs of her hands hanging at her sides and the breeze that played across her face, cooling her.

It was warm in her dream, the sun high overhead and cutting through a gap in the tall jungle canopy. Summer, maybe, she speculated, and near noon. She wanted it to be summer and so guessed that it was—it was her dream and she could make it whatever season she wanted. But it wasn't too hot. She'd sweated enough the past few days.

Beads of water on the big acacia leaves hinted that it had rained recently. Annja hadn't been caught in it, though, as she was thoroughly dry; she'd had enough of rain recently in real life that it didn't need to intrude on her dream. She didn't hear anything, but thought that she should.

Then sounds intruded, all of them pleasant, the chirp of the small green tree frogs that had sprung up on the trunks, the musical chitter of a little monkey, the cry of a bird circling overhead and the gentle hush of the leaves nudging one another in the breeze.

Paradise.

And she was floating in it.

Primitive and beautiful, as she imagined the land must have been to the ancient Hoabinhiam people.

The hunter-gatherers were near the mountains, and so she added those craggy peaks to the vista, towering up and artfully sculpted by her mind, covered with thick jungle growth and not yet bearing the scars of trails and ruts from Jeeps, and not yet rubbed clean of cave paintings by tourists needing to touch the past.

Annja would have pronounced the scene "amazing," but she had no voice in the dream. Only the creatures and the wind and the leaves made sound, and she considered that just as well. She'd talked so much lately—to Officer Johnson, to the people at the consulate and, before that, to Luartaro. Should he be here, in her dream? She could make Luartaro give back the jewels he'd taken from the treasure cavern. Couldn't she do whatever she wanted, as she was making this up as she floated along?

In answer to her thoughts Luartaro appeared a short distance in front of her. He was clean-shaven and in pressed clothes that hung perfectly on his rugged frame. Zakkarat stepped out from behind him, ruining her romantic thoughts.

Zakkarat's clothes were slick with mud and blood and a knife protruded from the center of his chest. Bullet holes riddled his torso, the design an arrow that pointed to a sign that had materialized: Bird Show.

Annja blinked and tried to dismiss Zakkarat, as she dismissed her sword when it was no longer needed. Zakkarat looked at her with empty eyes and reached out, thick gold rings on each of his fingers.

Go away, she ordered the walking corpse but no sound came out.

Zakkarat melted into the ferns. Luartaro followed, the colors of him smearing like an ice-cream cone dropped on hot pavement. The monkey howled mournfully, and Annja looked up to see it hop from the tree above her and race toward the mountains.

"Free me," the monkey called to her. "Free me. Free me. Free me."

Annja glided after it, curious where the dream would take her. She passed beneath a spreading tree covered in bright pink and white blooms. It looked like a dogwood, out of place in the jungle. There were willows, too, like the massive old trees she remembered from her youth in New Orleans, some with vines growing so profusely on them they looked like giant green mushrooms.

Farther in pursuit of the monkey, which seemed to have slowed to accommodate her lazy pace, she heard wind chimes. Clinky-clanky and almost tinny, not as pleasantly musical as the glass chimes that used to hang in the orphanage's yard. The sound grew louder and she looked up.

Not wind chimes…dog tags, hanging from a dead branch and dripping blood. She floated out from underneath them and hurried after the monkey.

The mountains were easy to climb in her wraith-like state, and the vines that seemed to grab at her feet passed harmlessly through her. The scents were more intense as she rose, the flowers the strongest. They were mostly native Thai flowers: bunnak, phikun, lotus and chumhet-yai, some of which were edible and had medicinal purposes. But there were out-of-place blooms, too: tulips, daffodils and crocuses.

Annja loved the smell of flowers, and she was certain she picked up a trace of bougainvillea. The bright magenta and purple flowers were native to South America, and she remembered that they grew profusely outside Luartaro's office window in Argentina.

The plant was discovered in the mid-1700s, Luartaro had told her, by a French botanist accompanying an explorer named Louis Antoine de Bougainville. She saw the beautiful thorny vine between a gap in the trees and she glided toward it, hovering and inhaling the fragrance. The bougainvillea's thorns were normally tipped by a black, waxy material. But these were coated with dried blood.

Annja shuddered and looked closer. Bougainvillea thrived in moist soil. There'd been a few pink-flowered ones across the street from the orphanage in New Orleans. She'd also seen some in the gardens of the *wat* the cabdriver had taken her past in Chiang Mai. The flowers were all over the world now—in warm climes. The plant in her dream was especially vibrant…and disturbing.

She thought she saw something in the leaves. Peering closer still, a face stared back at her. It had been almost indistinguishable at first from the foliage. A young man's face, smooth and unlined but covered with stripes of green and black paint that made the whites of his eyes stand out starkly. The mouth was set in a determined scowl. There were other faces, too, all painted, and all with sweat beads on their foreheads.

The monkey called to her, and she turned to see it hanging by its feet and holding something so she could see. A skull? No, just part of one. The monkey's fingers traced designs on it, and dark symbols appeared as it filled with a black substance. The monkey pointed at the symbol for Papa Ghede.

It was her skull bowl, and it cracked into pieces when the monkey dropped it and scrambled farther up the mountain.

Annja followed it.

She crested a rise and teetered at the edge of a gaping maw yawning up from the ground. Light flickered from inside, revealing mounds of treasure. Luartaro and Zakkarat were there, stuffing their pockets. It was almost comical how their pockets bulged with coins and jewelry, their cheeks, too, just like chipmunks that had stuffed walnuts away for later.

Put it back, Annja tried to tell them, but with no voice.

Luartaro understood. His expression haunted and sad, he opened his pockets and spilled the contents on the stone floor. He grew thinner as the coins continued to spew, Zakkarat kneeling and scooping them up. Thinner and thinner until he was little more than a skeleton.

"Free me, Annja," he implored as he melted into the stone, the broken skull bowl marking the place where he had stood.

"Free me," Zakkarat said. A heartbeat later, he was gone, too.

She tried to wish them back; it was her dream and she could paint it the colors she wanted. But they didn't return. And moments later the treasure vanished, too, leaving her alone at the top of the mountain, staring down at the green of the Thailand jungle. Thunder boomed, but there were no clouds. It boomed again and again, and she thought that maybe the sound was a drum beating. It came from down below, on the other side of the river that had magically appeared.

Annja went toward the sound, feeling the trees pass through her and sensing her heart beating in time with the thunderous drum. She stepped in time with it, walking over the water and following the bird-show sign. The breeze had stopped, taking the coolness with it.

She started to sweat.

My dream, she thought, make the heat go away.

But the opposite happened. The heat became more intense, the sun beating down in time with the drum, the leaves withering in what had become Sahara-like temperatures. The drum thrummed louder and Annja threw her diaphanous hands over her ears and tried to hum to blot it out, a tune she'd remembered Luartaro humming.

Leaves drifted to the ground around and through her, and branches curled and darkened in the oppressive heat. She felt the rings of sweat grow on her chest and under her arms and she smelled the smoke in the air—all the perfume from the bougainvillea gone. The wisps of smoke writhed like snakes and trailed away, beckoning.

She followed, still stepping in time with the drum.

The forest died and the trunks became blackened slashes that crumbled and then reformed into squat stone buildings. The smoke-snakes thickened and formed streets that radiated out from the center of a village like the spokes of a wheel. In the middle of the ring a fire burned; it was the source of the oppressive heat.

The drum quieted, to be replaced by the crackling and pops of the wood.

There was a figure in the middle of the blaze, burning and crying, and forever finding a place in history as a martyr.

Annja had dreamed of Joan and the fire before.

This had turned into a nightmare.

Bring back the bougainvillea and the gold coins and the little monkey that threw the remnants of the skull bowl, she thought.

The fire raged higher, the embers spitting away and sparkling like shards of silver, all flying through the crowd that had instantly appeared and streaked toward Annja.

The heat hurt her, it was that severe, and the shards that pelted her stung horribly.

Her face hurt the most, her right cheek swollen and aching. Why did it hurt so much? Her wrists, too, something squeezing them. Her shoulders…something digging into them.

The shards?

Embers from the fire?

Pieces of Joan?

Fingernails?

The village vanished and in place of burning Joan was a man with an expression twisted in anger.

"Wake up, Annja Creed," he said.

25

Annja was happy to be free of the nightmare, but aghast at the reality that had replaced it. She was in the back room of the antiques shop, trussed up in an uncomfortable straight-backed chair, her wrists and ankles tied with an electrical cord that dug painfully into her skin.

The air was heavy with the residue of cigarette smoke and the papery scents of packing material. A blackened window was open a few inches and the odors of the garbage in the alley came in with the rain.

The older man with stooped shoulders was at the desk, the younger man hovering over him this time. They had her fanny pack and were studying her passport, which was how they knew her name. The business cards she'd had in her fanny pack were crumpled on the floor at their feet. Her backpack sat nearby.

"She is the one," the younger man insisted, stabbing a finger at the passport and then pointing at Annja. "I tell you, Kim. This Annja Creed from New York City is the one who killed Dak and Soon in the mountains."

The man leaning over her, Kim, struck her hard on the cheek with his fist. "Annja Creed of New York City. She is a long way from the United States of America, and a long way from our mountains. Why is she here in our shop?" The question was asked with so much force that his spittle peppered her face. "Why is she here, so far from the cave she had no business being in? And she has no business being here!" He dug his fingers into her shoulders, the pain competing with the ache in her cheek.

"She had our card, Uncle. See?" He pointed to the cards on the floor. "She had all of them."

"What are you, Annja Creed?" Kim's eyes were hot black coals burning into hers. "Are you a thief? Did you come here to steal from thieves, Annja Creed from New York City?" His command of English was excellent, but it was thick with an Asian accent and she had to struggle to understand some of his words. He grabbed at her arm and felt her muscles. "Are you security? Were you hired to recover some relic that had found its way into my shop?"

A piece of information she'd just gained. The man Kim was the owner of this antiques store, maybe of all the stores she'd had cards for.

"You are not police, Annja Creed. The police were here an hour ago and left us alone. What…are…you?"

When she didn't answer, he struck her face again and again. She tasted blood in her mouth and felt it spill over her lower lip. He'd loosened at least one of her teeth. Her tongue felt thick and swollen.

"What are you?" This time he hit her in the stomach.

"An archaeologist," she managed. "I am an archaeologist." She'd give him that much.

He made a rumbling sound and took a step back. Behind him, the men at the desk picked through her wallet and looked at her broken camera. She'd kept it rather than toss it, putting the memory card back in, thinking the camera shell would protect the card.

"I am an archaeologist," she insisted. "I was in the caves looking for the teak coffins." It was the truth, and her voice was steady in telling it. "On vacation, I went to the caves to see the coffins. That I found your… treasure…was an accident."

"Pfah! You expect us to believe that?" He balled both of his hands and swung at the air with so much strength she felt a breeze in front of her face. "What are you, Annja Creed? A special agent of some government?"

"The business cards were Dak's, Uncle. I recognize his handwriting. She must have taken the cards from Dak after she killed him."

Kim hit her in the stomach again. "I want to know just what you have learned about our…business, Annja Creed. I want—"

"She is trained, Uncle," the younger man cut in. "I saw her dance like Bruce Lee. She had a sword and—"

A cell phone buzzed, and Kim turned away from Annja and walked into the shop. He spoke quickly in Vietnamese, and then switched to English as if he was now talking to someone else.

"The police were here, Sandman, but I convinced them nothing was wrong. I am merely an antiques dealer who struggles to pay his rent. They came in the front and looked through the shop. They did not see the Jeep and the crates in it." He paused, obviously listening to the individual on the other end of the call. "I have a spy here," he continued. "One that I am making less pretty by the moment. One who discovered our operation."

Annja had to strain to hear him over the quiet discussion of the two other men. They were futilely trying to get her camera to work so they could call up the pictures she'd taken. A large fly buzzed around the older man's head.

"A woman, this spy. My nephew Nang says she was at the cave and killed Soon and Dak with a sword. Pfah! Nang said there were two other men with her, one dead. I will find out where the last one is, and then I will kill her. No loose ends, Sandman. I will take care of her, my old friend, and I will see you soon. Tell my father I will bring him that case of Singha lager he asked for, and—"

Annja didn't need to see her reflection to know that her face was bruising and swelling. Her legs throbbed and her feet were numb, the cord around her ankles tied too tight. She thrust the noises of the shop—Kim's conversation…he was on his second call now, and the snarls of the two men cursing over her broken digital camera—all to the back of her mind. Out on the street a car honked repeatedly, and she ignored that, too.

Instead, she closed her eyes and concentrated on her sword.

She reached out and felt the pommel form against her numb hands that were still tied behind her back.

She opened her eyes to see the men using a tool on her camera with some measure of success by their happy reactions. The sword held awkwardly behind her, she shifted her grip and turned it so the blade was against the cord and the pommel rested on the floor. She started cutting and almost immediately felt the circulation in her hands improve. The cords might have been strong, but they were like warm butter to the ancient blade. The cords fell to the floor, the men not hearing the slight sound because they were so preoccupied with an image they'd managed to call up on the viewer of the camera.

Annja brought the sword around in front of her, her sore shoulders practically screaming in protest at being moved. Then she cut the cord holding her ankles to the chair.

"Nang—" the older man warned the other. "She is—"

"Free!" Nang shouted. He tugged open the top drawer and reached inside it as Annja stood. She fought a wave of dizziness that threatened to spill her to the floor.

Her legs felt like lead, asleep, and her feet still were numb and clumsy, but she forced them forward, turning the blade as she went and striking the flat of it against the older man's side. He fell with the second blow, the wind knocked out of him.

Nang drew an old pistol out of the drawer, and with a shaky hand waved it at her. "Kim! She is free! Kim!" He fired, the shot going wild and ricocheting off the counter behind her. A second shot also missed.

Annja held the sword in one hand. The other shot out and grabbed the gun barrel, yanking it out of Nang's hand and hurling it toward the back door.

"Down!" she yelled.

He dropped to his knees.

"Down!"

He flopped to his stomach and laced his fingers behind his head like a thug in a police movie might. She would have knocked him unconscious, but she heard heavy footfalls and the squeak of old hinges. Kim had come back, his fleshy face contorted with rage.

"What are you?" he demanded.

She took a step toward him, both hands tight on the pommel, sword up perpendicular to the floor. The fly that had been pestering the old man had switched targets to Annja now. It landed on her arm and she wriggled to chase it away.

"What are you? A demon?" He retreated into the shop, and she rushed after him. "Where did the sword come from?"

In the light that filtered in through the smudged front windows and seeped in from the back room, she made out tall elaborate urns; statues of long-legged birds with wings tucked close to their sides; old swords on a rack with dingy, tasseled guards; and graceful ladies in painted gowns that pooled around their bases. The shelves were narrow and filled with ceramic figurines that looked delicate and valuable, and old.

She spotted Kim ducking behind a shelf filled with terra-cotta pieces that could have come from a dig.

The rest of the details were lost in the shadows and in her hurry to catch the man.

26

Faint sounds indicated Kim was making another call. "Get here now!" he whispered to someone. Then he snapped the phone closed and turned down another aisle.

Annja stalked him, brushing by a lamp styled after an old Tiffany. The shop apparently carried an assortment from different places and time periods. How much of it was authentic? And how many pieces were forgeries and knockoffs...if any? The antiquities she'd seen in the cavern had certainly been real.

She didn't hear him anymore, but she saw his shoes at the base of a unit of shelves. He'd taken them off to be quiet. A smart, vile man. He'd moved quietly behind her before to clock her on the head without warning. She studied the statues against the wall, looking for one that might be breathing; it would be a good place to hide.

Nothing. They looked stiff like department-store mannequins, though much more intricate and valuable. Annja breathed shallowly and stepped slowly, careful not to let her clothes rustle or catch against the unfinished wood of the shelves.

Where are you? she thought. He'd called her a demon, but he was that—a man who trafficked in treasures and who had a highly illegal operation in place. She'd heard him on the phone telling whoever was on the other end that he would kill her. A demon in man's clothing. How extensive was the smuggling? Annja needed to take him alive; she had too many questions that demanded answers.

Annja reached the end of the aisle, which was near the front of the shop. Holding her breath, she looked around the shelf. Still nothing. A glance at the front windows showed that the grime she'd thought was on the outside was actually on the inside, as if it had been smeared with something to make it difficult to see much…or at least to see any of the pretty details. The door had three dead-bolt locks on it and a wire that ran up one side. There was a motion sensor and a security camera that looked pretty high-tech in comparison to the building and its furnishings.

Maybe the entirety of the store was a front. Maybe the place was always closed to the run-of-the-mill customer. Annja retraced her steps, heading to the back of the shop. He'd probably doubled back to the other room. Or else he—

It was the faintest of sounds, and had she not been paying especially close attention, she wouldn't have noticed. Wood squeaked, like weight was shifting on it. Her head snapped up just as a figure jumped off the top shelf. She leaped away as his blade whistled in the musty air and sliced off a hank of her hair.

He followed her, kicking as he went, landing a solid

blow to her arm as she ducked beneath his sword, then kicking out with his other foot as she spun away between terra-cotta warrior statues. She couldn't identify the style of martial arts he employed. It looked like karate, but it had elements of *qwan ki do*, which consisted mostly of jumping and scissor techniques with the hands and feet. The manner in which he used his sword also hinted at *qwan ki do*, which she'd studied briefly in New York a summer ago.

He came at her as she darted out from between the statues and dropped beneath his next kick. He held the sword in his right hand and performed a praying-mantis move, then followed it with rapid lightning thrusts with the heel of his left hand. The quick moves were intended to overwhelm her and smacked of karate or *kenpo*.

He shifted from one foot to the next, always kicking or punching or slashing and keeping her off balance. He knocked over a shelf of melon-size monkey carvings, and Annja cringed. She'd not been fighting back, only defending, on three counts. She wanted to study his technique and look for an opening; she didn't want to damage anything in the shop—the objects might be irreplaceable—and she didn't want to kill him.

She wouldn't kill him; she was adamant about that.

He shifted into an animal fighting style, leopard kung fu. Annja knew an old Chinese man who taught it in Central Park on Wednesday mornings. Like the other methods her attacker employed, leopard kung fu emphasized speed and angular attacks. He wasn't trying to rely on strength, which his frame hinted he had plenty of, but rather on his quickness and trying to outsmart her.

"Why block when you can kick?" the old Chinese

man had posed to Annja and his other students. "Why defend when you can attack?"

Her opponent focused on elbow jabs now, catching her on the shoulder as she brought her sword up, then focusing on a series of low kicks that though she avoided them drove her back into a counter covered with brass bells of various sizes. Many of them tipped, filling the air with a brief musical cacophony that managed to distract Kim.

Annja raised herself and rolled over the top of the counter, deftly avoiding a teetering brass urn and the next series of off-tempo sword swings that shattered the glass top and set the remaining bells clanking.

She made a move to slip around the corner, but instead vaulted it, planting her left hand on the intact edge of the countertop and bringing the sword up with her right. Her opponent was mixing martial-arts styles, so she did, too, landing a knee to his chin and at the same time hooking her leg around his sword arm, avoiding his blade and setting him off balance. She'd studied him just long enough to pick up a few flaws in his otherwise adept practice.

"Don't...want...to...ruin...anything," she told him through clenched teeth.

"Priceless antiques, all of these things," he returned as he took a step back and wiped blood off his lip with the back of his free hand.

Not all of them, she observed. Some didn't look all that old. Still, the lighting wasn't good enough for her to make an appraiser's judgment.

"Worth a fortune, all of them, New York City spy." His breath wasn't labored, evidence of what good shape he was in.

As she maneuvered around him and the closest high shelf, he drove at her again, using a series of lightning-fast low kicks, two of which connected with her shin. He had no way of knowing she'd been shot in that leg and that it was still sore.

Annja cried out, and he grinned, thinking it was his kicks that had hurt her.

"All of these things more valuable than you, New York City spy." He held the sword up high, the tip of the blade touching a dangling light fixture and disturbing a spiderweb that clung to it. He brought it down hard, the veins bulging along the sides of his neck, reminding Annja of the ropy roots of an acacia tree just beneath the soil.

She hooked her blade up at the last minute, the edges of the two weapons meeting with a shrill, scraping sound. In the back of her mind she saw the shards of silver arcing away from the fire that burned Joan of Arc, and she worried that the sword would again shatter and be forced to find a new wielder to make it whole.

But her sword withstood the blow, and instead Kim's snapped. He howled angrily.

"A fortune!" He tossed the broken blade behind him and clenched his fists, veins standing out on the backs of his hands, knuckles white. "A *katana* from the Muromachi period. Nearly seven hundred years old, that sword you ruined!"

"I believe you're the one who ruined it," she countered, turning her blade so the flat of it would strike him when he presented an opening. "My sword isn't quite that old. But it's getting there."

She performed a foot drop, fan kick and spinning kick, striking him soundly across the center of his chest with the sword as she danced around him and the edge of a tall, narrow case of antique hairpins and brooches.

Kim retaliated with an eagle claw and an overleap kick, still not tiring. A part of Annja reveled in the fight, the exertion blotting out the pain in her cheek from where he'd punched her repeatedly and the ache in her ankles and wrists from being tied so tight with the cord. Her breathing was deep and even, and she was aware of everything around her—the closeness of the antiques, which she tried so hard to avoid; Kim, who feinted and punched as she weaved through the shelves and matched him maneuver for maneuver; and the men in the back room, one of whom was moaning and stirring.

Annja would have to finish this soon before the odds worsened. She'd left the nephew's gun in that room.

"So you know who I am and where I am from. Give me the same luxury. Who are you?" It was a simple enough question, and Annja enjoyed banter during a fight, particularly one well matched like this.

"Kim Pham."

"Where are you from, Kim Pham?"

He smiled, showing off-colored teeth. Another smoker from the stains, though probably not a heavy one given his agility and stamina. "Bac Ninh Province."

Annja had no idea where that was. "In Northern Thailand?"

He shook his head as he took the praying-mantis stance. "Vietnam. Why is this so important? Why does a dead woman want to know about me? A soon to be very dead woman."

The last comment tipped her off. She glanced to the back of the shop, where Kim's nephew leaned against the door frame, one hand cradling the side of his head, the other holding the gun he'd retrieved.

Annja dipped down and reversed her grip on the sword, pommel facing out as she rammed it with all her strength into Kim's stomach. He was a big man, but it wasn't fat she connected with. The muscles were thick, and she'd hit him just hard enough to rattle him a little. Fortunately, she was close enough to him that his nephew was afraid to shoot.

She drove the pommel against him again and again, recalling how he'd pummeled her with his fists minutes ago when she'd been tied in the chair. The air rushed from his lungs and he doubled forward, hands clawing at the air and then finding her shoulders. He suddenly gripped her throat in a choke hold and slammed the back of her head against the shelf behind her. Something toppled off and crashed on the floor.

"Bitch!" Kim cursed. "That was Ming! Look what you did!"

Annja jabbed him again with the pommel, this time under his arm, using all the strength she could summon. He gasped and relaxed his grip. She dropped beneath his arms, came up at him from the other side and kicked him in the groin.

"My fault? That's two antiques you've claimed I broke. You're a thief *and* a liar!" Annja struck him once more with the flat of the blade, crouching when he doubled over again and using him for cover against his nephew. "I've been trying not to break anything."

When he cursed at her this time, it was in Vietnamese.

"And it's not polite to talk in a language I can't understand." Feeling a little better, and her feet no longer tingling, Annja had gotten her moxie back.

She lured him toward the front of the shop, farther from the nephew with the gun. As much as Annja didn't want to be shot, she worried that the young man, who had proven to have a lousy aim, might shoot his uncle. She needed Kim alive to answer her questions.

They continued to parry each other's blows, but Annja was gaining on him and he was finally tiring. Sweat grew under his arms and appeared on his forehead, and his eyes narrowed with hate. That was good; hate made people careless. Kim knocked over only two more pieces before she had him at the front door. Red-faced, he sputtered at her in Vietnamese and looked like a pile-driving machine aiming his fists at her and striking the door instead.

He cracked it down the middle, like a karate practitioner splitting a block of wood, and set off an alarm. It was her turn to curse.

The police didn't need to find her at this shop; she was supposed to be at their office answering questions. Now she'd have a lot more to answer…if they spotted her here. She wasn't guilty of anything, but she'd knocked out an old man and entered a closed store. If nothing else, the police would detain her. Maybe they would even charge her with something.

A new sense of urgency took over, and she dismissed the sword, wanting both hands free. Kim's eyes grew wide when he saw the blade disappear, then they closed in unconsciousness as she delivered an uppercut to his jaw, cracking it and sending him backward against an old piece of pottery that split in two.

"All right," Annja pronounced. "That was my fault."

She glanced at the price tag and whistled. "But I'm not paying for what I broke." She grabbed him by the shirt and pulled him down an aisle toward the back of the shop, stopping and peeking around the end to see the nephew still in the door frame, holding the gun with both hands now in an effort to steady himself.

"I'd drop the gun," she called to him. "Unless you want to end up like your uncle Kim."

He dropped the gun.

"And I'd back up a bit."

He complied.

Annja wanted to put some distance between him and the gun.

"Nang, right? I heard Kim call you Nang."

He nodded.

"Be a good fellow, Nang, and put your hands behind your head."

He got to his knees for good measure.

She tugged Kim behind the back counter and picked up the gun, emptying the bullets and tossing them in an urn that had been serving as someone's spittoon. She'd intended to question Kim, but he was soundly out.

"Nang, I've got a few questions, and it would be in your best interest to answer them. You understand English fine, yes?"

Another nod.

Annja pointed at the chair she'd been tied to.

"Sit and make yourself uncomfortable."

27

The phone on the desk was an old rotary model that was practically an antique. She used it to call the consulate, where she talked to Rose Walters. She told Annja that Pete was out of the building. After providing the antiques shop's address and giving a quick recap of her activities, leaving out the sword fight, she hung up and turned her attention to her prisoner.

"How old are you, Nang?"

He replied, "Twenty-two," after she repeated the question with a trace of venom in her voice.

He looked a little older than that. She would have put him at thirty. Maybe smuggling was a hard life. "Old enough that you should know not to get mixed up in something like this. Old enough not to wave a gun around unless you really know how to use it."

"I can use a gun," he retorted.

"Oh, you can pull the trigger. You just can't aim." Or maybe he just didn't want to kill anyone. Maybe he could find redemption.

She put her palm against his chest, the little use of

force serving as well as if she'd set a heavy anvil on him. He didn't budge, and the sweat beads multiplied on his face. She could hear his ragged breath, and the snores of the old man she'd propped up against the wall; she hoped she hadn't hurt him too badly. She didn't hear sirens, and she thought she would have by now, from the alarm she'd tripped in the other room.

"The police aren't coming, are they?" she asked.

Nang shook his head.

"Who is?"

He shrugged and she pushed harder against him.

"Men who work for my uncle," he said. "The alarm summons them."

"How many?"

Another shrug. He shook nervously. "I…I do not know. I just know that if trouble comes, the men come. They should be here soon."

She removed her hand and stepped back. He looked at his lap, not wanting to meet her angry gaze. Kim was still unconscious, and she had no way to tell how long he would be out.

"Nang, I want to be gone before those men you mentioned arrive. Understand?"

A quick nod. He still avoided looking at her face.

"So you're going to talk quickly. Then I'll be away and you can go about your business." She paused. "I don't want to hurt you. But if I have to—"

"What do you want to know?"

"Who is behind all of this?"

His shrug was more exaggerated this time.

Annja growled from deep in her throat and stepped to the desk, sticking her passport and wallet back in her fanny pack and strapping it on. She picked the crumpled business cards off the floor and flattened them as best as she could, then stuffed them back in her pocket. She took her camera, too, which they seemed to have repaired or at least jury-rigged to view the pictures.

"Try again," she said. "Who is behind this?"

Nang set his chin against his chest and mumbled something.

"Pardon…I couldn't hear you."

"Lanh Vuong."

The name didn't mean anything to her.

"Is that the Sandman? I heard your uncle talk to someone named the Sandman."

"No."

"So who is Lanh Vuong?"

He let out a great sigh, sounding like sand blowing in the dry wind. "An old and powerful man," he began. "An important one where I come from."

"Tell me more."

He hesitated a bit too long, and she closed her fist.

"Where is Lanh Vuong?"

"Hue."

She didn't need to pull the card out of her pocket. She remembered that one of the business cards was for an antiques store in Hue, Vietnam.

"Vietnam?" Annja wanted to be sure.

"Hue, Vietnam."

The desk had maps stacked on the corner. She pushed against his chest again and turned her back on him, searching through the maps and finding one produced by *National Geographic* in 1967 that showed Vietnam, Laos, Thailand and part of Burma.

"You're Vietnamese, right, Nang?" Annja looked over her shoulder to see him nod. "Then I've got a new idea." Grabbing a selection of maps, and the only set of keys she saw on the desk, she slung her backpack over her shoulders, returned to Nang and tugged him up by his collar.

He looked noticeably paler, and his face was even sweatier.

"You're coming with me," she said.

He started shaking, and she let out a disappointed sigh. She'd thought a smuggler should have a little more backbone.

"To…Hue? Going…to…Hue?"

It was her turn to nod. She nudged him out the back door and toward the muddy Jeep, just as a silver Hilux Vigo pulled into the far side of the alley. A four-door pickup, it was pristine enough to have just been driven off the showroom floor. Its windows were tinted, but Annja could make out three shapes inside.

"Lovely. I'll bet those are the men who work for your uncle." She shoved him into the Jeep's passenger side, jumped behind the wheel, sitting on the maps she'd grabbed, and prayed one of the keys fit in the ignition. Annja didn't want another fight right now.

She fumbled with the keys as two of the men leaped out of the Hilux, the driver staying behind the wheel. One man headed to the shop's back door, the other came barreling at the Jeep, pulling a gun out of his waistband.

The second key worked, and the Jeep's engine roared, tires spinning and throwing clumps of dirt at the man.

"The seat belt," Annja shouted. "Put it on! Now!"

Nang groped for the belt as Annja slammed her foot on the gas pedal and shot down the alley, right front fender catching a garbage can and sending it and its smelly contents flying.

"Duck!"

Nang hunched down as much as the belt allowed. The windshield shattered as bullets struck it. The shooter was using a silencer.

At the end of the alley she jerked the wheel hard right and swerved to avoid a parked car. Traffic wasn't heavy in this part of the city, and she took advantage of a near-empty street as she raced south. A few more turns, a cut through an alley, the silver truck gaining on her, and she found herself going west on Si Donchai Road, where a steady stream of cars headed in both directions and exhaust filled the air and settled heavily on her tongue.

She slammed her hand against the steering wheel in frustration as she weaved around a late-model Honda Civic and found herself smack behind a tour bus. She heard tires squeal behind her, and a glance in the rear-view mirror showed the pickup bullying the Civic onto the sidewalk.

"They will kill us!" Nang's knuckles were white on the dashboard.

"I will do my best to not let that happen." Annja spun the wheel to the right, cutting across the opposite lane of traffic and nearly being sideswiped by a minivan. More tires squealed, including the Jeep's. Cars started honking, and in the distance she heard a siren.

"The police!" Nang looked relieved and frightened at the same time.

Annja was confident she could talk herself out of trouble; she'd done it many times before. But having an unwilling passenger could be considered kidnapping.

Then there was the issue of car theft, breaking and entering at the shop, beating up the old man—it would take a while to talk herself out of this.

The truck swerved right behind her. Only two shapes were visible inside, one leaning out the passenger window—the man who'd shot at them in the alley. Everything was happening too fast for Annja to get a good look at him, but his yellow shirt and his shaved head stood out. He fired at them again, the bullet striking the rear of the Jeep.

Her heart pounded; she realized he was aiming at the jerricans in the back. He could blow them up with a well-placed shot.

"Hold on!" she shouted.

Annja hadn't needed to tell Nang that. He'd dug his fingernails into the dashboard and was gritting his teeth. His eyes were needle slits and he took in great gulps of the exhaust-filled air. One hand on the steering wheel, she flailed about with the other, finding her seat belt and pulling it across her lap, shimmying by a Land Rover and past a Camry, praying all the while that the gunmen didn't shoot an innocent driver. She clicked the belt and felt only a little safer.

Sirens wailed louder and she reached a stretch where traffic was thinner. She floored the gas pedal and the Jeep surged faster, and then was bumped from behind. A glance in the mirror showed the grille of the pickup. It conveniently had no license plate.

"They will kill us! They will—"

"Shut up," Annja warned. She didn't need Nang's distraction.

The truck veered to the left, coming alongside the Jeep. Annja kept one hand on the wheel and extended the other, calling for her sword and finding it difficult to grip the pommel with the blade meeting resistance from the wind and the speed.

Nang screamed and Annja swiped down with the blade, aiming for the gun in the man's hand and instead connecting with his arm. It had the same effect—the gun clattered away on the pavement, disappearing beneath a black BMW. The truck smashed into the Jeep's side, and Annja had to compensate to keep from being pushed off the road.

"Bridge!" Nang warned.

Annja divided her attention between the road, the threatening pickup, oncoming traffic and now the bridge, which narrowed the road to a single lane. Below, the water sparkled like sapphire glass spun between the dirt-brown banks.

"C'mon, c'mon, c'mon," she coaxed the Jeep as she pressed the gas pedal as far down as it would go and inched past the truck. At least the passenger was inside the truck now, holding his injured arm. The driver was another matter; she spotted a gun in his hand. But he had to jump in behind her in the face of now-one-lane traffic.

"We will die!" Nang cried.

"Everyone dies," Annja said. "But I won't let us die today."

The Jeep rode up on the sidewalk as she jockeyed for a better position to see the truck behind her. The passenger was on a cell phone; she couldn't make out more than that because of the tinting to the windows. The driver had his arm out the window, gun against the door.

More sirens wailed, and she picked out three distinct

sounds. At least three police cars were coming. Before they reached the end of the bridge a fourth was added to it. Car horns blared as she took an off-ramp at full speed, tilting the Jeep up on its right wheels and nearly tossing Nang from his seat, despite the seat belt. She raced past a motorcycle that spun out in her wake and watched in horror as the silver truck headed straight for the motorcycle.

"God, please don't," she prayed, her stomach rising into her throat. The biker's death would be on her hands.

A maintenance worker on the side of the road pumped his fist and shouted at her as she continued to look in her rearview mirror.

The truck driver veered to the right to avoid the motorcyclist. His tires screamed in protest and the truck briefly rose up on its right tires like a stunt car before rolling on its side, sparks from the metal scraping against the pavement shooting up like fireworks.

Annja jabbed the gas pedal again and switched lanes, driving straight west again and leaving Chiang Mai and the increasing number of sirens behind.

28

"Nang, I want you to tell me all about Lanh Vuong. You were going to do that, remember, before we were rudely interrupted by your uncle's thugs."

Nang was still shaking from the wild ride in the city. She'd pulled onto a narrow road that cut through farmland. She wanted to avoid any major routes for a while, as plenty of witnesses would have described her and the Jeep to police.

"Lanh Vuong," she repeated. "Tell me about him."

"I called him Uncle Lanh when I was a boy, but he was not a true uncle."

"Go on." She stopped and let the engine idle, and she unhooked her seat belt and stood, pulling the maps out from under her. If she hadn't sat on them, they would have blown out. Other papers had, and she'd nearly lost the jerricans and her backpack with the skull pieces, too. Stretching forward, she knocked the glass out of the window frame, making it easier to see. "I'd guess it was a 9 mm," she mused as she began to drive again.

"Lanh Vuong is an important—" Nang picked

through his brain for the appropriate word "—exporter of goods from Vietnam."

"Smuggler," Annja corrected under her breath. "How did he get in the business, Nang?" An odd question for her to ask, she thought, but something niggled at a corner of her mind.

"Because of the Vietnam War, I think. Before I was born, before my father and Uncle Kim were born, Uncle Lanh was a soldier in the North Vietnamese army. An important one, a colonel. He was in his forties then, and he led many men to battle."

So he was in his eighties, or perhaps ninety now, definitely an old man, Annja thought. She waited, listening to the wind blow across the hood and welcoming it cooling her. It dried the sweat on her face; she'd sweated rather profusely during the erratic race from the antiques shop and out of Chiang Mai.

"Uncle Lanh was captured by American fighting men in the war. Some of his men were captured also, and all of them were put in a prison in South Vietnam. A bad prison, Uncle Kim told me. For forty years."

Annja's eyebrows rose. "Forty years?" How was that possible? She'd thought prisoners on both sides were released after the war, though to this day reports lingered of MIA American soldiers still rumored to be held in the heart of the country.

"Papers were lost, and the prison changed hands," Nang said. "Uncle Kim said Lanh was supposed to be free after the war, but the lost papers kept him in prison. Until the prison closed and everyone left inside was freed."

"A forgotten man," Annja said.

"A bitter man with no love left for his country. Vietnam was bad to my uncle Lanh."

"So he took from it," she surmised. "In the past few years of his freedom, he has taken relics."

"What is the wrong in that? Uncle Lanh was owed for all the years in prison. A lifetime he spent in a cell."

"Uncle Lanh is a thief and a smuggler," Annja said. And probably worse. Those in the operation under him showed no compunction against killing, so likely Lanh hadn't, either.

"There were places, Uncle Kim said, where ancient golden treasures were hidden during the war. Monks did not want the temple riches to fall into American hands and so they hid them in the jungle. Uncle Lanh knew of the places, and much of it was still there when he got out of prison. So Uncle Lanh and a few of the soldiers who served under him regained the treasures and sold them to wealthy men in other countries. Getting them out of Vietnam was the dangerous part, he once told me. But he had ways, and people looked the other way when he gave them gold. He sent the gold to Laos and Thailand, to hidden places in the mountains. Then buyers were found and the treasures moved on. And when those treasures were gone he found more."

Nang kept talking without more prodding, as if he wanted someone to know about Lanh and the operation. He spoke about it with a sense of pride and clearly believed that it was all justified because of the prison time Lanh had served.

"He took things from temples. Not a lot at any one time, but all together a lot since his freedom. Also from a museum once, he told me. And from burial places. Uncle Kim said the dead did not need their gold. Lahn needed the gold, though, gold and diamonds and emeralds. Uncle Lahn said he would be dead soon enough because he was so old, and that he would enjoy the gold while he still lived. It became, I think, the only thing he loved. Gold and money. Everything else he hated."

"You don't need to be involved with all of this, Nang. The world is full of opportunities and—"

"This is what my family does. This is all I know," he said angrily.

And this is all *I* know, she thought. Seeing something through to its end, putting the last piece of the puzzle into place and righting any wrongs along the way. It wasn't all she knew before she picked up the sword, but it was her life now. Along her previous path she would have made a few phone calls and let some international authorities find Lanh Vuong. She would never have been involved in a chase scene on Chiang Mai's streets, or a sword fight in the antiques store. She certainly wouldn't have been driving across Thailand, and now Laos, and within several hours into Vietnam.

"But I do not hate like my uncle Lanh does. I do not hate everything. You, though, I hate you."

Had Lanh Vuong hated enough during the war to use the skull bowl? Annja wondered.

"Read this map to me." Annja sat the one of Northern Vietnam on Nang's lap. "Read about Hue. Tell me all about Hue."

She genuinely did want to know about the city she was driving to, and she wanted to keep his mind occupied at the same time.

Nang was clearly terrified of her, and she did nothing to ease that feeling. She'd left the gun in the back room of the antiques shop and appeared unarmed to him. He'd seen the sword during the race through Chiang Mai's streets, but she didn't have it now, so it would seem that she'd dropped it when the Jeep nearly flipped over. Still, he made no move to escape or call for help as they took a narrow road over the border in Laos and passed a farmer leading an ox.

The map shook in his hands.

Annja felt bad for him…but not bad enough to let him out of the Jeep. Annja might need his help to translate and to find the antiques shop in Hue, which he'd admitted to visiting on more than one occasion to see his "uncle" Lanh.

Her stomach rumbled, apparently taking issue with the food she'd bought a half hour earlier and wolfed down. Annja had wanted to keep her strength up and so had ordered, in effect, three meals. Next to a gas station was a noodle shop, and her reluctant passenger had ordered *neua gai,* steamed chicken on rice. She'd been hungrier, ordering the same, plus *loog chin plaa,* fish meatballs, which had a softer texture than beef meatballs, and *giaw plaa,* dumplings stuffed with chopped fish. Normally, Annja had a cast-iron stomach, but with every rut and bump in the road she hit, her meal threatened to make a reappearance.

"It is seven hundred kilometers," Nang said, oblivious to her discomfort. "From Chiang Mai to Hue."

"Good to know." Annja had filled up the tank, and the two jerricans in the back; she didn't know when the next service station would present itself. "Tell me more."

"Hue has a population of…" He paused and leaned forward, trying to read the tiny print as they bounced along. "Three hundred and fifty thousand, a little more. It covers five thousand square kilometers."

A big city. Good thing she'd brought Nang with her, after all, as navigating a large foreign city she'd never been to might be daunting.

"It has many districts. Phong Dien, Quang Dien, A Luoi, Nam Dong, Huong Thuy, Vang…"

She let his voice trail to the back of her mind. She'd pay more attention when the subject became more interesting or relevant.

She knew the dirt road they drove down was not on her map, but that she'd eventually come to something larger that would be. The grass that lined the edges was tall and broad and a brilliant green that gave way to paler green trees in the distance with wide, sweeping fronds. It was more of the primitive beauty that she'd noted around the Thins village, but the village she approached looked much poorer. The homes were made of severely weathered planks that looked as if a strong wind would take them down. Several of them were two levels high with rickety-looking outer stairs leading to the second floor. The villagers who made their way between the buildings were dressed simply, many of them in white, and none of the men wearing shirts.

The next village looked little different, though there were children playing. They wore colorful shorts and shirts that had seen better days.

"This part of the country is poor," Nang told her.

The road narrowed and rice fields appeared on both sides. Men and women worked them, and a boy led an ox across the road, forcing Annja to slow. There were puddles and deep ruts, and the Jeep bounced with the passing miles. Far to the south were forested mountains wreathed in gray clouds. One formation looked like the humps on a camel's back.

"Nang, tell me some more about Hue."

"Uncle Kim would take me to the palaces on the bank of the Perfume River when I was a child. Emperors and mandarins had built them. More than a hundred very old buildings along that river. Tombs of the Nguyen kings there also. Lanh took from some of those tombs. My favorite was the Khai Dinh tomb, but the Gia Long and Minh Mang I also remember." He was relaxing, talking about the city, but only a little. The map still shook in his hands. "Good food in Hue—mostly vegetables, though. Beautiful pagodas. Tourists like the pagodas. He took me to Da Nang also, my uncle Kim. It is north of Hue and not as rainy. Hue is a very rained-on city."

Lovely, Annja thought. An opportunity to find myself in another torrential downpour. She'd been rained on quite enough the past few days, and the clouds over the Laos mountains looked as if they could open up at any moment.

"Anything else?"

He gave her a blank look.

"Is there anything else you can tell me about the city?"

"I attended school there. It was the capital of the Nguyen lords."

She had no idea what that was, nor was she particularly interested. But she wanted to keep him talking. "Go on, Nang."

"Hue was the national capital until near the end of the Second World War. That was when Bao Dai abdicated as emperor and a new government was established."

"That would be the communist one."

"Saigon in the south became the new capital. And

Hanoi in the north. Saigon is called Ho Chi Minh City now."

"Hue looks like it sits on the border between North and South Vietnam." Annja had noticed that from craning her neck and looking at the map when he had it opened.

"The Battle of Hue was in 1968, the year my older brother was born. The city was hurt very bad by American bombs. Only in recent times are some of the buildings being restored. But some will never be fixed."

She came to a wider road and took it, snaking around a rice field and passing an impressive-looking temple. Her stomach had finally settled down, and she wished she had bought some candy bars or nuts at the gas station. At least she'd picked up a few cans of Cheerwine cherry cola and a six-pack of Red Bull. They'd cost her four or five times what she would have paid for them in New York. She reached behind Nang's seat.

"Want one?" She gave him a cola and pulled out two Red Bulls for herself.

It was hot, even after the sun set, and despite their speed clouds of gnats stayed with the Jeep, sticking to her skin. She liked the smell of the country, though mostly what she picked up was damp earth. It was preferable to the smog of Chiang Mai and the ugly odors of the antiques shop and the alley.

She let herself breathe deep.

"You are not going to let me go, are you? You are going to kill me and leave my flesh to rot," Nang said.

Annja stayed silent. Let him remain in fear of her to keep him cooperative. She didn't like herself very much at this moment. Several moments later, she said, "We'll see, Nang. We'll see."

29

To avoid a checkpoint along the road, Annja cut across a field, nearly miring the Jeep in mud. Her passport might have sufficed to get her across the border without too many questions, but she couldn't risk Nang causing problems.

She took him into the restroom with her when they stopped at a gas station a few miles over the Vietnam border. It was a small town, and the station had been ready to close. The owner accepted her Thailand baht, but charged her extra because he would lose some money in converting it to dong. She'd needed Nang to translate for her, and she hoped he hadn't said anything foolish like, "Help, I've been kidnapped by a mad woman."

She loaded up on candy bars and chips, which was all the fare for sale, and ushered Nang back into the Jeep, watching him while she filled the tank. If her calculations were correct, she wouldn't have to stop for gas again until they were headed back out of the country. Correction, she thought, until *she* was headed back. She'd leave Nang in Hue and hope against hope that he would find a different calling than smuggling. Maybe he would have to if she could catch Lanh Vuong and return him to prison.

"Are you married, Nang?"

"No."

"Is there someone you—"

"No."

She wondered how Luartaro was doing and if he'd been able to return to the treasure cave with the authorities. She wished she could have called him from the antiques store to tell him what was going on and where she was going. Maybe if there was a consulate in Hue she would stop and try to reach him.

When Nang fell asleep, she coasted to the side of the road and extricated the map from his hands. She found a small flashlight in the glove box and used it to check her route. Annja was proficient at reading maps, but the inset map for Hue was tiny and listed only major roads. She would wake Nang when they reached the city.

Hue sat in central Vietnam, perched on the bank of the Huong River and a dozen miles inland from the port of Bien Dong. She guessed it was a little more than four hundred miles south of Hanoi, which she knew would have a consulate or embassy.

"Nang, tell me more about this city." Annja nudged him awake. He looked angry at being disturbed. "What is that?" She pointed to an ornate building at the edge of the city, set back from a main road she turned on.

"Hue has many monuments, and that is one of them. I do not know the name. But that building, that one—" He waved his arm at a much larger structure, the ornate top of which rose higher than all the buildings around it. Through gaps in the other buildings, she saw that the massive one was walled. "That one is called the Citadel. Once there was an entire city inside it, a forbidden place where only emperors and their concubines and guards were permitted. The punishment for trespassing was death. It is a tourist attraction now." He paused. "You are going to kill me, are you not?"

"And what is that building?"

"The Thien Mu Pagoda, the largest one in Hue. It is the symbol of the city. Some of the royal tombs are behind it. The tombs were built while the rulers still lived. Some look like miniature palaces."

Several blocks later he pointed out Quoc Hoc High School, Hai Ba Trung High School, a series of old French-style buildings, mandarin houses and the Hue Museum of Royal Fine Arts.

Annja spotted several businesses that were still open, despite the late hour. Some had signs in English and French for the tourists. One advertised all-night foot massages, another *banh khoai* and *com hen,* which Nang explained were savory pancakes and mussels served on rice.

Annja was hungry again and ate the last candy bar.

"How far are we from the antiques store, Nang?"

He was shaking again; the neon lights of the bars they drove by showed that he was sweating profusely.

"Tell me the best way to get there."

In halting words, he did.

It was in an old part of the city; the buildings looked beat up, and half the ones on the block were closed and boarded up. There was a tavern on the corner, the only business open along the street, with a winking light that advertised Bia Hoi beer. Laughter spilled out of its propped open door, but it looked as if the patrons were sparse—so were the cars on the street. She circled the block, seeing the antiques store in the middle, and found an alley to pull into.

"You will kill me now?"

"Does your uncle Lanh speak English?"

"And French. He learned in prison."

"Does he live nearby?"

Nang looked up. There was a low light in one of the windows. "He owns the building, the block. He lives up there, above his store."

"Get out." She reached over and unsnapped his seat belt. "Get out."

He slid out, stumbling in his nervousness.

"Go home, Nang. Go somewhere."

He stared at her, barely visible in the light that spilled into the alley from a lamppost.

"I'm not going to kill you. I'm not going to hurt you. Just—" She didn't have to say anything else. He took off running, turning the corner past the alley, his feet slapping against the sidewalk. "I hope I don't regret that," she said to herself.

Nang could well stop somewhere, the tavern even, and call Lanh to warn him…or call some of his uncle's muscle. He probably would call, but hopefully after she'd concluded her business and was headed back out of the city. Better she got rid of Nang now than worry about him while she confronted the smuggling mastermind.

She could make out next to nothing in the alley; the light coming from the far end was faint like the first hint of dawn. There were backs of buildings and staircases leading to second floors, and plenty of insects that she couldn't see but could hear and feel all around her.

Not a single light burned in any windows in the back.

There were stairs directly behind the antiques shop, sturdy and narrow and incongruous to the rickety appearance of the front of the building. As she climbed, the clouds of gnats and mosquitoes following her, she touched the sword with her thoughts. Hopefully she wouldn't need it against a man in his eighties or nineties, but she would be prepared nonetheless. The steps were not steep; in fact, they were lower than usual, perhaps made to accommodate an old man's failing legs.

At the top, the door looked sturdy and resisted her attempts to force it open. Finally, she summoned the sword, and carefully used the blade to worry at the hinges until she could get it open. Unless he was deaf, he had to have heard her. She noticed as she passed through the door frame that she'd tripped a silent alarm.

"Wonderful," she muttered. It would either be keyed to a police station or private security firm, or perhaps— like the antiques store in Chiang Mai—to thugs who would come roaring up with guns ready.

The kitchen was dark, but she could pick through the shadows enough to make her way toward the doorway. The kitchen smelled of dirty dishes and food that had been left out. She wrinkled her nose and picked up the scent of something far worse.

Insects were thick inside the apartment, too.

"No." She entered a hall and felt around for a light switch, turning it on and holding the sword out in front of her.

He was lying on the couch as if he'd fallen asleep, a newspaper flat against his chest and flies buzzing around his face. He'd been dead for at least a few days. Annja dismissed the sword and cupped her hand over her nose, trying to cut the smell. She saw a chair near the couch and dropped into it.

Lanh Vuong had been a small man who looked ancient. The wrinkles were deep, and the skin thin like parchment, the hands twisted with arthritis to the point they looked like the claws of a bird—claws that were thick with gold rings. Three thick gold chains hung around his bloated neck. She looked away from the corpse, feeling the candy bars rise.

Annja felt sick to her stomach, and cheated of answers. She'd driven through three countries to confront him and to demand answers about the skull bowl and the smuggling operation. She'd dragged a frightened henchman with her—who might at this very moment be calling in thugs.

Lanh Vuong's death had robbed her of any feeling of completion.

"No. No. No. No." She sat there for several minutes, then pushed herself up and looked around for a phone, still cupping her hand over her nose.

Annja got a good look at the furniture. Beautiful antiques, every piece, many hinting at a French origin, and most of it well maintained. The carpet was threadbare in places, however, partially covered up by an expensive-looking Turkish rug that dominated the center of the living room. The apartment was small—the living room, kitchen, single bedroom and a bath all compact. There was another room, this with a stackable washer-dryer and a desk. The message light on the telephone blinked red.

Annja sat at the desk, the smells of laundry soap helping to cut the odor of the old man's corpse. She remembered the phone number of the consulate in Chiang

Mai and once again called it. Lanh Vuong would not mind if she added to his phone bill. She wanted to call the lodge, too, and see if someone there would get Luartaro for her. But it was late, too late for an indulgence like that.

After being transferred from person to sleepy person, Annja was connected to Pete Schwartz.

"I'm surprised you're still working," she said. "Oh, it's because of me, isn't it? Sorry. Really, I am sorry." She quickly related the story of her mad dash to Vietnam, leaving out her borrowing of Nang. "I wasn't sure who to call about all of this."

She had no contacts in Hue or Hanoi, and no computer to connect to her network of internet associates. Lanh Vuong didn't have a computer that she'd seen, though there might be one downstairs in the antiques store. That would be her next stop. She didn't want to take the time to search the apartment.

"And I didn't want to call the police just yet, Pete." She'd have too much explaining to do.

Pete told her there was a U.S. Consulate General in Ho Chi Minh City, and an embassy in Hanoi—both too far away to be convenient, though he gave her phone numbers for some men he knew there and told her to call them—immediately.

"I'm coming back to Chiang Mai," Annja said. "I'll be leaving soon. Hey, you don't need to yell at me." She wanted to look through the antiques store below for… what? Maybe for any records of the smuggling operation or artifacts. Maybe for a list of names of people buying the relics or working for Lanh Vuong. Maybe a laptop or hard drive she could take with her and dig through later. Something to put the last pieces of the puzzle in place.

"Yes, I'm coming right back. Right away," she told Pete when he pressed her to leave and to let the local authorities sort things out—not a "vacationing American archaeologist with a nose for trouble looking to get herself tossed in a foreign jail."

"You can stop yelling. I'm heading back now," Annja said.

Well, soon, she thought. A trip downstairs first. She considered calling the lodge to find Luartaro, again dismissing the notion because of the late hour. She considered calling the consulate or the embassy, too, as Pete had suggested, as well as Doug Morrell to see if a crew was on its way to Thailand to film the teak coffins.

Instead, she pushed the button to listen to Lanh Vuong's messages. She figured she might learn just how many days ago he died based on the age of the messages. It was an old-style answering machine, with a cassette tape in it. She didn't think they made those anymore. The tape was full.

There were nineteen messages, the first was five days ago, so he'd not been dead longer than that. Most of them were in Vietnamese, and she could pick out only a few words, not enough to yield anything useful. But there were four messages in English, all from the same man—Sandman, he called himself.

"I'm worried about you, old man," Sandman said. The voice was scratchy and distorted because the tape had been used so much. "You haven't returned a single call."

Another message said, "I wanted to tell you this face-to-face, but you're obviously not around. Something's rotten inside."

The next said, "Old man…pick up the phone. Are you there?"

The last was from the previous day. Sandman was worried about his friend and would have someone stop by to check on him tomorrow…which would be later that day. It was after midnight.

Annja paced in the tight confines of the room. She should leave—after a quick look downstairs—hop in the Jeep and return to Chiang Mai to tie up any loose ends with the authorities and the consulate. She shouldn't cool her heels in a dead man's apartment waiting for someone called the "Sandman."

She left the apartment, turning off the lights as she went, stopping to look in the refrigerator and taking out a block of cheese and a bottle of ginger ale. The rest of the items looked either fuzzy with the first hints of mold or unidentifiable. She took the back staircase down, eating the cheese as she went. It was sharp cheddar, and it helped to cut the smell of Lanh's corpse.

She retrieved a small flashlight from the Jeep. The back door to the antiques shop required a little work to open, and she managed to bypass the alarm—it was an older security device that anyone with a little thought could dismantle. She closed the door behind her and flicked on the flashlight.

A shiver coursed through her.

At the top of a hutch-style desk across a crowded and cramped back room sat a skull bowl.

30

The bowl was stoppered, and Annja held the base of the flashlight in her mouth as she worried away at the waxy seal. There were no voices in her head this time, just a desire to see what was inside.

Four more dog tags were stuck in an inch of dried blood. She pried the tags out and stuck them in her pocket and left the bowl sitting on the desk; it would be leaving with her, along with any others she found.

She squeezed past a bank of file cabinets. There was no computer out in the open in the office, or in the first three large drawers she opened, and so she suspected the old man kept all of his records on paper; he'd been from another era, after all. She stepped back and opened one of the file cabinets; the drawer had only a few folders in it. Riffling through some of the pages, she saw the writing was all in Vietnamese. Worthless to her at the moment.

"So much for hauling away any evidence," she muttered. Still, she pulled out one file and placed it next to the skull bowl; she'd have someone translate it later.

Then Annja entered the shop. It was similar to the setup of the shop in Chiang Mai. There was a comfortable sameness to all old buildings—a showroom and a back office, with a restroom tucked to the side for the employees and patrons.

The odors were intense. She was far enough below the apartment that she no longer smelled Lanh, but she picked up the strong scents of old things—wood and clay, cloth, relics threatened by mildew and the years in general. Annja relished these kinds of smells and wanted to turn on the ceiling lights so she could get a better look. The beam of the flashlight was terribly inadequate.

There were packing crates at the back, and mounds of packing materials. They extended farther than she could see, and she realized that the antiques shop was much bigger than the outside storefront implied. It extended into the other boarded-up businesses and was virtually a warehouse of antiquities ready to be packed up and moved out to buyers in other countries.

The shelves were unfinished plywood, but they were massive and braced to support the weight of the objects spaced out across them. Busts, urns, statues and more stretched farther than the flashlight beam. Annja could not help herself; she had to take a closer look at some of the works.

One shelf was filled with what to her practiced archaeological eye looked to be artifacts from the Champa culture in Binh Dinh's coastal central province, hundreds upon hundreds of years old. They included ancient bowls, cups and vases made of fire-hardened clay. They were museum pieces, especially the soccer-ball-size containers covered with reliefs of a sea monster called a *makara,* and a mythological *naga.*

Another shelf was filled with a collection of jewelry pieces from the holy land of Cat Tien, including figurines of deities made from terra-cotta, silver, gold and bronze.

There were stone tools that were clearly prehistoric. Annja would have liked to take them back for study to determine what region they came from and just how old they were. It wouldn't hurt to take one small piece, she told herself. She reached for a stone ax and stopped herself. She was upset that Luartaro had taken jewelry and who knew what else from the treasure cave. She had no right to take anything.

She edged toward a gap in the aisles, where some large objects took up a considerable section of floor. An ancient cart with intact wheels captivated her. Nearby was a large bronze drum she guessed was at least two thousand years old. These large treasures were priceless archaeological treasures that Annja knew should be displayed in a major museum.

It was a crime against the world to smuggle these things. Annja recalled reading an article several months earlier about two Chinese men arrested in Vietnam with a truck full of antiquities they were taking across the border. She wondered if they'd been part of this operation.

The artifacts had been Vietnamese—a bronze drum, dozens of earrings, statues and ceramic jars. She rubbed her forehead, smearing dirt and the gnats that had stuck there. She was feeling so many things at the same time—anger that people would steal from history and deprive the public of an opportunity to see these relics and deny archaeologists the opportunity to study them; elation that she'd uncovered what obviously had been a massive smuggling operation; fear that some of the parties involved were still out there and could resume the nefarious practice; worry that the authorities might not properly handle all these priceless things.

She pulled in a deep breath, taking the dusty air into her lungs and relishing the oldness. Her breathing was loud in the stillness of the building. That and the shush-shushing of her shoes against the plank wood floor were the only sounds. The tavern was too distant, and the walls and shelves of this place kept its music and laughter at bay. There was no traffic on the street at this hour in this part of the city.

Annja wouldn't be returning to Chiang Mai right away, as she'd told Pete. She would stay in Hue a day or two, call the American consulate and embassy, contact Doug and beg him to send a second film crew here and call the various experts she knew in the field of ancient Vietnamese relics. She wouldn't be able to see everything through, but she could put things in motion, and that would give her a better sense of accomplishment and closure. She'd done nothing illegal, save drive a Jeep from Chiang Mai that didn't belong to her…and temporarily force Nang to accompany her. She would talk her way out of trouble—she was good at that.

Annja glided down the next aisle, seeing bronze jewelry dully gleam in her flashlight beam. She wanted pictures! She reached to her fanny pack as she heard an engine roar and gravel crunch. Someone had arrived out back. The pictures would have to wait.

She summoned the sword and hurried to the back of the shop, leaving her flashlight on a shelf. She'd meet them outside, refusing to risk even one relic being ruined in the fight that was to come.

And Annja knew there would be a fight. It wasn't the police she slipped through the office to meet. Either Nang had summoned Lanh's thugs or the alarm she'd tripped upstairs had called them. She stepped out the back door and clung to the shadows up against the wall.

Two men got out of a dark SUV, and a van pulled up behind it, turning off its headlights and disgorging four more men. Neither driver door had opened, so there were at least two more people that she couldn't see.

The only light in the alley filtered down from a lamp-post at the far end. It was nearly as dark as a cave. She couldn't make out any details regarding the men, though her instincts told her they were well armed. They looked like moving splotches of black against the gray of the walls and the vehicles—shadows upon shadows. She stared at the man heading to the door she'd just exited. All she could tell was that he was bigger than her.

The man behind him started up the steps to Lanh's dwelling.

Common sense told her she should creep along the wall and get out of there. The odds were too great and the visibility too poor. Alive and away, she could report what she'd seen and retell what had happened in the past few days.

But common sense was rarely Annja's friend, and so she angled the blade so the flat of it was out, pivoting slightly. Her feet made a sound against the gravel that alerted the closest man. He stopped and stared at the wall, and she wondered if his eyes were more acute than hers and he could actually see her. But then the moment passed and he reached for the doorknob, and she swung the blade up with all her strength behind it.

Annja drove the flat of the blade against his neck, and he collapsed on the stoop, dropping something that made a metallic sound. He grabbed at his throat, hacking. She hit him again just as the man who'd started up the stairs retreated and called to the others.

Annja had managed to take one out without spilling blood, but she'd alerted the rest to her presence. The odds were five-to-one now, plus the two drivers and hopefully no more. Seven-to-one, she decided. She'd faced worse.

They shouted to one another in Vietnamese, one word in English ringing out and making her heart jump. *Sandman*. The van's lights snapped back on and caught Annja in a midleap kick at the man who'd just come off the stairs. The heel of her right foot landed solidly against the small of his back and sent him forward into another of his fellows.

Though the light wasn't bright, it momentarily blinded Annja, and she slammed her eyes shut as she planted her right foot and spun with a roundhouse kick that connected with the same man. She kicked him one more time and heard him drop, and then she opened her eyes to see two men pointing guns at her.

Her eyes better adjusted, she could tell that the men were a mix of young and middle-aged Asians, all with some bulk to them, and all wearing jackets despite the summer heat. They shimmered in the headlights like ghosts fazing in and out.

The one closest to her shouted that she should drop the sword, and she considered sending it away to find a peaceful resolution. But she noticed that the guns were sleek, recent models—all with silencers—and she was confident they would kill her quietly. She dropped to a crouch as bullets whispered above her head, and then she somersaulted forward, the gravel from the alley biting at the top of her head and the back of her neck. Rising right in front of the men, she swept the sword in hard, cutting through the jacket of the man on her right and into his rib cage. He howled as she dragged the blade in deeper, killing him.

Bullets whizzed by her ear as she stepped in close to the falling corpse and wrenched the sword free, driving the pommel up into the chin of the man who'd been standing shoulder to shoulder with him, cracking his jaw and breaking teeth. A slug slammed into her left arm, feeling like a piece of fire imbedded in her flesh.

Annja bit down hard on her lower lip in a failed effort to keep from crying out, tasting her own blood in her mouth and feeling a surge of adrenaline. This was a fight she shouldn't have picked, should have listened instead to her common sense. But since she'd started it, she knew she'd have to finish it quickly if she wanted to keep breathing.

The man whose jaw she'd broken swung his gun on her, firing just as she sidestepped it and she felt a bullet graze her right arm. She drew her sword down to her side and thrust it up at an angle, essentially skewering him. More whisper-hisses sounded, none of the bullets striking her, but hitting the man she'd skewered and the side of the van.

What were the odds now?

Her mind raced as she twirled away from the two she'd just dropped and rushed to the back of the van, buying her cover.

Four-to-one?

Had she counted right and cut the number in half? Was this a war she could possibly win?

Her arms burned from the bullets, and her chest felt on fire from the exertion. She stepped around to the other side of the van, nearly running into a man who'd just emerged from an open side door.

How many were there? An army?

Without hesitation, she drove the tip of the blade into his stomach, her charging momentum sending it in deeper and out his back. When he fell, she dropped with him, planting her knee on his chest and pulling hard to free the sword. She jumped to her feet and ran to the front of the van, darting around it just as someone hugging the shadows by the SUV opened fire.

31

This is madness, Annja thought. It was madness thinking she could fight all these men, madness that anyone would smuggle artifacts precious to all of humanity, madness that Zakkarat died.

"Madness!" Annja screamed the word as she charged a man coming around the other side of the van. She held her sword as if it was a lance and ran him through. "Madness!"

She fell on him, using the momentum to spring up, turn and tug the sword out of his gut.

What were the odds now? Better, but by how much? How many men had she dropped? Had more come out of the van or SUV?

She was close to two more men, so close that another two she spotted didn't fire, not wanting to risk their fellows. The closest two flanked her, and she used it to her advantage, ramming her elbow back into the shorter one, catching him squarely in the chest. She stepped back with him when he doubled over, striking him the same way a second time, hearing his gun drop. The move had bought her just enough space to bring her sword up on the man in front of her. One slice finished him.

Annja was spattered with blood and the insects had become a second skin, stuck to her sweat. The wound in her left arm continued to feel like fire, her right arm stinging where she'd been grazed. Sweat poured off her, from the heat of the summer night and all the fighting. She saw only two men left standing, and they yelled at each other, again. "Sandman" was repeated several times.

She heard a siren, but it was distant and receding, attending to another matter and leaving this private war to her and the remaining thugs. Both of them fired, missing because she was moving so fast and the shadows from the van helped cloak her, darting and weaving and never staying still for even a heartbeat. The slugs hit the side of the van, one of them breaking a headlight and making everything murkier.

Annja preferred that, not wanting to see too closely the faces of the men she was going to have to kill. She was haloed by the sole headlight, backlit like a movie monster as her feet churned to eat up the distance, feeling another bullet graze her left arm, and changing her grip so she held the sword only in her right hand.

Blood flowed down her left arm, that hand practically useless now, and mingled with the sweat as she hollered, "Madness!" once more and swung her weapon with all of her waning strength. She'd aimed high, and with one blow killed one of the men. Spinning from the energy of the swing, she followed through and struck the second, felling him, too.

She slouched forward, panting, holding her left arm

in close to her body, the fire of it fading and turning to numbness. She needed a hospital. But more than that she needed to end this war and finish the puzzle. Gulping in the humid, bug-filled air she turned and staggered toward the SUV. A man climbed out, taller than the others, thinner, and with hair so pale it looked like mist. In the light from the SUV's dome she saw that he wasn't Vietnamese, and that his deeply lined face was so pale it branded him a Caucasian.

"Sandman," she guessed.

"And you are a madwoman."

She couldn't argue with that. "Hands out to your sides." She raised the sword for emphasis, and he complied. She listened for any movement, either from the few men she'd knocked out rather than killed or from the vehicles, hinting that there were still more inside.

"You are impressive," he said after a few moments had passed. "An army unto yourself. I should have not dismissed Nang's ramblings so easily. He called you a pretty demon. I should have brought twice this many men."

"Who are you?"

"Sandman, as you know," he said. His face was an emotionless mask, cold and empty. "It is the only name I've used in, well, quite a long while."

Annja put him in his sixties.

"Tell me about this, about all of this." She pointed the sword behind her to the back of the antiques store. She had plenty of other questions, but she'd start there.

He gave a great shrug of his shoulders, and she realized that beneath the long coat he wore, he was frail and rail-thin. "What about it?" he said after another few minutes had passed.

In the silence she'd heard nothing but her own labored breathing and the buzzing of the damnable insects. Then somewhere out on the street a car horn honked.

"The smuggling," she started. "The cave in Northern Thailand." She paused. "All the guns. Vietnam and all of this!"

He leaned against the side of the SUV and dropped his hands to his sides. "Did you kill Lanh?"

Annja pointed the sword at his chest. "No. But he is dead. I don't think anyone killed him."

"He hadn't been well," he said. "It was only a matter of time. It's only a matter of time for all of us, actually."

She narrowed her eyes and her voice dripped with ire. "Tell…me…about…all…of…this."

"That could take a bit."

"I'm not going anywhere. And neither are you."

"Apparently not." He let out a long sigh. "I suppose 'all of this' started shortly after the Vietnam War. A police action, they called it. I'm sure the war was long over before you were born."

Annja listened, concentrating to stay on her feet and refusing to give in to the pain and blood loss.

"I survived the war, and I didn't go home. The gold was too tempting, you see. And I found things in Vietnam to my liking."

He explained that he'd been a soldier with a rifle company that had come across a stash of relics on a tour during 1966. A collection of golden Buddhas had been hidden by monks who feared that Americans would overrun their temple and take the holy objects. He took what he could carry with him and deserted, finding a few other soldiers who'd also fled their units, living from village to village and learning the language and customs.

"It was a small operation at first. We'd carry a few bits of holy treasure into China and make a tidy profit, reinvest it. Eventually, we set up a corporation of sorts in Saigon. We spread enough money around to get some police to look the other way, appeared to support the communist government, stuck to the shadows. Never sent too much across the border at any one time."

He shook his head sadly, the gesture making his mist-like hair appear to float around his face. "Times have changed. The government is cracking down on smuggling. It seems some people want to keep the relics here. But we never sent too much at any one time, tried not to be noticed."

Annja remembered the article about the men arrested in China transporting Vietnamese artifacts.

"It looked like a significant haul stashed in the mountains," she said. "I'd say that was 'too much.' And *I* noticed."

He gave another shrug. "Things have been complicated recently. More Western influence, more people concerned about the national relics and history, more guards watching the borders. If they only knew how much is gone, scattered across the globe. Most of it's gone when you think about it—beyond the considerable inventory in that warehouse and the pittance in a few… antiques stores."

Annja shuddered at the loss of history.

"Yes, Lanh and I saw to it that there's really not all that much left. Pity, I suppose. But it couldn't be helped—it was the best way to earn a fortune that I could think of."

One of the men she'd knocked out groaned and tried to rise, but he fell flat again and stopped moving.

"How did you get involved with him? Lanh Vuong?"

He smiled fondly, the first trace of emotion he'd shown. "During the war, actually. That was the first time I met him. We ran afoul of a dink base he was in charge of, and he had the audacity to capture us. I expected to spend the rest of the war in some slimy slope-head prison. But I made friends with some of them. I'd learned enough of the language at that point to get by. I bargained my freedom with Lanh for the location of a temple stash. He always did like gold."

Annja felt the bile rise in her stomach. This man was making her physically sick recounting what he'd done.

"The short version is that Lanh released me and two of my friends. There were four others, but he wanted some souls to take back with him. As we were running away, his camp was taken by American Marines—we managed to avoid the Marines, not wanting to end up in some U.S. prison for desertion. Neither did we want to end up dead. There were a lot of bullets flying that day. I learned later that Lanh had been grabbed by the Marines and tossed into a cell in the south. Many, many years, he was stuck there. Later our paths crossed again."

Annja felt dizzy, from lack of sleep, loss of blood and from listening to the sordid doings of a former U.S. soldier. The Sandman had successfully turned her stomach.

"It was an accident, really, our meeting again. Lanh had found my smuggling network, and he had far more contacts than I did. He was running a few operations of his own from behind bars. When he finally got back up north, we combined our resources. Became friends, I suppose, or as close to friends as our kind can be."

She hissed and stepped close, dismissing the sword as she brought her right hand up and grabbed his throat, feeling a few gold chains hanging there and dangling down beneath his shirt. There was another chain, with a familiar feel to it, and this she yanked free.

"And you come clean to me," she said, feeling his dog tags in her fingers. "Why? Why spill your guts about this?"

He looked surprised. "Why? Because you asked. Because you've won this war." He swallowed hard and she eased up and gave him a little breathing room. "And because I'll be joining Lanh soon. Something's rotten inside."

She remembered those exact words from one of his answering-machine messages to Lanh.

"Something horribly rotten. Cancer of the pancreas, the doctor told me. He gives me a month at the most. Hurts like hell. War is old men dying in the fullness of their promise while there is still madness in this world. War is hell."

"Which is where you'll end up," Annja said. She swung him around and pushed him toward the back of the shop. He was easy to push, frail and weak, and his hands were twisted from arthritis. "Go in." She intended to make sure he spent whatever days he had left rotting in a cell somewhere.

Annja flipped on the lights, wanting to better see the inside.

"Records?" she asked.

He gave a clipped laugh. "Never bothered with them.

Lanh, neither. Not records on our…real dealings, anyway."

She pointed to the skull bowl she'd left on the desk and fought a crashing wave of dizziness. "What do you know about that?"

"Oh, the skulls? Only that Lanh liked them. Said he put souvenirs from the war in them. Said he picked them up in the States before the war. Must have had a dozen of them. Talked to them like they were childhood imaginary friends. Rubbed them like a magic genie's lamp and called them Papa Ghede."

Annja nudged him up one aisle and down the next. She found eight more skull bowls among the treasures on the shelves, all filled with dried blood and dog tags. She forced him to carry some of them to the back room.

Free, she thought when she broke all of the seals.

There were eight bowls, plus the one on the desk made nine. And the one from the mountain made ten. Two were unaccounted for, if indeed he'd had a dozen. All of them were filled with dog tags.

She looked at the Sandman's dog tag. Sanduski, Merle M., Catholic.

"Pretty demon, what did you do with that sword you were waving around?"

Annja shoved him into a chair.

"That sword looked old. I could probably find a buyer who'd give you a sweet dollar for it, pretty demon. Set it up for you if you let me walk out the door. I've only got a few weeks, anyway. I'll be dead before any trial. No need to put me through that, huh?" He rubbed at a spot on his pant leg. "So, about that sword…"

She clocked him on the side of the head to knock him out and reached for the phone, calling the Chiang

Mai consulate again because in her fuzziness it was the only number she could remember.

ANNJA WOKE UP TWO DAYS later in a hospital bed in the heart of Hue, Pete from the consulate at her side and three Americans in suits with him. "From the Ho Chi Minh consulate," he explained, gesturing to them. "Some of the fellows I'd asked you to call."

The room was simple, but at least it was private. The bed was small, and there was no television, radio or phone. Annja scowled at the IV drip in her bandaged arm.

"You lost a lot of blood," Pete said. "And picked up a nasty infection. The nurse said you were covered with mud and blood when they brought you in."

Annja would find out later just who brought her in and who called the authorities—probably Pete for the latter. "There were some unusual bowls in the antiques store. Made of skulls and—" Annja started to say.

"I don't know anything about the antiques store, other than that you were found in it…along with a collection of U.S. servicemen's dog tags that were turned over to the Ho Chi Minh consulate. Found more dog tags in a carry bag in a Jeep."

"There was a man with me, in the antiques store."

"Ah, that would be Mr. Merle Sanduski. I do know about him." Pete rocked back on his heels. "He's on the floor below you."

"He's a—"

"Crook. And a deserter from the military from a long time back."

"A smuggler," she said.

"I gathered that. There's a guard outside his door,

and they say he's going to prison, probably for the rest of his life."

For however many weeks he has left, Annja thought. "How about me? Am I going—"

"To prison?" Pete laughed. "I've no doubt that you should…for something. Quite a few bodies you leave in your wake. Are you sure you're only an archaeologist? But they're calling you a hero, stopping the biggest relic ring in all of Vietnam. Apparently, they've been after Sanduski for years. He was a slippery fellow. So, no, you're not going to jail."

Pete reached into a big briefcase he'd sat on the floor and pulled out a laptop and a cell phone and put them on her bedside table.

"Thank you," she said.

"There are some news reporters downstairs, and a couple of TV crews. The doctors are keeping them at bay, but they'll eventually get up here. Reporters always do."

Annja frowned. "There are some people I want to talk to, but I'd rather avoid the news."

Pete laughed louder. "That isn't going to happen."

She ran her fingers over the laptop. "Will this—"

"They have Wi-Fi here. Yeah, it'll work." He pointed to the phone. "That is prepaid, so take care with your calls, because when that one is empty, you're on your own."

Annja smiled. She was always on her own.

She had to admit that she felt much better than she had in days. A glance under the covers revealed that her leg had been rebandaged, and her left arm was in a loose sling. She felt a little pulling from the stitches where the bullets had been.

"We'll leave you be for a while," Pete said. "But we'll be back after dinner. Some reports to fill out, plenty of questions to ask, that sort of thing." He tipped his head and spun around in military fashion, walking out of the room with the other men nodding politely to her and following.

Annja punched in the number for the lodge and asked the man at the front desk if he would please find Luartaro.

"He checked out, Miss Creed. Early yesterday. He and his film crew packed up and took the bus to the city and the airport. But he left a note for you."

Annja asked him to read it.

Dear Annja:
What a remarkable, memorable, hell of a vacation this has been. I must get back, however—the next class session is starting soon and I've got to prepare for it. We have to package and sell the film from the spirit caves. I have offers from a few networks already.

I hope you don't mind, dear heart, but when you went off to Chiang Mai without me, I contacted a local film crew and had a go at the story myself. Some of the water receded and we got excellent shots of those bodies in the teak coffins. We made history.

I'm sure if you and your crew ever show up you can concoct a monster for your program.

I would like to see you again, sweet Annja, in your country or in mine. Please stay in touch.
Love, Lu

Annja hung up the phone and flopped her head back on the pillow. She couldn't blame him...not really. The previously undiscovered teak coffins with the human remains were the real treasure of the spirit caves. She'd wanted them for a *Chasing History's Monsters* special, but she was fine with Luartaro getting the credit. Annja had more than enough hours in the spotlight, and apparently would be getting more if the television crews downstairs had their way.

She still was bothered that Luartaro took the ancient jewelry from the cave...and she would stay in touch with him, if only to discuss that and come to some resolution.

And there was the matter of the skull bowl in a museum in Florida. She'd travel there to make sure it didn't have a seal and dog tags.

A knock on the door interrupted her musings.

A nurse opened it a crack. "I speak English," she announced.

"Yes?"

"You have a visitor, Miss Creed."

Annja groaned. She didn't want to deal with the media yet. She shook her head. "No. I need my rest."

"I understand." She started to back out. "He is a Frenchman. Said he came a long way. But he can wait. I will tell him to come back—"

"Wait." Annja sat up a little straighter. "You can send Roux in." She had a lot to tell him.

epilogue

Vietnam, July 1966

Lightning flashed and the ground rocked again and again. Above the patter of the driving rain, the whisper-hiss of machine-gun fire reached inside the old stone building.

Sanduski risked a glance outside to see mud spitting up around the feet of his sergeant.

Gary Thomsen screamed when the bullets chewed into his legs, and he fell face forward.

"Wallem!" he managed before he hit the mud. "Company. Moore, get out here. We've got…"

Wallem and Moore were the first soldiers out the door, raising their rifles and firing as they went. Sanduski hung back. He'd gotten a look at the Vietnamese force out there.

At least two dozen…and that was his guess without counting or getting a real good look. And that meant there were more. There were always ones that you couldn't see. This was his second tour, and he intended to get out of it alive.

As the rest of the men raced out, all of them firing and hollering, some of them screaming as bullets slammed into them, Sanduski edged deeper into the building. There was a large Buddha at the back, decorated in gold and silver and just big enough to squat behind. He hid just as the firing stopped.

He held his breath when he heard footsteps. They were faint against the sound of the rain. Men talked, in a language Sanduski didn't understand. Slope heads. And that meant Thomsen, Moore, Wallem and all of the others were dead.

The Vietcong talked among themselves, pacing and moving things around, and finally leaving.

Sanduski let out a breath carefully. His legs cramped from the position, but he didn't dare move. He didn't move for what he guessed was a few hours.

When it had gotten so dark that he couldn't see anything, he stood, rubbing at his numb legs to get the feeling back and stumbling forward and into one statue after another. He could hardly walk; his legs weren't cooperating.

At last he found the opening and cautiously looked out. It had stopped raining, and there were just enough stars overhead so that he could see the bodies of his fellows. Not a single VC corpse—they'd either taken their fallen or Thomsen and the others hadn't scored a single hit.

Sanduski went from one body to the next, discovering that the VC had taken the treasure; however, they missed a diamond ring that Thomsen had taken. The gem was the size of a big sunflower seed. Sanduski plucked it loose and then went to collect the dog tags.

But there weren't any.

"Damn slope heads took 'em," he said to no one.

He hadn't seen Lanh Vuong carefully pluck each tag loose and put a bullet in the head of each soldier…just to be sure they were dead.

He hadn't seen the colonel collect blood from each man and say a twisted prayer to Papa Ghede.

Sanduski returned to the building, where he hid until dawn. Then he picked up enough small pieces of treasure to fill his pockets and pack and headed down the trail to the east.

"'War is always the same,'" he said. "'It is young men dying in the fullness of their promise.' I promise it won't get me."

The
Don Pendleton's
Executioner®
POWDER BURN

American officials are targeted by a Colombian cartel...

When a ruthless Colombian drug lord launches a deadly campaign targeting DEA agents and U.S. diplomats, Mack Bolan is called in to infiltrate and destroy the chain of command. Bolan knows he must shut down the operation quickly but the cartel's leader has declared war on anyone who stands in his way. There's just one flaw in the plan—no one expected the Executioner!

GOLD EAGLE®

Available February wherever books are sold.

www.readgoldeagle.blogspot.com

GEX387

JAMES AXLER

DEATH LANDS®

Playfair's Axiom

The warriors of a shattered world forge new rules for survival...

When J. B. Dix is gravely wounded in the concrete jungle of St. Louis, Ryan and his group become captive guests of a local barony. Freedom lies in the success of a deal: recapture a runaway teen, daughter of the ailing baron. But the gruesome manipulation of the holy man with the power means the group is in a life-and-death race....

Available March wherever books are sold.